Don’t Tell! February 17

Don’t tell a bunch of ugly people it’s not foreal.

Chapter 1: Zero

Clinging Vines

White girls come in all colors.

Every kiss begins with ass. The F-factor “Sweetheart." He hid it in his condom. They called him Sweet Pea. The both of them. They hate what it was. He fought, not like yourself.

YOu care deeply, not like themselves. And that’s what it was. They tried to glue his ear back on. Do yo’ understand?

We Kill the People, they sacrifice, then they eat their souls. It's called recycling. The murder rate was up in Toral Town, Alaska. They just did not care.

From extreme cold that enters through the door so that has a temperature of zero, the house was at least four stories tall, square windows on each wall so it looks of a typical colonial home. It was a blue Hound blue, screen siding panels made of wood and standings past one-hundred years to everyone who tries to be there, everyone tries to want the name of the house. It kept everyone, sent everyone, everyone wanted to wake up there.

I did. I ran to the window on the dry hardwood floors, and I ran down the hall full of leafy green carpet. Lee ran through the waves of all of the air that collided with how it ripped through my grapes. Yes, I fell on the floor rolling about like I'm literally on caution that a bear was shocked at a nurse. I never will sit there again, and ever since, he's such a bad session during the holidays. But I just seen a ladybug. There was nothing but nor'eastern zero degree temperatures on the magazines of the year before. Expired, so the fireplace had to be used for my wet hair, snapping rancid, crinkled away. Photographs all of the past, of a present, lay on the table in front of the fireplace, made of oakwood. Why was it cold like zero in that house? The furnace had broken, never to be fixed, so we called the house Zero.

My name is Akwa Aqua. It means Wednesday blue or Wednesday water, something that will stop prettying him down. What does that mean? We were a family of eight. The girls got all of the pretty names, while the boys got names less than, shall we say pretty, and let's just say not to do with anything, but they were not pretty. Because of that my brothers couldn't get as bad as they wanted to be. In so many ways, no one gave a darn.

Between comfort and discomfort is this 7th day of September of the year of our Lord, 2001. Right after the Y2K scare and no mention of apps on cell-phones to replace good-old-fashioned search-engines. It is glorious, fun year cast in beer-time, so quickly. There was no storm today. I could not see the floor of my door. Everyday it's winter in Alaska.

Imperturbably beary is what you must be there. My favorite musical people has to be my sister, just to keep them away from things to see what they'd do. Will it benefit society? It's called stupidity knowledge. before bear became all that she was in the store she started singing in high school and making records she's performed all over the world cleaning Japan she has very solid tympanic Club beats that could be played to her sultry jazz .

I first realize Billy bear she handed me a tape of a record a song. Like so many musical people she had a special vibrato Special Air a voice tune it just comes up through the air things. She is done inspiring and plastic her spirit is the LIE of love togetherness an extreme training Guelph complete imperturbe Lee Berry her life is been so balanced I just called her the Ampere terribly Barry she has been sitting I know existence for difference she likes sitting in the breeze and believe is an impenetrable day so let's all try to be infertile early Berry and this is where I'll begin my journey to be like my idol I will be in future we bury in so many ways let's start out On the 1st of December.

I was born in the middle of the month timing disco's at its height it was an air of sophistication I could just go on and on there to so many people I don't see why shutter success stop being poor success is being happy to get to a point of imperturbability Barry happiness mimosa's jovial is the honey dripping from a bear right after hurts hibernation during the cold cold existence of the planet Earth there are some for which Life Goes On there's some for which there's a different Tale the bear has no Tales of this every years the summer every year is the honey this girl is what so many try to be to not give it from anyting to walk through those bitter snooze so many people must do to be blinded my passion warmed by the strength of your ability strength to go and do it's almost animal is human to fail so many half can any of us be in Pretoria blueberry any of us have that drive their focus then one tunnel vision life it makes it hibernate through the dark days history rest upon our souls mini rester gifted and blessed is it gift people strike is not being the bear being the human causes are suffering that we mistreat that they will suffer this is the tale as so many others human suffering The Berry people seem so sweet they just

picked the Bears right off a tree berries put them in
there a little dresses and scoop them up and bowls and
rush them in bowls symbols of Pies there others just
we'll catch that when of sophistication and Air what
will never be lift sway how will it be can we all try a
real animals some of us just choose to be God can we all
be in picture of Lee Barry can we all just ignore the
superfluous strenuous activities hell on Earth we all
Drive the existence of poverty existence of well does it
take the money that's something she's never been abridge
stuff and something of a circumstance provide to her
tell unbridled ability money is cast upon them to be the
animal they are they exist as no other no one can seem
to not hurt yep they will never not help despair pull
through he people shoot at it they always preserve it
it's mistake simplicity it's snowing this to enjoy the
wall to wrap up in the warmth of oneself to endure the
cold this is story of many tales of many people try to
accomplish such a thing so many ways so many jacket ways
find ourselves why bear freeing ourselves to be the
humane this is what many will never do so much easier
how to do a kickover tent 2Pac to steal one's honey
steal one's food does the bear often do that in cases of

hunger what happens when the Bears not hungry what happens is plentiful the garden is semen really feel sorry for the bear do they ever wondered when there is not sufficient and provided fattened will there ever be a time will exist is this the question I choose to stay on the side of the rich the money The Castaways steripen girls anchor avarice Envy walk two roads been with the poor the unlikely perhaps ignored and the wealth I can't tell you what money. Sweetheart here's looking at the well to do the Wella biters all the success here's to that I'm staying in for terribly Barry Oh that men can do .

Early stage of life I have to say that coming down from many peaceful days it's not a immature are small at the beach for

Chapter 2: We Won't Look Like This

the world. No tornado Valley this what anyting what bow down to. Plus, adieu what is the easiest. I don't see it from the start I don't spread the legs of secession and meager attitudes. there's a life and happiness, steadiness, or failure.

I stayed at home in this dedication to life study. I want to tell about the song Take My Love From the berry imperatively berry girl it just is what people take. they must be loved someone must love it sure someone must be love. How much did be for who must love must they be what is week unless they be able to Strong has a case what does not impose what is not in search of the ugly of the swing and they hating Brothers.

Mist Berryessa name before thinks that music is not like art not like Tom had it Tom was an artist he did the cover the spot it's what disconnects the book and the world father this is the picture of me pictures of men a woman disconnecting happiness where did smothered the colors run it's the tears eliminate the breast of one side the funny Parable heartbeat just pulls us into the point of dying here you see a woman on the cover is a dead woman she cannot whisper a letter of this book.

she can say anything to lay down I never walk. It's just something shocking to let the readers understand the point of life it's not to be that is to live they're two totally different words don't look similar whatsoever I think today's paper called the car moves where we live Poland match match difference between the dying and living in the book called shoe the orange rain by Rachel K. Martin well this will hit the foot like a nail in Jesus on the cross. she killed the ground, was a slave 2 the mundane, or was everyone I did not care about the Hills of grass. Complete waste of words. what's this woman a prostitute? what she crown debutante person beauty queen of high school Rich Roll? was she all things of stupidity unknowingness ignorance or hid ugly imagine and she started.

let's just cover up this life in the grave let's throw the dirt do you disagree? what's rice on the high side paints. It's good to not feel like a zero.

Chapter 2: We Won’t Look Like This

Required to run towards the track . Chloe did with chicken we thought you'd want looks like this Daphne could save your life.

Chapter 2: We Won’t Look Like This

How do we not look this way is it because it's Halloween to you it's because you can't see them the running everywhere this one in particular this one goes through Michelle mentioned in the Poetry of choosing your own trying there's something much like a spider on the wall just in the introvignes much like yourself reading interpreting songs like what I consider amuse hear it . to me this is the point of life one cannot get through when cannot pass through it without fighting it without chewing Dan taking that last breath. is that how it is the last moment the last breath we clench her teeth trying to survive a horrible World horrible tide change and Michelle was just a coaster the poet that must live within that moment but last poem has many different phases of change of the death of the dying as I mentioned in the last buck to the orange rain as you split and diet of course this means US Mini Splits a Bittersweet taste is in the orange rind 1 West recall supposed to leave us or last 10 to 15 seconds of Life flashing before eyes in these different frames these different stanzas of the poetry depicts all of those emotions racing before becoming free of ourselves when we come raging spirits everlasting life and a r motorcycles oh the last book was more about trying to chew to live eventually we get to the last year I think that's where this book will pick up movie about all that resides in the reflection of one's life at that last moment those last days Rising for the last challenge what will it be like for anyone Harrison introspection when's fall back people give so much advice how is it to look backwards and tell yourself or you will go for it no more. We won't look like this first of all like we are we want looks like we used to when you were sick dying decrepit weathering fattening whatever the case may be will become something that cannot recover to become the death supposedly we were big pile of dust he'll be thrown out to sea is this more of it was just an interest faction into what we will face something will will will be borne by.

We ran together Chloe we had every feeling that the last three days or empty and Shiloh of white snow ice, performance shows knives healthy walking bodies and medical and poverty togetherness much worse find sunny I need a. let's go think of moving for it. I will be there?

It's been quite a herring experience they just keep sitting there watching me will invisible people I

watching you ain't heavy things in me that you and I
feel their tactile you cannot see the sale practically
breaking every bone in my body pinched they just keep
taking all of my air and weighing me down odesse
torturous all day and they keep me up all night I get no
rest my eyes are peeled they're black and they are ready
explosions all over the TV and nothing phases they're
more than bothering me this is completely Concerta done
bothering me she went to the back what's 2 two tier and
that was all she does is Justin find the 2-day anymore
of the two deer used to come around back I think someone
hit and crush the deer and split it off to the side like
a big pile of reverie organs and blood the head of used
to recognize so dearly when her go baby dad Aerotek such
a beautiful picture that captured in time she said that
was promised a the road a little baby doll left
motherless they're practically skin and bone I just fed
them she barely had nutrients and she tried to use all
of them as much as she could feed her baby deer animals
their highest extent to keep themselves in there
offspring live people cannot do the same.

I heard it's racing is pounding his true knocking knocking as if wanting to be raped I think I have your heart he said it's putting me everywhere that you're never going to be what you say don't understand or appreciate themselves they don't want you to not really anything cuz you did not have this problem they want me to sit there and be there in and then you and Father's day but this isn't expanding to anyone that can guess what it seems people don't want to be bothered and I think of any way to bother me that care about him being agitated and extremes they've gone to the bothering you and that's better. now question art I thought. the news of sunny day and every computer I walk in front of was there when I left the building. I could see the smoke coming out of the windows watch the TV and explosions. I'm in bed watching too finally just relaxing to a week ago and it was with just one more time. December went by so quickly and I just wanted to go and make it through the last year at of my job app. And I always felt just like it was had just happened but I was just going to pray for the first time. I just for a little a little yeah fresh air my father and I didn't run many travels at through the Midwest as much as we went through more in St Louis we saw the downtown area we saw the malls that's been closed a lot of the Sea Breeze old friends used to live places that the houses are not as well kept you probably are now condemned you are perhaps someone else is living there there's this not really a place where a lot of people are still states structured it's not like living in New Orleans just had its pride and its culture for many many years. drove me to school quite a bit that is only when and if the last time he dropped me off it was a very Rocky rainy morning I said hello to have then he drove off to the Sun.

medium sized statue woman with all of these cat like I appearance perm straighten hair I'm sorry my pigtails blow in the Wind he went further and further into the Sun. That was him going to the start of his day every day started with a Sun Ray and going away to begin my beach walk into start of my new school year. Seemed like he was going into the sun to me Style of course he was not driving into the sun just a figure of speech for your child and you're not too tall can't see too far over the hell seems like that's where he's gay.

of course it's a whole different culture to be involved in different kinds of weather and different kinds of States Midwest pretty humdrum you ever winter spring or summer or fall more of the summer in the winter is definite the fall in the spring 10 do Collide somewhat but the leaves do fall by the end of September. squinting outside of the window I looked at how everyone was little dots down from an airplane there's so many people about because it was the July 4th holiday and all the sudden there was planking and clashing airplanes flying and firecrackers going. can hear loads and loads a fireworks when their direction under the arch I get my daughter look at this time. My mind was empty with no hope for anyting a few hours went by and I saw a big cloud in the sky jumped Define it was on the floor.

Chapter 3: We Just Don’t Care

He met a friend and yet we couldn't go through Finding Nemo it was a coffee all black coffee everyday black coffee Olympic cream in the coffee Willow thought you was black it was dark and made him crazy he went looking for anyone finally came up Iraq we found his child in a Ciroc you're really funny story Stanley Charlie found any survivors how she kept hiding from him somebody for children who don't want to be you're off and running I didn't see what the point of it is till they get to the point. Lucy Wizards daughter's name and she spoke unhinged address of the clock as it sat on the wall S4 had school in the plants and everything that we saw stay consistent we were together we're overwhelmed to begin every day but there was no where we were going we were all very happy to finally be junior high in front of all of the bag sickle writers they all took a plunge it was just the sun rise of the Cascades when she was in the big Village running and soon to be in the middle of September for bats were the roads were all the problems has one set there I thought well when I go to Houston Texas or something while we didn't want to sit Africa bigger place but the car couldn't go anywhere it's just broken down there always just imagine you what we might do and he was still looking for his daughter still trying to figure out what to be there by funny name for Lucy means like can see the light of it

The leftover people were all scattered throughout the yard. After every day he had ended we did not get to ignore the cold feet that cat walking towards the other ones. Many of them wanted to join the others and pray for all of their cold feet to bow to their heads in the Forum of a monstrous pleasure so they'd all set there we had to take a trip to New Orleans and people did not think this was a good idea they did not like their feet being sick isn't not like anything they were going to be reaching for many many many many many many feet.

the day before they all had left to go to Spencer's store and buy the most expensive sheets. They were never going to be put never pack from the rooms they're never going to be not broken and they just wanted to feel as if they jumped off of their beds Temple Run.

the night before of what's his call this December 2018 7 in the morning it was the most beautiful day. The snow still nothing moved nothing was alert. The only thing that could have been better was seeing the dogs air blow out of his nose from extreme cold that enter through the door so that has. The house was at least four stories Square Windows in each wall you so looks of a typical Colonial home it was a blue Hound blue screen siding panels made of wood and standings past hundred year everyone try to be there everyone try to want to the name of the house kept everyone sent everyone wanted to wake up there.

I did I ran to the window and I ran down the hall and gressive Lee ran through the waves of all of the air that collided with how it ripped through my grapes yes I fell on the floor rolling about like I'm literally on caution bear I was shocked at the nurse and I ever sit there again and ever since since he's such a bad as before session can you during the holidays. But I just seen a ladybug there was nothing Easter magazines at the year before expired so the fireplace have to be used for wet hair and snapping acid crinkled away photographs all the past of a present.

Chapter 4: We Just Hope You Give A Damn

Stop prettying him down. He had to stay pretty and not do anything. He couldn't get as bad as he wanted to be. In so many ways no one gives a darn

between comfort and discomfort is the title
It says September 7th this is the year 2019 this is a fun year there's a glorious year deercast beerfeast time went by so quickly There was no storm today I could not see the floor my house standing as w between comfort and discomfort is the title Everyday it's winter.

New line Monday
Blue Line and that you can see the indent and you just Uline
this is our switch to this is our switch to do indignant
indent

Chapter 4: We Just Hope You Give A Damn

Imperturbably beary. My favorite musical people has to be my sister Billy bear. before bear became all that she was in the store she started singing in high school and making records she's performed all over the world cleaning Japan she has very solid tympanic Club beats that could be played to her sultry jazz .

I first realize Billy bear she handed me a tape of a record a song. Like so many musical people she had a special vibrato Special Air a voice tune it just comes up through the air things. She is done inspiring and plastic her spirit is the LIE of love togetherness an extreme training Guelph complete imperturbe Lee Berry her life is been so balanced I just called her the Ampere terribly Barry she has been sitting I know existence for difference she likes sitting in the breeze and believe is an impenetrable day so let's all try to be infertile early Berry and this is where I'll begin my journey to be like my idol I will be in future we bury in so many ways let's start out On the 1st of December.

I was born in the middle of the month timing disco's at its height it was an air of sophistication I could just go on and on there to so many people I don't see why shutter success stop being poor success is being happy to get to a point of imperturbability Barry happiness mimosa's jovial is the honey dripping from a bear right after hurts hibernation during the cold cold existence of the planet Earth there are some for which Life Goes On there's some for which there's a different Tale the bear has no Tales of this every years the summer every year is the honey this girl is what so many try to be to not give it from anyting to walk through those bitter snooze so many people must do to be blinded my passion warmed by the strength of your ability strength to go and do it's almost animal is human to fail so many half can any of us be in Pretoria blueberry any of us have that drive their focus then one tunnel vision life it makes it hibernate through the dark days history rest upon our souls mini rester gifted and blessed is it gift people strike is not being the bear being the human causes are suffering that we mistreat that they will suffer this is the tale as so many others human suffering The Berry people seem so sweet they just picked the Bears right off a tree berries put them in there a little dresses and scoop them up and bowls and rush them in bowls symbols of Pies there others just we'll catch that when of sophistication and Air what will never be lift sway how will it be can we all try a real animals some of us just choose to be God can we all be in picture of Lee Barry can we all just ignore the superfluous strenuous activities hell on Earth we all Drive the existence of poverty existence of well does it take the money that's something she's never been abridge stuff and something of a circumstance provide to her tell unbridled ability money is cast upon them to be the animal they are they exist as no other no one can seem to not hurt yep they will never not help despair pull through he people shoot at it they always preserve it it's mistake simplicity it's snowing this to enjoy the wall to wrap up in the warmth of oneself to endure the cold this is story of many tales of many people try to accomplish such a thing so many ways so many jacket ways find ourselves why bear freeing ourselves to be the humane this is what many will never do so much easier how to do a kickover tent 2Pac to steal one's honey steal one's food does the bear often do that in cases of hunger what happens when the Bears not hungry what happens is plentiful the garden is semen really feel sorry for the bear do they ever wondered when there is not sufficient and provided fattened will there ever be a time will exist is this the question I choose to stay on the side of the rich the money The Castaways steripen girls anchor avarice Envy walk two roads been with the poor the unlikely perhaps ignored and the wealth I can't tell you what money. Sweetheart here's looking at the well to do the Wella biters all the success here's to that I'm staying in for terribly Barry Oh that men can do .

Early stage of life I have to say that coming down from many peaceful days it's not a immature are small at the beach for the world. No tornado Valley this what anyting what bow down to. Plus, adieu what is the easiest. I don't see it from the start I don't spread the legs of secession and meager attitudes. there's a life and happiness, steadiness, or failure.

I stayed at home in this dedication to life study. I want to tell about the song Take My Love From the berry imperatively berry girl it just is what people take. they must be loved someone must love it sure someone must be love. How much did be for who must love must they be what is week unless they be able to Strong has a case what does not impose what is not in search of the ugly of the swing and they hating Brothers.

Mist Berryessa name before thinks that music is not like art not like Tom had it Tom was an artist he did the cover the spot it's what disconnects the book and the world father this is the picture of me pictures of men a woman disconnecting happiness where did smothered the colors run it's the tears eliminate the breast of one side the funny Parable heartbeat just pulls us into the point of dying here you see a woman on the cover is a dead woman she cannot whisper a letter of this book.

she can say anything to lay down I never walk. It's just something shocking to let the readers understand the point of life it's not to be that is to live they're two totally different words don't look similar whatsoever I think today's paper called the car moves where we live Poland match match difference between the dying and living in the book called shoe the orange rain by Rachel K. Martin well this will hit the foot like a nail in Jesus on the cross. she killed the ground, was a slave 2 the mundane, or was everyone I did not care about the Hills of grass. Complete waste of words. what's this woman a prostitute? what she crown debutante person beauty queen of high school Rich Roll? was she all things of stupidity unknowingness ignorance or hid ugly imagine and she started.

let's just cover up this life in the grave let's throw the dirt do you disagree? what's rice on the high side paints. It's good to not feel like a zero.

Chapter 2: We Won't Look Like This

Required to run towards the track . Chloe did with chicken we thought you'd want looks like this Daphne could save your life.

Chapter 2: We Won’t Look Like This

How do we not look this way is it because it's Halloween to you it's because you can't see them the running everywhere this one in particular this one goes through Michelle mentioned in the Poetry of choosing your own trying there's something much like a spider on the wall just in the introvignes much like yourself reading interpreting songs like what I consider amuse hear it . to me this is the point of life one cannot get through when cannot pass through it

Chapter 5: This Is How Much He Cares

without fighting it without chewing Dan taking that last breath. is that how it is the last moment the last breath we

clench her teeth trying to survive a horrible World horrible tide change and Michelle was just a coaster the poet that must live within that moment but last poem has many different phases of change of the death of the dying as I mentioned in the last buck to the orange rain as you split and diet of course this means US Mini Splits a Bittersweet taste is in the orange rind 1 West recall supposed to leave us or last 10 to 15 seconds of Life flashing before eyes in these different frames these different stanzas of the poetry depicts all of those emotions racing before becoming free of ourselves when we come raging spirits everlasting life and a r motorcycles oh the last book was more about trying to chew to live eventually we get to the last year I think that's where this book will pick up movie about all that resides in the reflection of one's life at that last moment those last days Rising for the last challenge what will it be like for anyone Harrison introspection when's fall back people give so much advice how is it to look backwards and tell yourself or you will go for it no more. We won't look like this first of all like we are we want looks like we used to when you were sick dying decrepit weathering fattening whatever the case may be will become something that cannot recover to become the death supposedly we were big pile of dust he'll be thrown out to sea is this more of it was just an interest faction into what we will face something will will will be borne by.

We ran together Chloe we had every feeling that the last three days or empty and Shiloh of white snow ice, performance shows knives healthy walking bodies and medical and poverty togetherness much worse find sunny I need a. let's go think of moving for it. I will be there?

It's been quite a herring experience they just keep sitting there watching me will invisible people I watching you ain't heavy things in me that you and I feel their tactile you cannot see the sale practically breaking every bone in my body pinched they just keep taking all of my air and weighing me down odesse torturous all day and they keep me up all night I get no rest my eyes are peeled they're black and they are ready explosions all over the TV and nothing phases they're more than bothering me this is completely Concerta done bothering me she went to the back what's 2 two tier and that was all she does is Justin find the 2-day anymore of the two deer used to come around back I think someone hit and crush the deer and split it off to the side like a big pile of reverie organs and blood the head of used to recognize so dearly when her go baby dad Aerotek such

a beautiful picture that captured in time she said that was promised a the road a little baby doll left motherless they're practically skin and bone I just fed them she barely had nutrients and she tried to use all of them as much as she could feed her baby deer animals their highest extent to keep themselves in there offspring live people cannot do the same.

I heard it's racing is pounding his true knocking knocking as if wanting to be raped I think I have your heart he said it's putting me everywhere that you're never going to be what you say don't understand or appreciate themselves they don't want you to not really anything cuz you did not have this problem they want me to sit there and be there in and then you and Father's day but this isn't expanding to anyone that can guess what it seems people don't want to be bothered and I think of any way to bother me that care about him being agitated and extremes they've gone to the bothering you and that's better. now question art I thought. the news of sunny day and every computer I walk in front of was there when I left the building. I could see the smoke coming out of the windows watch the TV and explosions.

I'm in bed watching too finally just relaxing to a week ago and it was with just one more time. December went by so quickly and I just wanted to go and make it through the last year at of my job app. And I always felt just like it was had just happened but I was just going to pray for the first time. I just for a little a little yeah fresh air my father and I didn't run many travels at through the Midwest as much as we went through more in St Louis we saw the downtown area we saw the malls that's been closed a lot of the Sea Breeze old friends used to live places that the houses are not as well kept you probably are now condemned you are perhaps someone else is living there there's this not really a place where a lot of people are still states structured it's not like living in New Orleans just had its pride and its culture for many many years. drove me to school quite a bit that is only when and if the last time he dropped me off it was a very Rocky rainy morning I said hello to have then he drove off to the Sun.

medium sized statue woman with all of these cat like I appearance perm straighten hair I'm sorry my pigtails blow in the Wind he went further and further

into the Sun. That was him going to the start of his day every day started with a Sun Ray and going away to begin my beach walk into start of my new school year. Seemed like he was going into the sun to me Style of course he was not driving into the sun just a figure of speech for your child and you're not too tall can't see too far over the hell seems like that's where he's gay.

of course it's a whole different culture to be involved in different kinds of weather and different kinds of States Midwest pretty humdrum you ever winter spring or summer or fall more of the summer in the winter is definite the fall in the spring 10 do Collide somewhat but the leaves do fall by the end of September. squinting outside of the window I looked at how everyone was little dots down from an airplane there's so many people about because it was the July 4th holiday and all the sudden there was planking and clashing airplanes flying and firecrackers going. can hear loads and loads a fireworks when their direction under the arch I get my daughter look at this time. My mind was empty with no hope for anyting a few hours went by and I saw a big cloud in the sky jumped Define it was on the floor.

rom extreme cold that enter through the door so that has. The house was at least four stories Square Windows in each wall you so looks of a typical Colonial home it was a blue Hound blue screen siding panels made of wood and standings past hundred year everyone try to be there everyone try to want to the name of the house kept everyone sent everyone wanted to wake up there.

I did I ran to the window and I ran down the hall and gressive Lee ran through the waves of all of the air that collided with how it ripped through my grapes yes I fell on the floor rolling about like I'm literally on caution bear I was shocked at the nurse and I ever sit there again and ever since since he's such a bad as before session can you during the holidays. But I just seen a ladybug there was nothing Easter magazines at the year before expired so the fireplace have to be used for wet hair and snapping acid crinkled away photographs all the past of a present.

Chapter 4: We Just Hope You Give A Damn

Chapter 6: Fine

Stop prettying him down. He had to stay pretty and not do anything. He couldn't get as bad as he wanted to be. In so many ways no one gives a darn

between comfort and discomfort is the title
It says September 7th this is the year 2019 this is a fun year there's a glorious year deercast beerfeast time went by so quickly There was no storm today I could not see the floor my house standing as w between comfort and discomfort is the title
Everyday it's winter.

New line Monday
Blue Line and that you can see the indent and you just Uline
this is our switch to this is our switch to do indignant
indent

Chapter 1: Zero

Imperturbably beary. My favorite musical people has to be my sister Billy bear. before bear became all that she was in the store she started singing in high school and making records she's performed all over the

world cleaning Japan she has very solid tympanic Club beats that could be played to her sultry jazz .

I first realize Billy bear she handed me a tape of a record a song. Like so many musical people she had a special vibrato Special Air a voice tune it just comes up through the air things. She is done inspiring and plastic her spirit is the LIE of love togetherness an extreme training Guelph complete imperturbe Lee Berry her life is been so balanced I just called her the Ampere terribly Barry she has been sitting I know existence for difference she likes sitting in the breeze and believe is an impenetrable day so let's all try to be infertile early Berry and this is where I'll begin my journey to be like my idol I will be in future we bury in so many ways let's start out On the 1st of December.

I was born in the middle of the month timing disco's at its height it was an air of sophistication I could just go on and on there to so many people I don't see why shutter success stop being poor success is being happy to get to a point of imperturbability Barry happiness mimosa's jovial is the honey dripping from a bear right after hurts hibernation during the cold cold

existence of the planet Earth there are some for which Life Goes On there's some for which there's a different Tale the bear has no Tales of this every years the summer every year is the honey this girl is what so many try to be to not give it from anyting to walk through those bitter snooze so many people must do to be blinded my passion warmed by the strength of your ability strength to go and do it's almost animal is human to fail so many half can any of us be in Pretoria blueberry any of us have that drive their focus then one tunnel vision life it makes it hibernate through the dark days history rest upon our souls mini rester gifted and blessed is it gift people strike is not being the bear being the human causes are suffering that we mistreat that they will suffer this is the tale as so many others human suffering The Berry people seem so sweet they just picked the Bears right off a tree berries put them in there a little dresses and scoop them up and bowls and rush them in bowls symbols of Pies there others just we'll catch that when of sophistication and Air what will never be lift sway how will it be can we all try a real animals some of us just choose to be God can we all be in picture of Lee Barry can we all just ignore the

superfluous strenuous activities hell on Earth we all
Drive the existence of poverty existence of well does it
take the money that's something she's never been abridge
stuff and something of a circumstance provide to her
tell unbridled ability money is cast upon them to be the
animal they are they exist as no other no one can seem
to not hurt yep they will never not help despair pull
through he people shoot at it they always preserve it
it's mistake simplicity it's snowing this to enjoy the
wall to wrap up in the warmth of oneself to endure the
cold this is story of many tales of many people try to
accomplish such a thing so many ways so many jacket ways
find ourselves why bear freeing ourselves to be the
humane this is what many will never do so much easier
how to do a kickover tent 2Pac to steal one's honey
steal one's food does the bear often do that in cases of
hunger what happens when the Bears not hungry what
happens is plentiful the garden is semen really feel
sorry for the bear do they ever wondered when there is
not sufficient and provided fattened will there ever be
a time will exist is this the question I choose to stay
on the side of the rich the money The Castaways steripen
girls anchor avarice Envy walk two roads been with the

poor the unlikely perhaps ignored and the wealth I can't tell you what money. Sweetheart here's looking at the well to do the Wella biters all the success here's to that I'm staying in for terribly Barry Oh that men can do .

Early stage of life I have to say that coming down from many peaceful days it's not a immature are small at the beach for the world. No tornado Valley this what anyting what bow down to. Plus, adieu what is the easiest. I don't see it from the start I don't spread the legs of secession and meager attitudes. there's a life and happiness, steadiness, or failure.

I stayed at home in this dedication to life study. I want to tell about the song Take My Love From the berry imperatively berry girl it just is what people take. they must be loved someone must love it sure someone must be love. How much did be for who must love must they be what is week unless they be able to Strong has a case what does not impose what is not in search of the ugly of the swing and they hating Brothers.

Mist Berryessa name before thinks that music is not like art not like Tom had it Tom was an artist he did the cover the spot it's what disconnects the book and the world father this is the picture of me pictures of men a woman disconnecting happiness where did smothered the colors run it's the tears eliminate the breast of one side the funny Parable heartbeat just pulls us into the point of dying here you see a woman on the cover is a dead woman she cannot whisper a letter of this book.

she can say anything to lay down I never walk. It's just something shocking to let the readers understand the point of life it's not to be that is to live they're two totally different words don't look similar whatsoever I think today's paper called the car moves where we live Poland match match difference between the dying and living in the book called shoe the orange rain by Rachel K. Martin well this will hit the foot like a nail in Jesus on the cross. she killed the ground, was a slave 2 the mundane, or was everyone I did not care about the Hills of grass. Complete waste of words. what's this woman a prostitute? what she crown debutante person beauty queen of high school Rich Roll? was she all things of stupidity unknowingness ignorance or hid ugly imagine and she started.

let's just cover up this life in the grave let's throw the dirt do you disagree? what's rice on the high side paints. It's good to not feel like a zero.

Chapter 2: We Won't Look Like This

Chapter 7: We'll See What We Must Do Now

Required to run towards the track . Chloe did with chicken we thought you'd want looks like this Daphne could save your life.

Chapter 2: We Won't Look Like This

How do we not look this way is it because it's Halloween to you it's because you can't see them the running everywhere this one in particular this one goes through Michelle mentioned in the Poetry of choosing your own trying there's something much like a spider on the wall just in the introvignes much like yourself reading interpreting songs like what I consider amuse hear it . to me this is the point of life one cannot get through when cannot pass through it without fighting it without chewing Dan taking that last breath. is that how it is the last moment the last breath we clench her teeth trying to survive a horrible World horrible tide change and Michelle was just a coaster the poet that must live within that moment but last poem has many different phases of change of the death of the dying as I mentioned in the last buck to the orange rain as you split and diet of course this means US Mini Splits a Bittersweet taste is in the orange rind 1 West recall supposed to leave us or last 10 to 15 seconds of Life flashing before eyes in these different frames these different stanzas of the poetry depicts all of those emotions racing before becoming free of ourselves when we come raging spirits everlasting life and a r motorcycles oh the last book was more about trying to chew to live eventually we get to the last year I think that's where this book will pick up movie about all that resides in the reflection of one's life at that last moment those last days Rising for the last challenge what will it be like for anyone Harrison introspection when's fall back people give so much advice how is it to look backwards and tell yourself or you will go for it no more. We won't look like this first of all like we are we want looks like we used to when you were sick dying decrepit weathering fattening whatever the case may be will become something that cannot recover to become the death supposedly we were big pile of dust he'll be thrown out to sea is this more of it was just an interest faction into what we will face something will will will be borne by.

We ran together Chloe we had every feeling that the last three days or empty and Shiloh of white snow ice, performance shows knives healthy walking bodies and medical and poverty togetherness much worse find sunny I need a. let's go think of moving for it. I will be there?

It's been quite a herring experience they just keep sitting there watching me will invisible people I watching you ain't heavy things in me that you and I feel their tactile you cannot see the sale practically breaking every bone in my body pinched they just keep taking all of my air and weighing me down odesse torturous all day and they keep me up all night I get no rest my eyes are peeled they're black and they are ready explosions all over the TV and nothing phases they're more than bothering me this is completely Concerta done bothering me she went to the back what's 2 two tier and that was all she does is Justin find the 2-day anymore of the two deer used to come around back I think someone hit and crush the deer and split it off to the side like a big pile of reverie organs and blood the head of used to recognize so dearly when her go baby dad Aerotek such a beautiful picture that captured in time she said that was promised a the road a little baby doll left motherless they're practically skin and bone I just fed them she barely had nutrients and she tried to use all of them as much as she could feed her baby deer animals their highest extent to keep themselves in there offspring live people cannot do the same.

I heard it's racing is pounding his true knocking knocking as if wanting to be raped I think I have your heart he said it's putting me everywhere that you're never going to be what you say don't understand or appreciate themselves they don't want you to not really anything cuz you did not have this problem they want me to sit there and be there in and then you and Father's day but this isn't expanding to anyone that can guess what it seems people don't want to be bothered and I think of any way to bother me that care about him being agitated and extremes they've gone to the bothering you and that's better. now question art I thought. the news of sunny day and every computer I walk in front of was there when I left the building. I could see the smoke coming out of the windows watch the TV and explosions. I'm in bed watching too finally just relaxing to a week ago and it was with just one more time. December went by so quickly and I just wanted to go and make it through the last year at of my job app. And I always felt just like it was had just happened but I was just going to pray for the first time. I just for a little a little yeah fresh air my father and I didn't run many travels at through the Midwest as much as we went through more in St Louis we saw the downtown area we saw the malls that's been closed a lot of the Sea Breeze old friends used to live places that the houses are not as well kept you probably are now condemned you are perhaps someone else is living there there's this not really a place where a lot of people are still states structured it's not like living in New Orleans just had its pride and its culture for many many years. drove me to school quite a bit that is only when and if the last time he dropped me off it was a very Rocky rainy morning I said hello to have then he drove off to the Sun.

medium sized statue woman with all of these cat like I appearance perm straighten hair I'm sorry my pigtails blow in the Wind he went further and further into the Sun. That was him going to the start of his day every day started with a Sun Ray and going away to begin my beach walk into start of my new school year. Seemed like he was going into the sun to me Style of course he was not driving into the sun just a figure of speech for your child and you're not too tall can't see too far over the hell seems like that's where he's gay.

of course it's a whole different culture to be involved in different kinds of weather and different kinds of States Midwest pretty humdrum you ever winter spring or summer or fall more of the summer in the winter is definite the fall in the spring 10 do Collide somewhat but the leaves do fall by the end of September. squinting outside of the window I looked at how everyone was little dots down from an airplane there's so many people about because it was the July 4th holiday and all the sudden there was planking and clashing airplanes flying and firecrackers going. can hear loads and loads a fireworks when their direction under the arch I get my daughter look at this time. My mind was empty with no hope for anyting a few hours went by and I saw a big cloud in the sky jumped Define it was on the floor.

Chapter 8: Please YOu are Obama

He met a friend and yet we couldn't go through Finding Nemo it was a coffee all black coffee everyday black coffee Olympic cream in the coffee Willow thought you was black it was dark and made him crazy he went looking for anyone finally came up Iraq we found his child in a Ciroc you're really funny story Stanley Charlie found any survivors how she kept hiding from him somebody for children who don't want to be you're off and running I didn't see what the point of it is till they get to the point. Lucy Wizards daughter's name and she spoke unhinged address of the clock as it sat on the wall S4 had school in the plants and everything that we saw stay consistent we were together we're overwhelmed to begin every day but there was no where we were going we were all very happy to finally be junior high in front of all of the bag sickle writers they all took a plunge it was just the sun rise of the Cascades when she was in the big Village running and soon to be in the middle of September for bats were the roads were all the problems has one set there I thought well when I go to Houston Texas or something while we didn't want to sit Africa bigger place but the car couldn't go anywhere it's just broken down there always just imagine you what we might do and he was still looking for his daughter still trying to figure out what to be there by funny name for Lucy means like can see the light of it

The leftover people were all scattered throughout the yard. After every day he had ended we did not get to ignore the cold feet that cat walking towards the other ones. Many of them wanted to join the others and pray for all of their cold feet to bow to their heads in the Forum of a monstrous pleasure so they'd all set there we had to take a trip to New Orleans and people did not think this was a good idea they did not like their feet being sick isn't not like anything they were going to be reaching for many many many many many many feet.

the day before they all had left to go to Spencer's store and buy the most expensive sheets. They were never going to be put never pack from the rooms they're never going to be not broken and they just wanted to feel as if they jumped off of their beds Temple Run.

the night before of what's his call this December 2018 7 in the morning it was the most beautiful day. The snow still nothing moved nothing was alert. The only thing that could have been better was seeing the dogs air blow out of his nose from extreme cold that enter through the door so that has. The house was at least four stories Square Windows in each wall you so looks of a typical Colonial home it was a blue Hound blue screen siding panels made of wood and standings past hundred year everyone try to be there everyone try to want to the name of the house kept everyone sent everyone wanted to wake up there.

I did I ran to the window and I ran down the hall and gressive Lee ran through the waves of all of the air that collided with how it ripped through my grapes yes I fell on the floor rolling about like I'm literally on caution bear I was shocked at the nurse and I ever sit there again and ever since since he's such a bad as before session can you during the holidays. But I just seen a ladybug there was nothing Easter magazines at the year before expired so the fireplace have to be used for wet hair and snapping acid crinkled away photographs all the past of a present.

Chapter 4: We Just Hope You Give A Damn

Stop prettying him down. He had to stay pretty and not do anything. He couldn't get as bad as he wanted to be. In so many ways no one gives a darn

between comfort and discomfort is the title
It says September 7th this is the year 2019 this is a fun year there's a glorious year deercast beerfeast time went by so quickly There was no storm today I could not see the floor my house standing as w between comfort and discomfort is the title Everyday it's winter.

New line Monday
Blue Line and that you can see the indent and you just Uline
this is our switch to this is our switch to do indignant
indent

Chapter 1: Zero

Imperturbably beary. My favorite musical people has to be my sister Billy bear. before bear became all that she was in the store she started singing in high school and making records she's performed all over the world cleaning Japan she has very solid tympanic Club beats that could be played to her sultry jazz .

I first realize Billy bear she handed me a tape of a record a song. Like so many musical people she had a special vibrato Special Air a voice tune it just comes up through the air things. She is done inspiring and plastic her spirit is the LIE of love togetherness an extreme training Guelph complete imperturbe Lee Berry her life is been so balanced I just called her the Ampere terribly Barry she has been sitting I know existence for difference she likes sitting in the breeze and believe is an impenetrable day so let's all try to be infertile early Berry and this is where I'll begin my journey to be like my idol I will be in future we bury in so many ways let's start out On the 1st of December.

I was born in the middle of the month timing disco's at its height it was an air of sophistication I could just go on and on there to so many people I don't see why shutter success stop being poor success is being happy to get to a point of imperturbability Barry happiness mimosa's jovial is the honey dripping from a bear right after hurts hibernation during the cold cold existence of the planet Earth there are some for which Life Goes On there's some for which there's a different

Tale the bear has no Tales of this every years the summer every year is the honey this girl is what so many try to be to not give it from anyting to walk through those bitter snooze so many people must do to be blinded my passion warmed by the strength of your ability strength to go and do it's almost animal is human to fail so many half can any of us be in Pretoria blueberry any of us have that drive their focus then one tunnel vision life it makes it hibernate through the dark days history rest upon our souls mini rester gifted and blessed is it gift people strike is not being the bear being the human causes are suffering that we mistreat that they will suffer this is the tale as so many others human suffering The Berry people seem so sweet they just picked the Bears right off a tree berries put them in there a little dresses and scoop them up and bowls and rush them in bowls symbols of Pies there others just we'll catch that when of sophistication and Air what will never be lift sway how will it be can we all try a real animals some of us just choose to be God can we all be in picture of Lee Barry can we all just ignore the superfluous strenuous activities hell on Earth we all Drive the existence of poverty existence of well does it take the money that's something she's never been abridge stuff and something of a circumstance provide to her tell unbridled ability money is cast upon them to be the animal they are they exist as no other no one can seem to not hurt yep they will never not help despair pull through he people shoot at it they always preserve it it's mistake simplicity it's snowing this to enjoy the wall to wrap up in the warmth of oneself to endure the cold this is story of many tales of many people try to accomplish such a thing so many ways so many jacket ways find ourselves why bear freeing ourselves to be the humane this is what many will never do so much easier how to do a kickover tent 2Pac to steal one's honey steal one's food does the bear often do that in cases of hunger what happens when the Bears not hungry what happens is plentiful the garden is semen really feel sorry for the bear do they ever wondered when there is not sufficient and provided fattened will there ever be a time will exist is this the question I choose to stay on the side of the rich the money The Castaways steripen girls anchor avarice Envy walk two roads been with the poor the unlikely perhaps ignored and the wealth I can't tell you what money. Sweetheart here's looking at the well to do the Wella biters all the success here's to that I'm staying in for terribly Barry Oh that men can do .

Early stage of life I have to say that coming down from many peaceful days it's not a immature are small at the beach for the world. No tornado Valley this what anyting what bow down to. Plus, adieu what is the easiest. I don't see it from the start I don't spread the legs of secession and meager attitudes. there's a life and happiness, steadiness, or failure.

I stayed at home in this dedication to life study. I want to tell about the song Take My Love From the berry imperatively berry girl it just is what people take. they must be loved someone must love it sure someone must be love. How much did be for who must love must they be what is week unless they be able to Strong has a case what does not impose what is not in search of the ugly of the swing and they hating Brothers.

Mist Berryessa name before thinks that music is not like art not like Tom had it Tom was an artist he did the cover the spot it's what disconnects the book and the world father this is the picture of me pictures of men a woman disconnecting happiness where did smothered the colors run it's the tears eliminate the breast of one side the funny Parable heartbeat just pulls us into the point of dying here you see a woman on the cover is a dead woman she cannot whisper a letter of this book.

she can say anything to lay down I never walk. It's just something shocking to let the readers understand the point of life it's not to be that is to live they're two totally different words don't look similar whatsoever I think today's paper called the car moves where we live Poland match match difference between the dying and living in the book called shoe the orange rain by Rachel K. Martin well this will hit the foot like a nail in Jesus on the cross. she killed the ground, was a slave 2 the mundane, or was everyone I did not care about the Hills of grass. Complete waste of words. what's this woman a prostitute? what she crown debutante person beauty queen of high school Rich Roll?

was she all things of stupidity unknowingness ignorance or hid ugly imagine and she started.

let's just cover up this life in the grave let's throw the dirt do you disagree? what's rice on the high side paints. It's good to not feel like a zero.

Chapter 2: We Won't Look Like This

Required to run towards the track . Chloe did with chicken we thought you'd want looks like this Daphne could save your life.

Chapter 2: We Won't Look Like This

How do we not look this way is it because it's Halloween to you it's because you can't see them the running everywhere this one in particular this one goes through Michelle mentioned in the Poetry of choosing your own trying there's something much like a spider on the wall just in the introvignes much like yourself reading interpreting songs like what I consider amuse hear it . to me this is the point of life one cannot get through when cannot pass through it without fighting it without chewing Dan taking that last breath. is that how it is the last moment the last breath we clench her teeth trying to survive a horrible World horrible tide change and Michelle was just a coaster the poet that must live within that moment but last poem has many different phases of change of the death of the dying as I mentioned in the last buck to the orange rain as you split and diet of course this means US Mini Splits a Bittersweet taste is in the orange rind 1 West recall supposed to leave us or last 10 to 15 seconds of Life flashing before eyes in these different frames these different stanzas of the poetry depicts all of those emotions racing before becoming free of ourselves when we come raging spirits everlasting life and a r motorcycles oh the last book was more about trying to chew to live eventually we get to the last year I think that's where this book will pick up movie about all that resides in the reflection of one's life at that last moment those last days Rising for the last challenge what will it be like for anyone Harrison introspection when's fall back people give so much advice how is it to look backwards and tell yourself or you will go for it no more. We won't look like this first of all like we are we want looks like we used to when you were sick dying decrepit weathering fattening whatever the case may be will become something that cannot recover to become the death supposedly we were big pile of dust he'll be thrown out to sea is this more of it was just an interest faction into what we will face something will will will be borne by.

We ran together Chloe we had every feeling that the last three days or empty and Shiloh of white snow ice, performance shows knives healthy walking bodies and medical and poverty togetherness much worse find sunny I need a. let's go think of moving for it. I will be there?

It's been quite a herring experience they just keep sitting there watching me will invisible people I watching you ain't heavy things in me that you and I feel their tactile you cannot see the sale practically breaking every bone in my body pinched they just keep taking all of my air and weighing me down odesse torturous all day and they keep me up all night I get no rest my eyes are peeled they're black and they are ready explosions all over the TV and nothing phases they're more than bothering me this is completely Concerta done bothering me she went to the back what's 2 two tier and that was all she does is Justin find the 2-day anymore of the two deer used to come around back I think someone hit and crush the deer and split it off to the side like a big pile of

Chapter 10: Ohh! Don't Say That

reverie organs and blood the head of used to recognize so dearly when her go baby dad Aerotek such a beautiful picture

that captured in time she said that was promised a the road a little baby doll left motherless they're practically skin and bone I just fed them she barely had nutrients and she tried to use all of them as much as she could feed her baby deer animals their highest extent to keep themselves in there offspring live people cannot do the same.

I heard it's racing is pounding his true knocking knocking as if wanting to be raped I think I have your heart he said it's putting me everywhere that you're never going to be what you say don't understand or

appreciate themselves they don't want you to not really anything cuz you did not have this problem they want me to sit there and be there in and then you and Father's day but this isn't expanding to anyone that can guess what it seems people don't want to be bothered and I think of any way to bother me that care about him being agitated and extremes they've gone to the bothering you and that's better. now question art I thought. the news of sunny day and every computer I walk in front of was there when I left the building. I could see the smoke coming out of the windows watch the TV and explosions. I'm in bed watching too finally just relaxing to a week ago and it was with just one more time. December went by so quickly and I just wanted to go and make it through the last year at of my job app. And I always felt just like it was had just happened but I was just going to pray for the first time. I just for a little a little yeah fresh air my father and I didn't run many travels at through the Midwest as much as we went through more in St Louis we saw the downtown area we saw the malls that's been closed a lot of the Sea Breeze old friends used to live places that the houses are not as well kept you probably are now condemned you are perhaps someone else is living there there's this not really a place where a lot of people are still states structured it's not like living in New Orleans just had its pride and its culture for many many years. drove me to school quite a bit that is only when and if the last time he dropped me off it was a very Rocky rainy morning I said hello to have then he drove off to the Sun.

medium sized statue woman with all of these cat like I appearance perm straighten hair I'm sorry my pigtails blow in the Wind he went further and further into the Sun. That was him going to the start of his day every day started with a Sun Ray and going away to begin my beach walk into start of my new school year. Seemed like he was going into the sun to me Style of course he was not driving into the sun just a figure of speech for your child and you're not too tall can't see too far over the hell seems like that's where he's gay.

of course it's a whole different culture to be involved in different kinds of weather and different kinds of States Midwest pretty humdrum you ever winter spring or summer or fall more of the summer in the winter is definite the fall in the spring 10 do Collide somewhat but the leaves do fall by the end of September. squinting outside of the window I looked at how everyone was little dots down from an airplane there's so many people about because it was the July 4th holiday and all the sudden there was planking and clashing airplanes flying and firecrackers going. can hear loads and loads a fireworks when their direction under the arch I get my daughter look at this time. My mind was empty with no hope for anyting a few hours went by and I saw a big cloud in the sky jumped Define it was on the floor.

vvvrom extreme cold that enter through the door so that has. The house was at least four stories Square Windows in each wall you so looks of a typical Colonial home it was a blue Hound blue screen siding panels made of wood and standings past hundred year everyone try to be there everyone try to want to the name of the house kept everyone sent everyone wanted to wake up there.

I did I ran to the window and I ran down the hall and gressive Lee ran through the waves of all of the air that collided with how it ripped through my grapes yes I fell on the floor rolling about like I'm literally on caution bear I was shocked at the nurse and I ever sit there again and ever since since he's such a bad as before session can you during the holidays. But I just seen a ladybug there was nothing Easter magazines at the

year before expired so the fireplace have to be used for wet hair and snapping acid crinkled away photographs all the past of a present.

Chapter 4: We Just Hope You Give A Damn

Stop prettying him down. He had to stay pretty and not do anything. He couldn't get as bad as he wanted to be. In so many ways no one gives a darn

between comfort and discomfort is the title
It says September 7th this is the year 2019 this is a fun year there's a glorious year deercast beerfeast time went by so quickly There was no storm today I could not see the floor my house standing as w between comfort and discomfort is the title Everyday it's winter.

New line Monday
Blue Line and that you can see the indent and you just Uline
this is our switch to this is our switch to do indignant
indent

Chapter 1: Zero

Imperturbably beary. My favorite musical people has to be my sister Billy bear. before bear became all that she was in the store she started singing in high school and making records she's performed all over the world cleaning Japan she has very solid tympanic Club beats that could be played to her sultry jazz .

I first realize Billy bear she handed me a tape of a record a song. Like so many musical people she had a special vibrato Special Air a voice tune it just comes up through the air things. She is done inspiring and plastic her spirit is the LIE of love togetherness an extreme training Guelph complete imperturbe Lee Berry her life is been so balanced I just called her the Ampere terribly Barry she has been sitting I know existence for difference she likes sitting in the breeze and believe is an impenetrable day so let's all try to be infertile early Berry and this is where I'll begin my journey to be like my idol I will be in future we bury in so many ways let's start out On the 1st of December.

I was born in the middle of the month timing disco's at its height it was an air of sophistication I could just go on and on there to so many people I don't

see why shutter success stop being poor success is being happy to get to a point of imperturbability Barry happiness mimosa's jovial is the honey dripping from a bear right after hurts hibernation during the cold cold existence of the planet Earth there are some for which Life Goes On there's some for which there's a different Tale the bear has no Tales of this every years the summer every year is the honey this girl is what so many try to be to not give it from anyting to walk through those bitter snooze so many people must do to be blinded my passion warmed by the strength of your ability strength to go and do it's almost animal is human to fail so many half can any of us be in Pretoria blueberry any of us have that drive their focus then one tunnel vision life it makes it hibernate through the dark days history rest upon our souls mini rester gifted and

Chapter 11: Really? This Is Us?

blessed is it gift people strike is not being the bear being the human causes are suffering that we mistreat that they will suffer this is the tale as so many others human suffering The Berry people seem so sweet they just picked the Bears right off a tree berries put them in there a little dresses and scoop them up and bowls and rush them in bowls symbols of Pies there others just we'll catch that when of sophistication and Air what will never be lift sway how will it be can we all try a real animals some of us just choose to be God can we all be in picture of Lee Barry can we all just ignore the superfluous strenuous activities hell on Earth we all Drive the existence of poverty existence of well does it take the money that's something she's never been abridge stuff and something of a circumstance provide to her tell unbridled ability money is cast upon them to be the animal they are they exist as no other no one can seem to not hurt yep they will never not help despair pull through he people shoot at it they always preserve it it's mistake simplicity it's snowing this to enjoy the wall to wrap up in the warmth of oneself to endure the cold this is story of many tales of many people try to accomplish such a thing so many ways so many jacket ways find ourselves why bear freeing ourselves to be the humane this is what many will never do so much easier how to do a kickover tent 2Pac to steal one's honey steal one's food does the bear often do that in cases of hunger what happens when the Bears not hungry what happens is plentiful the garden is semen really feel sorry for the bear do they ever wondered when there is not sufficient and provided fattened will there ever be a time will exist is this the question I choose to stay on the side of the rich the money The Castaways steripen girls anchor avarice Envy walk two roads been with the poor the unlikely perhaps ignored and the wealth I can't tell you what money. Sweetheart here's looking at the well to do the Wella biters all the success here's to that I'm staying in for terribly Barry Oh that men can do .

Early stage of life I have to say that coming down from many peaceful days it's not a immature are small at the beach for the world. No tornado Valley this what anyting what bow down to. Plus, adieu what is the easiest. I don't see it from the start I don't spread the legs of secession and meager attitudes. there's a life and happiness, steadiness, or failure.

I stayed at home in this dedication to life study. I want to tell about the song Take My Love From the berry imperatively berry girl it just is what people take. they must be loved someone must love it sure someone must be love. How much did be for who must love must they be what is week unless they be able to Strong has a case what does not impose what is not in search of the ugly of the swing and they hating Brothers.

Mist Berryessa name before thinks that music is not like art not like Tom had it Tom was an artist he did the cover the spot it's what disconnects the book and the world father this is the picture of me pictures of men a woman disconnecting happiness where did smothered the colors run it's the tears eliminate the breast of one side the funny Parable heartbeat just pulls us into the point of dying here you see a woman on the cover is a dead woman she cannot whisper a letter of this book.

she can say anything to lay down I never walk. It's just something shocking to let the readers understand the point of life it's not to be that is to live they're two totally different words don't look similar whatsoever I think today's paper called the car moves where we live Poland match match difference between the dying and living in the book called shoe the orange rain by Rachel K. Martin well this will hit the foot like a nail in Jesus on the cross. she killed the ground, was a slave 2 the mundane, or was everyone I did not care about the Hills of grass. Complete waste of words. what's this woman a prostitute? what she crown debutante person beauty queen of high school Rich Roll? was she all things of stupidity unknowingness ignorance or hid ugly imagine and she started.

let's just cover up this life in the grave let's throw the dirt do you disagree? what's rice on the high side paints. It's good to not feel like a zero.

Chapter 2: We Won't Look Like This

Required to run towards the track . Chloe did with chicken we thought you'd want looks like this Daphne could save your life.

Chapter 2: We Won't Look Like This

How do we not look this way is it because it's Halloween to you it's because you can't see them the running everywhere this one in particular this one goes through Michelle mentioned in the Poetry of choosing your own trying there's something much like a spider on the wall just in the introvignes much like yourself reading

interpreting songs like what I consider amuse hear it .
to me this is the point of life one cannot get through
when cannot pass through it without fighting it without
chewing Dan taking that last breath. is that how it is
the last moment the last breath we clench her teeth
trying to survive a horrible World horrible tide change
and Michelle was just a coaster the poet that must live
within that moment but last poem has many different
phases of change of the death of the dying as I
mentioned in the last buck to the orange rain as you
split and diet of course this means US Mini Splits a
Bittersweet taste is in the orange rind 1 West recall
supposed to leave us or last 10 to 15 seconds of Life
flashing before eyes in these different frames these
different stanzas of the poetry depicts all of those
emotions racing before becoming free of ourselves when
we come raging spirits everlasting life and a r
motorcycles oh the last book was more about trying to
chew to live eventually we get to the last year I think
that's where this book will pick up movie about all that
resides in the reflection of one's life at that last
moment those last days Rising for the last challenge
what will it be like for anyone Harrison introspection

when's fall back people give so much advice how is it to look backwards and tell yourself or you will go for it no more. We won't look like this first of all like we are we want looks like we used to when you were sick dying decrepit weathering fattening whatever the case may be will become something that cannot recover to become the death supposedly we were big pile of dust he'll be thrown out to sea is this more of it was just an interest faction into what we will face something will will will be borne by.

We ran together Chloe we had every feeling that the last three days or empty and Shiloh of white snow ice, performance shows knives healthy walking bodies and medical and poverty togetherness much worse find sunny I need a. let's go think of moving for it. I will be there?

It's been quite a herring experience they just keep sitting there watching me will invisible people I watching you ain't heavy things in me that you and I feel their tactile you cannot see the sale practically breaking every bone in my body pinched they just keep taking all of my air and weighing me

Chapter 12: Who Cares?

down odesse torturous all day and they keep me up all night I get no rest my eyes are peeled they're black and they are

ready explosions all over the TV and nothing phases they're more than bothering me this is completely Concerta done bothering me she went to the back what's 2 two tier and that was all she does is Justin find the 2-day anymore of the two deer used to come around back I think someone hit and crush the deer and split it off to the side like a big pile of reverie organs and blood the head of used to recognize so dearly when her go baby dad Aerotek such a beautiful picture that captured in time she said that was promised a the road a little baby doll left motherless they're practically skin and bone I just fed them she barely had nutrients and she tried to use all of them as much as she could feed her baby deer animals their highest extent to keep themselves in there offspring live people cannot do the same.

I heard it's racing is pounding his true knocking knocking as if wanting to be raped I think I have your heart he said it's putting me everywhere that you're never going to be what you say don't understand or appreciate themselves they don't want you to not really anything cuz you did not have this problem they want me to sit there and be there in and then you and Father's day but this isn't expanding to anyone that can guess what it seems people don't want to be bothered and I think of any way to bother me that care about him being agitated and extremes they've gone to the bothering you and that's better. now question art I thought. the news of sunny day and every computer I walk in front of was there when I left the building. I could see the smoke coming out of the windows watch the TV and explosions. I'm in bed watching too finally just relaxing to a week ago and it was with just one more time. December went by so quickly and I just wanted to go and make it through the last year at of my job app. And I always felt just like it was had just happened but I was just going to pray for the first time. I just for a little a little yeah fresh air my father and I didn't run many travels at through the Midwest as much as we went through more

in St Louis we saw the downtown area we saw the malls that's been closed a lot of the Sea Breeze old friends used to live places that the houses are not as well kept you probably are now condemned you are perhaps someone else is living there there's this not really a place where a lot of people are still states structured it's not like living in New Orleans just had its pride and its culture for many many years. drove me to school quite a bit that is only when and if the last time he dropped me off it was a very Rocky rainy morning I said hello to have then he drove off to the Sun.

medium sized statue woman with all of these cat like I appearance perm straighten hair I'm sorry my pigtails blow in the Wind he went further and further into the Sun. That was him going to the start of his day every day started with a Sun Ray and going away to begin my beach walk into start of my new school year. Seemed like he was going into the sun to me Style of course he was not driving into the sun just a figure of speech for your child and you're not too tall can't see too far over the hell seems like that's where he's gay.

of course it's a whole different culture to be involved in different kinds of weather and different kinds of States Midwest pretty humdrum you ever winter spring or summer or fall more of the summer in the winter is definite the fall in the spring 10 do Collide somewhat but the leaves do fall by the end of September. squinting outside of the window I looked at how everyone was little dots down from an airplane there's so many people about because it was the July 4th holiday and all the sudden there was planking and clashing airplanes flying and firecrackers going. can hear loads and loads a fireworks when their direction under the arch I get my daughter look at this time. My mind was empty with no hope for anyting a few hours went by and I saw a big cloud in the sky jumped Define it was on the floor.

Chapter 3: We Just Don’t Care

He met a friend and yet we couldn't go through Finding Nemo it was a coffee all black coffee everyday black coffee Olympic cream in the coffee Willow thought you was black it was dark and made him crazy he went looking for anyone finally came up Iraq we found his child in a Ciroc you're really funny story Stanley Charlie found any survivors how she kept hiding from him somebody for children who don't want to be you're off and running I didn't see what the point of it is till they get to the point. Lucy Wizards daughter's name and she spoke unhinged address of the clock as it sat on the wall S4 had school in the plants and everything that we saw stay consistent we were together we're overwhelmed to begin

every day but there was no where we were going we were all very happy to finally be junior high in front of all of the bag sickle writers they all took a plunge it was just the sun rise of the Cascades when she was in the big Village running and soon to be in the middle of September for bats were the roads were all the problems has one set there I thought well when I go to Houston Texas or something while we didn't want to sit Africa bigger place but the car couldn't go anywhere it's just broken down there always just imagine you what we might do and he was still looking for his daughter still trying to figure out what to be there by funny name for Lucy means like can see the light of it

The leftover people were all scattered throughout the yard. After every day he had ended we did not get to ignore the cold feet that cat walking towards the other ones. Many of them wanted to join the others and pray for all of their cold feet to bow to their heads in the Forum of a monstrous pleasure so they'd all set there we had to take a trip to New Orleans and people did not think this was a good idea they did not like their feet

being sick isn't not like anything they were going to be reaching for many many many many many many feet.

the day before they all had left to go to Spencer's store and buy the most expensive sheets. They were never going to be put never pack from the rooms they're never going to be not broken and they just wanted to feel as if they jumped off of their beds Temple Run.

the night before of what's his call this December 2018 7 in the morning it was the most beautiful day. The snow still nothing moved nothing was alert. The only thing that could

Chapter 13: You're The Irish, So There

have been better was seeing the dogs air blow out of his nose from extreme cold that enter through the door so that has. The house was at least four stories Square Windows in each wall you so looks of a typical Colonial home it was a blue Hound blue screen siding panels made of wood and standings past hundred year everyone try to be there everyone try to want to the name of the house kept everyone sent everyone wanted to wake up there.

I did I ran to the window and I ran down the hall and gressive Lee ran through the waves of all of the air that collided with how it ripped through my grapes yes I fell on the floor rolling about like I'm literally on caution bear I was shocked at the nurse and I ever sit there again and ever since since he's such a bad as before session can you during the holidays. But I just seen a ladybug there was nothing Easter magazines at the year before expired so the fireplace have to be used for wet hair and snapping acid crinkled away photographs all the past of a present.

Chapter 4: We Just Hope You Give A Damn

Stop prettying him down. He had to stay pretty and not do anything. He couldn't get as bad as he wanted to be. In so many ways no one gives a darn

between comfort and discomfort is the title
It says September 7th this is the year 2019 this is a fun year there's a glorious year deercast beerfeast time went by so quickly There was no storm today I could not see the floor my house standing as w between comfort and discomfort is the title Everyday it's winter.

New line Monday
Blue Line and that you can see the indent and you just Uline
this is our switch to this is our switch to do indignant
indent

Chapter 1: Zero

Imperturbably beary. My favorite musical people has to be my sister Billy bear. before bear became all that she was in the store she started singing in high school and making records she's performed all over the world cleaning Japan she has very solid tympanic Club beats that could be played to her sultry jazz .

I first realize Billy bear she handed me a tape of a record a song. Like so many musical people she had a special vibrato Special Air a voice tune it just comes up through the air things. She is done inspiring and plastic her spirit is the LIE of love togetherness an extreme training Guelph complete imperturbe Lee Berry her life is been so balanced I just called her the Ampere terribly Barry she has been sitting I know existence for difference she likes sitting in the breeze and believe is an impenetrable day so let's all try to be infertile early Berry and this is where I'll begin my journey to be like my idol I will be in future we bury in so many ways let's start out On the 1st of December.

I was born in the middle of the month timing disco's at its height it was an air of sophistication I could just go on and on there to so many people I don't see why shutter success stop being poor success is being happy to get to a point of imperturbability Barry happiness mimosa's jovial is the honey dripping from a bear right after hurts hibernation during the cold cold existence of the planet Earth there are some for which Life Goes On there's some for which there's a different Tale the bear has no Tales of this every years the summer every year is the honey this girl is what so many try to be to not give it from anyting to walk through those bitter snooze so many people must do to be blinded my passion warmed by the strength of your ability strength to go and do it's almost animal is human to fail so many half can any of us be in Pretoria blueberry any of us have that drive their focus then one tunnel vision life it makes it hibernate through the dark days history rest upon our souls mini rester gifted and blessed is it gift people strike is not being the bear being the human causes are suffering that we mistreat that they will suffer this is the tale as so many others human suffering The Berry people seem so sweet they just picked the Bears right off a tree berries put them in there a little dresses and scoop them up and bowls and rush them in bowls symbols of Pies there others just we'll catch that when of sophistication and Air what will never be lift sway how will it be can we all try a real animals some of us just choose to be God can we all be in picture of Lee Barry can we all just ignore the superfluous strenuous activities hell on Earth we all Drive the existence of poverty existence of well does it take the money that's something she's never been abridge stuff and something of a circumstance provide to her tell unbridled ability money is cast upon them to be the animal they are they exist as no other no one can seem to not hurt yep they will never not help despair pull through he people shoot at it they always preserve it it's mistake simplicity it's snowing this to enjoy the wall to wrap up in the warmth of oneself to endure the cold this is story of many tales of many people try to accomplish such a thing so many ways so many jacket ways find ourselves why bear freeing ourselves to be the humane this is what many will never do so much easier how to do a kickover tent 2Pac to steal one's honey steal one's food does the bear often do that in cases of hunger what happens when the Bears not hungry what happens is plentiful the garden is semen really feel sorry for the bear do they ever wondered when there is not sufficient and provided fattened will there ever be a time will exist is this the question I choose to stay on the side of the rich the money The Castaways steripen girls anchor avarice Envy walk two roads been with the poor the unlikely perhaps ignored and the wealth I can't tell you what money. Sweetheart here's looking at the well to do the Wella biters all the success here's to that I'm staying in for terribly Barry Oh that men can do .

Early stage of life I have to say that coming down from many peaceful days it's not a immature are small at the beach for the world. No tornado Valley this what anyting what bow down to. Plus, adieu what is the easiest. I don't see it from the start I don't spread the legs of secession and meager attitudes. there's a life and happiness, steadiness, or failure.

I stayed at home in this dedication to life study. I want to tell about the song Take My Love From the berry imperatively berry girl it just is what people take. they must be loved someone must love it sure someone must be love. How much did be for who must love must they be what is week unless they be able to Strong has a case what does not impose what is not in search of the ugly of the swing and they hating Brothers.

Mist Berryessa name before thinks that music is not like art not like Tom had it Tom was an artist he did the cover the spot it's what disconnects the book and the world father this is the picture of me pictures of men a woman disconnecting happiness where did smothered the colors run it's the tears eliminate the breast of one side the funny Parable heartbeat just pulls us into the point of dying here you see a woman on

Chapter 14: If You Don't Want Us

the cover is a dead woman she cannot whisper a letter of this book.

she can say anything to lay down I never walk. It's just something shocking to let the readers understand the point of life it's not to be that is to live they're two totally different words don't look similar whatsoever I think today's paper called the car moves where we live Poland match match difference between the dying and living in the book called shoe the orange rain by Rachel K. Martin well this will hit the foot like a nail in Jesus on the cross. she killed the ground, was a slave 2 the mundane, or was everyone I did not care about the Hills of grass. Complete waste of words. what's this woman a prostitute? what she crown debutante person beauty queen of high school Rich Roll? was she all things of stupidity unknowingness ignorance or hid ugly imagine and she started.

let's just cover up this life in the grave let's throw the dirt do you disagree? what's rice on the high side paints. It's good to not feel like a zero.

Chapter 2: We Won't Look Like This

Required to run towards the track . Chloe did with chicken we thought you'd want looks like this Daphne could save your life.

Chapter 2: We Won't Look Like This

How do we not look this way is it because it's Halloween to you it's because you can't see them the running everywhere this one in particular this one goes through Michelle mentioned in the Poetry of choosing your own trying there's something much like a spider on the wall just in the introvignes much like yourself reading interpreting songs like what I consider amuse hear it . to me this is the point of life one cannot get through when cannot pass through it without fighting it without chewing Dan taking that last breath. is that how it is the last moment the last breath we clench her teeth trying to survive a horrible World horrible tide change and Michelle was just a coaster the poet that must live within that moment but last poem has many different phases of change of the death of the dying as I mentioned in the last buck to the orange rain as you split and diet of course this means US Mini Splits a

Bittersweet taste is in the orange rind 1 West recall supposed to leave us or last 10 to 15 seconds of Life flashing before eyes in these different frames these different stanzas of the poetry depicts all of those emotions racing before becoming free of ourselves when we come raging spirits everlasting life and a r motorcycles oh the last book was more about trying to chew to live eventually we get to the last year I think that's where this book will pick up movie about all that resides in the reflection of one's life at that last moment those last days Rising for the last challenge what will it be like for anyone Harrison introspection when's fall back people give so much advice how is it to look backwards and tell yourself or you will go for it no more. We won't look like this first of all like we are we want looks like we used to when you were sick dying decrepit weathering fattening whatever the case may be will become something that cannot recover to become the death supposedly we were big pile of dust he'll be thrown out to sea is this more of it was just an interest faction into what we will face something will will will be borne by.

We ran together Chloe we had every feeling that the last three days or empty and Shiloh of white snow ice, performance shows knives healthy walking bodies and medical and poverty togetherness much worse find sunny I need a. let's go think of moving for it. I will be there?

It's been quite a herring experience they just keep sitting there watching me will invisible people I watching you ain't heavy things in me that you and I feel their tactile you cannot see the sale practically breaking every bone in my body pinched they just keep taking all of my air and weighing me down odesse torturous all day and they keep me up all night I get no rest my eyes are peeled they're black and they are ready explosions all over the TV and nothing phases they're more than bothering me this is completely Concerta done bothering me she went to the back what's 2 two tier and that was all she does is Justin find the 2-day anymore of the two deer used to come around back I think someone hit and crush the deer and split it off to the side like a big pile of reverie organs and blood the head of used to recognize so dearly when her go baby dad Aerotek such

a beautiful picture that captured in time she said that was promised a the road a little baby doll left motherless they're practically skin and bone I just fed them she barely had nutrients and she tried to use all of them as much as she could feed her baby deer animals their highest extent to keep themselves in there offspring live people cannot do the same.

I heard it's racing is pounding his true knocking knocking as if wanting to be raped I think I have your heart he said it's putting me everywhere that you're never going to be what you say don't understand or appreciate themselves they don't want you to not really anything cuz you did not have this problem they want me to sit there and be there in and then you and Father's day but this isn't expanding to anyone that can guess what it seems people don't want to be bothered and I think of any way to bother me that care about him being agitated and extremes they've gone to the bothering you and that's better. now question art I thought. the news of sunny day and every computer I walk in front of was there when I left the building. I could see the smoke coming out of the windows watch the TV and explosions.

I'm in bed watching too finally just relaxing to a week ago and it was with just one more time. December went by so quickly and I just wanted to go and make it through the last year at of my job app. And I always felt just like it was had just happened but I was just going to pray for the first time. I just for a little a little yeah fresh air my father and I didn't run many travels at through the Midwest as much as we went through more in St Louis we saw the downtown area we saw the malls that's been closed a lot of the Sea Breeze old friends used to live places that the houses are not as well kept you probably are now condemned you are perhaps someone else is living there there's this not really a place where a lot of people are still states structured it's not like living in New Orleans just had its pride and its culture for many many years. drove me to school quite a bit that is only when and if the last time he dropped me off it was a very Rocky rainy morning I said hello to have then he drove off to the Sun.

medium sized statue woman with all of these cat like I appearance perm straighten hair I'm sorry my pigtails blow in the Wind he went further and further

into the Sun. That was him going to the start of his day every day started with a Sun Ray and going away to begin my beach walk into start of my new school year. Seemed like he was going into the sun to me Style of course he was not driving into the sun just a figure of speech for your child and you're not too tall can't see too far over the hell seems like that's where he's gay.

Chapter 15: Sister

of course it's a whole different culture to be involved in different kinds of weather and different kinds of States

Midwest pretty humdrum you ever winter spring or summer or fall more of the summer in the winter is definite the fall in the spring 10 do Collide somewhat but the leaves do fall by the end of September. squinting outside of the window I looked at how everyone was little dots down from an airplane there's so many people about because it was the July 4th holiday and all the sudden there was planking and clashing airplanes flying and firecrackers going. can hear loads and loads a fireworks when their direction under the arch I get my daughter look at this time. My mind was empty with no hope for anyting a few hours went by and I saw a big cloud in the sky jumped Define it was on the floor.

rom extreme cold that enter through the door so that has. The house was at least four stories Square Windows in each wall you so looks of a typical Colonial home it was a blue Hound blue screen siding panels made of wood and standings past hundred year everyone try to be there everyone try to want to the name of the house kept everyone sent everyone wanted to wake up there.

I did I ran to the window and I ran down the hall and gressive Lee ran through the waves of all of the air that collided with how it ripped through my grapes yes I fell on the floor rolling about like I'm literally on caution bear I was shocked at the nurse and I ever sit there again and ever since since he's such a bad as before session can you during the holidays. But I just seen a ladybug there was nothing Easter magazines at the year before expired so the fireplace have to be used for wet hair and snapping acid crinkled away photographs all the past of a present.

Chapter 4: We Just Hope You Give A Damn

Stop prettying him down. He had to stay pretty and not do anything. He couldn’t get as bad as he wanted to be. In so many ways no one gives a darn

between comfort and discomfort is the title
It says September 7th this is the year 2019 this is a fun year there's a glorious year deercast beerfeast time went by so quickly There was no storm today I could not see the floor my house standing as w between comfort and discomfort is the title
Everyday it's winter.

New line Monday
Blue Line and that you can see the indent and you just Uline
this is our switch to this is our switch to do indignant
indent

Chapter 1: Zero

Imperturbably beary. My favorite musical people has to be my sister Billy bear. before bear became all that she was in the store she started singing in high school and making records she's performed all over the

world cleaning Japan she has very solid tympanic Club beats that could be played to her sultry jazz .

I first realize Billy bear she handed me a tape of a record a song. Like so many musical people she had a special vibrato Special Air a voice tune it just comes up through the air things. She is done inspiring and plastic her spirit is the LIE of love togetherness an extreme training Guelph complete imperturbe Lee Berry her life is been so balanced I just called her the Ampere terribly Barry she has been sitting I know existence for difference she likes sitting in the breeze and believe is an impenetrable day so let's all try to be infertile early Berry and this is where I'll begin my journey to be like my idol I will be in future we bury in so many ways let's start out On the 1st of December.

I was born in the middle of the month timing disco's at its height it was an air of sophistication I could just go on and on there to so many people I don't see why shutter success stop being poor success is being happy to get to a point of imperturbability Barry happiness mimosa's jovial is the honey dripping from a bear right after hurts hibernation during the cold cold

existence of the planet Earth there are some for which Life Goes On there's some for which there's a different Tale the bear has no Tales of this every years the summer every year is the honey this girl is what so many try to be to not give it from anyting to walk through those bitter snooze so many people must do to be blinded my passion warmed by the strength of your ability strength to go and do it's almost animal is human to fail so many half can any of us be in Pretoria blueberry any of us have that drive their focus then one tunnel vision life it makes it hibernate through the dark days history rest upon our souls mini rester gifted and blessed is it gift people strike is not being the bear being the human causes are suffering that we mistreat that they will suffer this is the tale as so many others human suffering The Berry people seem so sweet they just picked the Bears right off a tree berries put them in there a little dresses and scoop them up and bowls and rush them in bowls symbols of Pies there others just we'll catch that when of sophistication and Air what will never be lift sway how will it be can we all try a real animals some of us just choose to be God can we all be in picture of Lee Barry can we all just ignore the

superfluous strenuous activities hell on Earth we all Drive the existence of poverty existence of well does it take the money that's something she's never been abridge stuff and something of a circumstance provide to her tell unbridled ability money is cast upon them to be the animal they are they exist as no other no one can seem to not hurt yep they will never not help despair pull through he people shoot at it they always preserve it it's mistake simplicity it's snowing this to enjoy the wall to wrap up in the warmth of oneself to endure the cold this is story of many tales of many people try to accomplish such a thing so many ways so many jacket ways find ourselves why bear freeing ourselves to be the humane this is what many will never do so much easier how to do a kickover tent 2Pac to steal one's honey steal one's food does the bear often do that in cases of hunger what happens when the Bears not hungry what happens is plentiful the garden is semen really feel sorry for the bear do they ever wondered when there is not sufficient and provided fattened will there ever be a time will exist is this the question I choose to stay on the side of the rich the money The Castaways steripen girls anchor avarice Envy walk two roads been with the

poor the unlikely perhaps ignored and the wealth I can't tell you what money. Sweetheart here's looking at the well to do the Wella biters all the success here's to that I'm staying in for terribly Barry Oh that men can do .

Early stage of life I have to say that coming down from many peaceful days it's not a immature are small at the beach for the world. No tornado Valley this what anyting what bow down to. Plus, adieu what is the easiest. I don't see it from the start I don't spread the legs of secession and meager attitudes. there's a life and happiness, steadiness, or failure.

Chapter 16: What?

I stayed at home in this dedication to life study. I want to tell about the song Take My Love From the berry

imperatively berry girl it just is what people take. they must be loved someone must love it sure someone must be love. How much did be for who must love must they be what is week unless they be able to Strong has a case what does not impose what is not in search of the ugly of the swing and they hating Brothers.

Mist Berryessa name before thinks that music is not like art not like Tom had it Tom was an artist he did the cover the spot it's what disconnects the book and the world father this is the picture of me pictures of men a woman disconnecting happiness where did smothered the colors run it's the tears eliminate the breast of one side the funny Parable heartbeat just pulls us into the point of dying here you see a woman on the cover is a dead woman she cannot whisper a letter of this book.

she can say anything to lay down I never walk. It's just something shocking to let the readers understand the point of life it's not to be that is to live they're two totally different words don't look similar whatsoever I think today's paper called the car moves where we live Poland match match difference between the dying and living in the book called shoe the orange rain by Rachel K. Martin well this will hit the foot like a nail in Jesus on the cross. she killed the ground, was a slave 2 the mundane, or was everyone I did not care about the Hills of grass. Complete waste of words. what's this woman a prostitute? what she crown debutante person beauty queen of high school Rich Roll? was she all things of stupidity unknowingness ignorance or hid ugly imagine and she started.

let's just cover up this life in the grave let's throw the dirt do you disagree? what's rice on the high side paints. It's good to not feel like a zero.

Chapter 2: We Won't Look Like This

Required to run towards the track . Chloe did with chicken we thought you'd want looks like this Daphne could save your life.

Chapter 2: We Won't Look Like This

How do we not look this way is it because it's Halloween to you it's because you can't see them the running everywhere this one in particular this one goes through Michelle mentioned in the Poetry of choosing your own trying there's something much like a spider on the wall just in the introvignes much like yourself reading interpreting songs like what I consider amuse hear it . to me this is the point of life one cannot get through when cannot pass through it without fighting it without chewing Dan taking that last breath. is that how it is the last moment the last breath we clench her teeth trying to survive a horrible World horrible tide change and Michelle was just a coaster the poet that must live within that moment but last poem has many different phases of change of the death of the dying as I mentioned in the last buck to the orange rain as you split and diet of course this means US Mini Splits a Bittersweet taste is in the orange rind 1 West recall supposed to leave us or last 10 to 15 seconds of Life flashing before eyes in these different frames these different stanzas of the poetry depicts all of those emotions racing before becoming free of ourselves when we come raging spirits everlasting life and a r motorcycles oh the last book was more about trying to chew to live eventually we get to the last year I think that's where this book will pick up movie about all that resides in the reflection of one's life at that last moment those last days Rising for the last challenge what will it be like for anyone Harrison introspection when's fall back people give so much advice how is it to look backwards and tell yourself or you will go for it no more. We won't look like this first of all like we are we want looks like we used to when you were sick dying decrepit weathering fattening whatever the case may be will become something that cannot recover to become the death supposedly we were big pile of dust he'll be thrown out to sea is this more of it was just an interest faction into what we will face something will will will be borne by.

We ran together Chloe we had every feeling that the last three days or empty and Shiloh of white snow ice, performance shows knives healthy walking bodies and medical and poverty togetherness much worse find sunny I need a. let's go think of moving for it. I will be there?

It's been quite a herring experience they just keep sitting there watching me will invisible people I watching you ain't heavy things in me that you and I feel their tactile you cannot see the sale practically breaking every bone in my body pinched they just keep taking all of my air and weighing me down odesse torturous all day and they keep me up all night I get no rest my eyes are peeled they're black and they are ready explosions all over the TV and nothing phases they're more than bothering me this is completely Concerta done bothering me she went to the back what's 2 two tier and that was all she does is Justin find the 2-day anymore of the two deer used to come around back I think someone hit and crush the deer and split it off to the side like a big pile of reverie organs and blood the head of used to recognize so dearly when her go baby dad Aerotek such a beautiful picture that captured in time she said that was promised a the road a little baby doll left motherless they're practically skin and bone I just fed them she barely had nutrients and she tried to use all of them as much as she could feed her baby deer animals their highest extent to keep themselves in there offspring live people cannot do the same.

I heard it's racing is pounding his true knocking knocking as if wanting to be raped I think I have your heart he said it's putting me everywhere that you're never going to be what you say don't understand or appreciate themselves they don't want you to not really anything cuz you did not have this problem they want me to sit there and be there in and then you and Father's day but this isn't expanding to anyone that can guess what it seems people don't want to be bothered and I think of any way to bother me that care about him being agitated and extremes they've gone to the bothering you and that's better. now question art I thought. the news of sunny day and every computer I walk in front of was there when I left the building. I could see the smoke coming out of the windows watch the TV and explosions. I'm in bed watching too finally just relaxing to a week ago and it was with just one more time. December went by so quickly and I just wanted to go and make it through the last year at of my job app. And I always felt just like it was had just happened but I was just going to pray for the first time. I just for a little a little yeah fresh air my father and I didn't run many travels at through the Midwest as much as we went through more in St Louis we saw the downtown area we saw the malls that's been closed a lot of the Sea Breeze old friends used to live places that the houses are not as well kept you probably are now condemned you are perhaps someone else is living there there's this not really a place where a lot of people are still states structured it's not like living in New Orleans just had its

Chapter 17: Do You Think They'll Go Anywhere Doing This

pride and its culture for many many years. drove me to school quite a bit that is only when and if the last time he dropped me off it was a very Rocky rainy morning I said hello to have then he drove off to the Sun.

medium sized statue woman with all of these cat like I appearance perm straighten hair I'm sorry my pigtails blow in the Wind he went further and further into the Sun. That was him going to the start of his day every day started with a Sun Ray and going away to begin my beach walk into start of my new school year. Seemed like he was going into the sun to me Style of course he was not driving into the sun just a figure of speech for your child and you're not too tall can't see too far over the hell seems like that's where he's gay.

of course it's a whole different culture to be involved in different kinds of weather and different kinds of States Midwest pretty humdrum you ever winter spring or summer or fall more of the summer in the winter is definite the fall in the spring 10 do Collide somewhat but the leaves do fall by the end of September.

squinting outside of the window I looked at how everyone was little dots down from an airplane there's so many people about because it was the July 4th holiday and all the sudden there was planking and clashing airplanes flying and firecrackers going. can hear loads and loads a fireworks when their direction under the arch I get my daughter look at this time. My mind was empty with no hope for anyting a few hours went by and I saw a big cloud in the sky jumped Define it was on the floor.

Chapter 3: We Just Don't Care

He met a friend and yet we couldn't go through Finding Nemo it was a coffee all black coffee everyday black coffee Olympic cream in the coffee Willow thought you was black it was dark and made him crazy he went looking for anyone finally came up Iraq we found his child in a Ciroc you're really funny story Stanley Charlie found any survivors how she kept hiding from him somebody for children who don't want to be you're off and running I didn't see what the point of it is till they get to the point. Lucy Wizards daughter's name and she spoke unhinged address of the clock as it sat on the wall S4 had school in the plants and everything that we saw stay consistent we were together we're overwhelmed to begin every day but there was no where we were going we were all very happy to finally be junior high in front of all of the bag sickle writers they all took a plunge it was just the sun rise of the Cascades when she was in the big Village running and soon to be in the middle of September for bats were the roads were all the problems has one set there I thought well when I go to Houston Texas or something while we didn't want to sit Africa bigger place but the car couldn't go anywhere it's just broken down there always just imagine you what we might do and he was still looking for his daughter still trying to figure out what to be there by funny name for Lucy means like can see the light of it

The leftover people were all scattered throughout the yard. After every day he had ended we did not get to ignore the cold feet that cat walking towards the other ones. Many of them wanted to join the others and pray for all of their cold feet to bow to their heads in the Forum of a monstrous pleasure so they'd all set there we had to take a trip to New Orleans and people did not think this was a good idea they did not like their feet being sick isn't not like anything they were going to be reaching for many many many many many many feet.

the day before they all had left to go to Spencer's store and buy the most expensive sheets. They were never going to be put never pack from the rooms they're never going to be not broken and they just wanted to feel as if they jumped off of their beds Temple Run.

the night before of what's his call this December 2018 7 in the morning it was the most beautiful day. The snow still nothing moved nothing was alert. The only thing that could have been better was seeing the dogs air blow out of his nose from extreme cold that enter through the door so that has. The house was at least four stories Square Windows in each wall you so looks of a typical Colonial home it was a blue Hound blue screen siding panels made of wood and standings past hundred year everyone try to be there everyone try to want to the name of the house kept everyone sent everyone wanted to wake up there.

I did I ran to the window and I ran down the hall and gressive Lee ran through the waves of all of the air that collided with how it ripped through my grapes yes I fell on the floor rolling about like I'm literally on caution bear I was shocked at the nurse and I ever sit there again and ever since since he's such a bad as before session can you during the holidays. But I just seen a ladybug there was nothing Easter magazines at the

year before expired so the fireplace have to be used for wet hair and snapping acid crinkled away photographs all the past of a present.

Chapter 4: We Just Hope You Give A Damn

Stop prettying him down. He had to stay pretty and not do anything. He couldn't get as bad as he wanted to be. In so many ways no one gives a darn

between comfort and discomfort is the title
It says September 7th this is the year 2019 this is a fun year there's a glorious year deercast beerfeast time went by so quickly There was no storm today I could not see the floor my house standing as w between comfort and discomfort is the title Everyday it's winter.

New line Monday
Blue Line and that you can see the indent and you just Uline
this is our switch to this is our switch to do indignant
indent

Chapter 1: Zero

Imperturbably beary. My favorite musical people has to be my sister Billy bear. before bear became all that she was in the store she started singing in high school and making records she's performed all over the world cleaning Japan she has very solid tympanic Club beats that could be played to her sultry jazz .

Chapter 18: We Took How You Did That

I first realize Billy bear she handed me a tape of a record a song. Like so many musical people she had a special vibrato Special Air a voice tune it just comes up through the air things. She is done inspiring and plastic her spirit is the LIE of love togetherness an extreme training Guelph complete imperturbe Lee Berry her life is been so balanced I just called her the Ampere terribly Barry she has been sitting I know existence for difference she likes sitting in the breeze and believe is an impenetrable day so let's all try to be infertile early Berry and this is where I'll begin my journey to be like my idol I will be in future we bury in so many ways let's start out On the 1st of December.

I was born in the middle of the month timing disco's at its height it was an air of sophistication I could just go on and on there to so many people I don't see why shutter success stop being poor success is being happy to get to a point of imperturbability Barry happiness mimosa's jovial is the honey dripping from a bear right after hurts hibernation during the cold cold existence of the planet Earth there are some for which Life Goes On there's some for which there's a different Tale the bear has no Tales of this every years the summer every year is the honey this girl is what so many try to be to not give it from anyting to walk through those bitter snooze so many people must do to be blinded my passion warmed by the strength of your ability strength to go and do it's almost animal is human to fail so many half can any of us be in Pretoria blueberry any of us have that drive their focus then one tunnel vision life it makes it hibernate through the dark days history rest upon our souls mini rester gifted and blessed is it gift people strike is not being the bear being the human causes are suffering that we mistreat that they will suffer this is the tale as so many others human suffering The Berry people seem so sweet they just picked the Bears right off a tree berries put them in there a little dresses and scoop them up and bowls and rush them in bowls symbols of Pies there others just we'll catch that when of sophistication and Air what will never be lift sway how will it be can we all try a real animals some of us just choose to be God can we all be in picture of Lee Barry can we all just ignore the superfluous strenuous activities hell on Earth we all Drive the existence of poverty existence of well does it take the money that's something she's never been abridge stuff and something of a circumstance provide to her tell unbridled ability money is cast upon them to be the animal they are they exist as no other no one can seem to not hurt yep they will never not help despair pull through he people shoot at it they always preserve it it's mistake simplicity it's snowing this to enjoy the wall to wrap up in the warmth of oneself to endure the cold this is story of many tales of many people try to accomplish such a thing so many ways so many jacket ways find ourselves why bear freeing ourselves to be the humane this is what many will never do so much easier how to do a kickover tent 2Pac to steal one's honey steal one's food does the bear often do that in cases of

hunger what happens when the Bears not hungry what happens is plentiful the garden is semen really feel sorry for the bear do they ever wondered when there is not sufficient and provided fattened will there ever be a time will exist is this the question I choose to stay on the side of the rich the money The Castaways steripen girls anchor avarice Envy walk two roads been with the poor the unlikely perhaps ignored and the wealth I can't tell you what money. Sweetheart here's looking at the well to do the Wella biters all the success here's to that I'm staying in for terribly Barry Oh that men can do .

Early stage of life I have to say that coming down from many peaceful days it's not a immature are small at the beach for the world. No tornado Valley this what anyting what bow down to. Plus, adieu what is the easiest. I don't see it from the start I don't spread the legs of secession and meager attitudes. there's a life and happiness, steadiness, or failure.

I stayed at home in this dedication to life study. I want to tell about the song Take My Love From the berry imperatively berry girl it just is what people take. they must be loved someone must love it sure someone must be love. How much did be for who must love must they be what is week unless they be able to Strong has a case what does not impose what is not in search of the ugly of the swing and they hating Brothers.

Mist Berryessa name before thinks that music is not like art not like Tom had it Tom was an artist he did the cover the spot it's what disconnects the book and the world father this is the picture of me pictures of men a woman disconnecting happiness where did smothered the colors run it's the tears eliminate the breast of one side the funny Parable heartbeat just pulls us into the point of dying here you see a woman on the cover is a dead woman she cannot whisper a letter of this book.

she can say anything to lay down I never walk. It's just something shocking to let the readers understand the point of life it's not to be that is to live they're two totally different words don't look similar whatsoever I think today's paper called the car moves where we live Poland match match difference between the dying and living in the book called shoe the orange rain by Rachel K. Martin well this will hit the

foot like a nail in Jesus on the cross. she killed the ground, was a slave 2 the mundane, or was everyone I did not care about the Hills of grass. Complete waste of words. what's this woman a prostitute? what she crown debutante person beauty queen of high school Rich Roll? was she all things of stupidity unknowingness ignorance or hid ugly imagine and she started.

let's just cover up this life in the grave let's throw the dirt do you disagree? what's rice on the high side paints. It's good to not feel like a zero.

Chapter 2: We Won't Look Like This

Required to run towards the track . Chloe did with chicken we thought you'd want looks like this Daphne could save your life.

Chapter 2: We Won't Look Like This

How do we not look this way is it because it's Halloween to you it's because you can't see them the running everywhere this one in particular this one goes through Michelle mentioned in the Poetry of choosing your own trying there's something much like a spider on the wall

just in the introvignes much like yourself reading interpreting songs like what I consider amuse hear it . to me this is the point of life one cannot get through when cannot pass through it without fighting it without chewing Dan taking that last breath. is that how it is the last moment the last breath we clench her teeth trying to survive a horrible World horrible tide change and Michelle was just a coaster the poet that must

Chapter 19: We're Animals

live within that moment but last poem has many different phases of change of the death of the dying as I mentioned in the last buck to the orange rain as you split and diet of course this means US Mini Splits a Bittersweet taste is in the orange rind 1 West recall supposed to leave us or last 10 to 15 seconds of Life flashing before eyes in these different frames these different stanzas of the poetry depicts all of those emotions racing before becoming free of ourselves when we come raging spirits everlasting life and a r motorcycles oh the last book was more about trying to chew to live eventually we get to the last year I think that's where this book will pick up movie about all that resides in the reflection of one's life at that last moment those last days Rising for the last challenge what will it be like for anyone Harrison introspection when's fall back people give so much advice how is it to look backwards and tell yourself or you will go for it no more. We won't look like this first of all like we are we want looks like we used to when you were sick dying decrepit weathering fattening whatever the case may be will become something that cannot recover to become the death supposedly we were big pile of dust he'll be thrown out to sea is this more of it was just an interest faction into what we will face something will will will be borne by.

We ran together Chloe we had every feeling that the last three days or empty and Shiloh of white snow ice, performance shows knives healthy walking bodies and medical and poverty togetherness much worse find sunny I need a. let's go think of moving for it. I will be there?

It's been quite a herring experience they just keep sitting there watching me will invisible people I watching you ain't heavy things in me that you and I feel their tactile you cannot see the sale practically breaking every bone in my body pinched they just keep taking all of my air and weighing me down odesse torturous all day and they keep me up all night I get no rest my eyes are peeled they're black and they are ready explosions all over the TV and nothing phases they're more than bothering me this is completely Concerta done bothering me she went to the back what's 2 two tier and that was all she does is Justin find the 2-day anymore of the two deer used to come around back I think someone hit and crush the deer and split it off to the side like a big pile of reverie organs and blood the head of used to recognize so dearly when her go baby dad Aerotek such a beautiful picture that captured in time she said that was promised a the road a little baby doll left motherless they're practically skin and bone I just fed them she barely had nutrients and she tried to use all of them as much as she could feed her baby deer animals their highest extent to keep themselves in there offspring live people cannot do the same.

I heard it's racing is pounding his true knocking knocking as if wanting to be raped I think I have your heart he said it's putting me everywhere that you're never going to be what you say don't understand or appreciate themselves they don't want you to not really anything cuz you did not have this problem they want me to sit there and be there in and then you and Father's day but this isn't expanding to anyone that can guess what it seems people don't want to be bothered and I think of any way to bother me that care about him being agitated and extremes they've gone to the bothering you and that's better. now question art I thought. the news of sunny day and every computer I walk in front of was there when I left the building. I could see the smoke coming out of the windows watch the TV and explosions. I'm in bed watching too finally just relaxing to a week ago and it was with just one more time. December went by so quickly and I just wanted to go and make it through the last year at of my job app. And I always felt just like it was had just happened but I was just going to pray for the first time. I just for a little a little yeah fresh air my father and I didn't run many travels at through the Midwest as much as we went through more in St Louis we saw the downtown area we saw the malls that's been closed a lot of the Sea Breeze old friends used to live places that the houses are not as well kept you probably are now condemned you are perhaps someone else is living there there's this not really a place where a lot of people are still states structured it's not like living in New Orleans just had its pride and its culture for many many years. drove me to school quite a bit that is only when and if the last time he dropped me off it was a very Rocky rainy morning I said hello to have then he drove off to the Sun.

medium sized statue woman with all of these cat like I appearance perm straighten hair I'm sorry my pigtails blow in the Wind he went further and further into the Sun. That was him going to the start of his day every day started with a Sun Ray and going away to begin my beach walk into start of my new school year. Seemed like he was going into the sun to me Style of course he was not driving into the sun just a figure of speech for your child and you're not too tall can't see too far over the hell seems like that's where he's gay.

of course it's a whole different culture to be involved in different kinds of weather and different kinds of States Midwest pretty humdrum you ever winter

spring or summer or fall more of the summer in the winter is definite the fall in the spring 10 do Collide somewhat but the leaves do fall by the end of September. squinting outside of the window I looked at how everyone was little dots down from an airplane there's so many people about because it was the July 4th holiday and all the sudden there was planking and clashing airplanes flying and firecrackers going. can hear loads and loads a fireworks when their direction under the arch I get my daughter look at this time. My mind was empty with no hope for anyting a few hours went by and I saw a big cloud in the sky jumped Define it was on the floor.

rom extreme cold that enter through the door so that has. The house was at least four stories Square Windows in each wall you so looks of a typical Colonial home it was a blue Hound blue screen siding panels made of wood and standings past hundred year everyone try to be there everyone try to want to the name of the house kept everyone sent everyone wanted to wake up there.

I did I ran to the window and I ran down the hall and gressive Lee ran through the waves of all of the air that collided with how it ripped through my grapes yes I

fell on the floor rolling about like I'm literally on caution bear I was shocked at the nurse and I ever sit there again and ever since since he's such a bad as before session can you during the holidays. But I just seen a ladybug there was nothing Easter magazines at the year before expired so the fireplace have to be used for wet hair and snapping acid crinkled away photographs all the past of a present.

Chapter 4: We Just Hope You Give A Damn

Stop prettying him down. He had to stay pretty and not do anything. He couldn't get as bad as he wanted to be. In so many ways no one gives a darn

between comfort and discomfort is the title

Chapter 20: Wow! We Don't Care

It says September 7th this is the year 2019 this is a fun year there's a glorious year deercast beerfeast time went by so quickly There was no storm today I could not see the floor my house standing as w between comfort and discomfort is the title Everyday it's winter.

New line Monday
Blue Line and that you can see the indent and you just Uline
this is our switch to this is our switch to do indignant
indent

Chapter 1: Zero

Imperturbably beary. My favorite musical people has to be my sister Billy bear. before bear became all that she was in the store she started singing in high school and making records she's performed all over the world cleaning Japan she has very solid tympanic Club beats that could be played to her sultry jazz .

I first realize Billy bear she handed me a tape of a record a song. Like so many musical people she had a special vibrato Special Air a voice tune it just comes up through the air things. She is done inspiring and plastic her spirit is the LIE of love togetherness an extreme training Guelph complete imperturbe Lee Berry her life is been so balanced I just called her the Ampere terribly Barry she has been sitting I know existence for difference she likes sitting in the breeze and believe is an impenetrable day so let's all try to be infertile early Berry and this is where I'll begin my journey to be like my idol I will be in future we bury in so many ways let's start out On the 1st of December.

I was born in the middle of the month timing disco's at its height it was an air of sophistication I could just go on and on there to so many people I don't see why shutter success stop being poor success is being happy to get to a point of imperturbability Barry happiness mimosa's jovial is the honey dripping from a bear right after hurts hibernation during the cold cold existence of the planet Earth there are some for which Life Goes On there's some for which there's a different Tale the bear has no Tales of this every years the summer every year is the honey this girl is what so many try to be to not give it from anyting to walk through those bitter snooze so many people must do to be blinded my passion warmed by the strength of your ability strength to go and do it's almost animal is human to fail so many half can any of us be in Pretoria blueberry any of us have that drive their focus then one tunnel vision life it makes it hibernate through the dark days history rest upon our souls mini rester gifted and blessed is it gift people strike is not being the bear being the human causes are suffering that we mistreat that they will suffer this is the tale as so many others human suffering The Berry people seem so sweet they just picked the Bears right off a tree berries put them in there a little dresses and scoop them up and bowls and rush them in bowls symbols of Pies there others just we'll catch that when of sophistication and Air what will never be lift sway how will it be can we all try a real animals some of us just choose to be God can we all be in picture of Lee Barry can we all just ignore the superfluous strenuous activities hell on Earth we all Drive the existence of poverty existence of well does it take the money that's something she's never been abridge stuff and something of a circumstance provide to her tell unbridled ability money is cast upon them to be the animal they are they exist as no other no one can seem to not hurt yep they will never not help despair pull through he people shoot at it they always preserve it it's mistake simplicity it's snowing this to enjoy the wall to wrap up in the warmth of oneself to endure the cold this is story of many tales of many people try to accomplish such a thing so many ways so many jacket ways find ourselves why bear freeing ourselves to be the humane this is what many will never do so much easier how to do a kickover tent 2Pac to steal one's honey steal one's food does the bear often do that in cases of hunger what happens when the Bears not hungry what happens is plentiful the garden is semen really feel sorry for the bear do they ever wondered when there is not sufficient and provided fattened will there ever be a time will exist is this the question I choose to stay on the side of the rich the money The Castaways steripen girls anchor avarice Envy walk two roads been with the poor the unlikely perhaps ignored and the wealth I can't tell you what money. Sweetheart here's looking at the well to do the Wella biters all the success here's to that I'm staying in for terribly Barry Oh that men can do .

Early stage of life I have to say that coming down from many peaceful days it's not a immature are small at the beach for the world. No tornado Valley this what anyting what bow down to. Plus, adieu what is the easiest. I don't see it from the start I don't spread the legs of

secession and meager attitudes. there's a life and happiness, steadiness, or failure.

I stayed at home in this dedication to life study. I want to tell about the song Take My Love From the berry imperatively berry girl it just is what people take. they must be loved someone must love it sure someone must be love. How much did be for who must love must they be what is week unless they be able to Strong has a case what does not impose what is not in search of the ugly of the swing and they hating Brothers.

Mist Berryessa name before thinks that music is not like art not like Tom had it Tom was an artist he did the cover the spot it's what disconnects the book and the world father this is the picture of me pictures of men a woman disconnecting happiness where did smothered the colors run it's the tears eliminate the breast of one side the funny Parable heartbeat just pulls us into the point of dying here you see a woman on the cover is a dead woman she cannot whisper a letter of this book.

she can say anything to lay down I never walk. It's just something shocking to let the readers understand the point of life it's not to be that is to

live they're two totally different words don't look similar whatsoever I think today's paper called the car moves where we live Poland match match difference between the dying and living in the book called shoe the orange rain by Rachel K. Martin well this will hit the foot like a nail in Jesus on the cross. she killed the ground, was a slave 2 the mundane, or was everyone I did not care about the Hills of grass. Complete waste of words. what's this woman a prostitute? what she crown debutante person beauty queen of high school Rich Roll? was she all things of stupidity unknowingness ignorance or hid ugly imagine and she started.

let's just cover up this life in the grave let's throw the dirt do you disagree? what's rice on the high side paints. It's good to not feel like a zero.

Chapter 2: We Won't Look Like This

Required to run towards the track . Chloe did with chicken we thought you'd want looks like this Daphne could save your life.

Chapter 2: We Won't Look Like This

Chapter 21: Ok, Rachel

How do we not look this way is it because it's Halloween to you it's because you can't see them the running everywhere this one in particular this one goes through Michelle

mentioned in the Poetry of choosing your own trying there's something much like a spider on the wall just in the introvignes much like yourself reading interpreting songs like what I consider amuse hear it . to me this is the point of life one cannot get through when cannot pass through it without fighting it without chewing Dan taking that last breath. is that how it is the last moment the last breath we clench her teeth trying to survive a horrible World horrible tide change and Michelle was just a coaster the poet that must live within that moment but last poem has many different phases of change of the death of the dying as I mentioned in the last buck to the orange rain as you split and diet of course this means US Mini Splits a

Bittersweet taste is in the orange rind 1 West recall supposed to leave us or last 10 to 15 seconds of Life flashing before eyes in these different frames these different stanzas of the poetry depicts all of those emotions racing before becoming free of ourselves when we come raging spirits everlasting life and a r motorcycles oh the last book was more about trying to chew to live eventually we get to the last year I think that's where this book will pick up movie about all that resides in the reflection of one's life at that last moment those last days Rising for the last challenge what will it be like for anyone Harrison introspection when's fall back people give so much advice how is it to look backwards and tell yourself or you will go for it no more. We won't look like this first of all like we are we want looks like we used to when you were sick dying decrepit weathering fattening whatever the case may be will become something that cannot recover to become the death supposedly we were big pile of dust he'll be thrown out to sea is this more of it was just an interest faction into what we will face something will will will be borne by.

We ran together Chloe we had every feeling that the last three days or empty and Shiloh of white snow ice, performance shows knives healthy walking bodies and medical and poverty togetherness much worse find sunny I need a. let's go think of moving for it. I will be there?

It's been quite a herring experience they just keep sitting there watching me will invisible people I watching you ain't heavy things in me that you and I feel their tactile you cannot see the sale practically breaking every bone in my body pinched they just keep taking all of my air and weighing me down odesse torturous all day and they keep me up all night I get no rest my eyes are peeled they're black and they are ready explosions all over the TV and nothing phases they're more than bothering me this is completely Concerta done bothering me she went to the back what's 2 two tier and that was all she does is Justin find the 2-day anymore of the two deer used to come around back I think someone hit and crush the deer and split it off to the side like a big pile of reverie organs and blood the head of used to recognize so dearly when her go baby dad Aerotek such

a beautiful picture that captured in time she said that was promised a the road a little baby doll left motherless they're practically skin and bone I just fed them she barely had nutrients and she tried to use all of them as much as she could feed her baby deer animals their highest extent to keep themselves in there offspring live people cannot do the same.

I heard it's racing is pounding his true knocking knocking as if wanting to be raped I think I have your heart he said it's putting me everywhere that you're never going to be what you say don't understand or appreciate themselves they don't want you to not really anything cuz you did not have this problem they want me to sit there and be there in and then you and Father's day but this isn't expanding to anyone that can guess what it seems people don't want to be bothered and I think of any way to bother me that care about him being agitated and extremes they've gone to the bothering you and that's better. now question art I thought. the news of sunny day and every computer I walk in front of was there when I left the building. I could see the smoke coming out of the windows watch the TV and explosions.

I'm in bed watching too finally just relaxing to a week ago and it was with just one more time. December went by so quickly and I just wanted to go and make it through the last year at of my job app. And I always felt just like it was had just happened but I was just going to pray for the first time. I just for a little a little yeah fresh air my father and I didn't run many travels at through the Midwest as much as we went through more in St Louis we saw the downtown area we saw the malls that's been closed a lot of the Sea Breeze old friends used to live places that the houses are not as well kept you probably are now condemned you are perhaps someone else is living there there's this not really a place where a lot of people are still states structured it's not like living in New Orleans just had its pride and its culture for many many years. drove me to school quite a bit that is only when and if the last time he dropped me off it was a very Rocky rainy morning I said hello to have then he drove off to the Sun.

medium sized statue woman with all of these cat like I appearance perm straighten hair I'm sorry my pigtails blow in the Wind he went further and further

into the Sun. That was him going to the start of his day every day started with a Sun Ray and going away to begin my beach walk into start of my new school year. Seemed like he was going into the sun to me Style of course he was not driving into the sun just a figure of speech for your child and you're not too tall can't see too far over the hell seems like that's where he's gay.

of course it's a whole different culture to be involved in different kinds of weather and different kinds of States Midwest pretty humdrum you ever winter spring or summer or fall more of the summer in the winter is definite the fall in the spring 10 do Collide somewhat but the leaves do fall by the end of September. squinting outside of the window I looked at how everyone was little dots down from an airplane there's so many people about because it was the July 4th holiday and all the sudden there was planking and clashing airplanes flying and firecrackers going. can hear loads and loads a fireworks when their direction under the arch I get my daughter look at this time. My mind was empty with no hope for anyting a few hours went by and I saw a big cloud in the sky jumped Define it was on the floor.

Chapter 3: We Just Don’t Care

Chapter 22: We Won’t Stop Telling You The Truth,MyFriend

He met a friend and yet we couldn't go through Finding Nemo it was a coffee all black coffee everyday black coffee Olympic cream in the coffee Willow thought you was black it was dark and made him crazy he went looking for anyone finally came up Iraq we found his child in a Ciroc you're really funny story Stanley Charlie found any survivors how she kept hiding from him somebody for children who don't want to be you're off and running I didn't see what the point of it is till they get to the point. Lucy Wizards daughter's name and she spoke unhinged address of the clock as it sat on the wall S4 had school in the plants and everything that we saw stay consistent we were together we're overwhelmed to begin every day but there was no where we were going we were all very happy to finally be junior high in front of all of the bag sickle writers they all took a plunge it was just the sun rise of the Cascades when she was in the big Village running and soon to be in the middle of September for bats were the roads were all the problems has one set there I thought well when I go to Houston Texas or something while we didn't want to sit Africa bigger place but the car couldn't go anywhere it's just broken down there always just imagine you what we might do and he was still looking for his daughter still trying to figure out what to be there by funny name for Lucy means like can see the light of it

The leftover people were all scattered throughout the yard. After every day he had ended we did not get to ignore the cold feet that cat walking towards the other ones. Many of them wanted to join the others and pray for all of their cold feet to bow to their heads in the Forum of a monstrous pleasure so they'd all set there we had to take a trip to New Orleans and people did not think this was a good idea they did not like their feet being sick isn't not like anything they were going to be reaching for many many many many many many feet.

the day before they all had left to go to Spencer's store and buy the most expensive sheets. They were never going to be put never pack from the rooms they're never going to be not broken and they just wanted to feel as if they jumped off of their beds Temple Run.

the night before of what's his call this December 2018 7 in the morning it was the most beautiful day. The snow still nothing moved nothing was alert. The only thing that could have been better was seeing the dogs air blow out of his nose from extreme cold that enter through the door so that has. The house was at least four stories Square Windows in each wall you so looks of a typical Colonial home it was a blue Hound blue screen siding panels made of wood and standings past hundred year everyone try to be there everyone try to want to the name of the house kept everyone sent everyone wanted to wake up there.

I did I ran to the window and I ran down the hall and gressive Lee ran through the waves of all of the air that collided with how it ripped through my grapes yes I fell on the floor rolling about like I'm literally on caution bear I was shocked at the nurse and I ever sit there again and ever since since he's such a bad as before session can you during the holidays. But I just seen a ladybug there was nothing Easter magazines at the year before expired so the fireplace have to be used for wet hair and snapping acid crinkled away photographs all the past of a present.

Chapter 4: We Just Hope You Give A Damn

Stop prettying him down. He had to stay pretty and not do anything. He couldn't get as bad as he wanted to be. In so many ways no one gives a darn

between comfort and discomfort is the title
It says September 7th this is the year 2019 this is a fun year there's a glorious year deercast beerfeast time went by so quickly There was no storm today I could not see the floor my house standing as w between comfort and discomfort is the title
Everyday it's winter.

New line Monday
Blue Line and that you can see the indent and you just Uline
this is our switch to this is our switch to do indignant
indent

Chapter 1: Zero

Imperturbably beary. My favorite musical people has to be my sister Billy bear. before bear became all that she was in the store she started singing in high school and making records she's performed all over the world cleaning Japan she has very solid tympanic Club beats that could be played to her sultry jazz .

I first realize Billy bear she handed me a tape of a record a song. Like so many musical people she had a

special vibrato Special Air a voice tune it just comes up through the air things. She is done inspiring and plastic her spirit is the LIE of love togetherness an extreme training Guelph complete imperturbe Lee Berry her life is been so balanced I just called her the Ampere terribly Barry she has been sitting I know existence for difference she likes sitting in the breeze and believe is an impenetrable day so let's all try to be infertile early Berry and this is where I'll begin my journey to be like my idol I will be in future we bury in so many ways let's start out On the 1st of December.

I was born in the middle of the month timing disco's at its height it was an air of sophistication I could just go on and on there to so many people I don't see why shutter success stop being poor success is being happy to get to a point of imperturbability Barry happiness mimosa's jovial is the honey dripping from a bear right after hurts hibernation during the cold cold existence of the planet Earth there are some for which Life Goes On there's some for which there's a different Tale the bear has no Tales of this every years the summer every year is the honey this girl is what so many

try to be to not give it from anyting to walk through
those bitter snooze so many people must do to be blinded
my passion warmed by the strength of your ability
strength to go and do it's almost animal is human to
fail so many half can any of us be in Pretoria blueberry
any of us have that drive their focus then one tunnel
vision life it makes it hibernate through the dark days
history rest upon our souls mini rester gifted and
blessed is it gift people strike is not being the bear
being the human causes are suffering that we mistreat
that they will suffer this is the tale as so many others
human suffering The Berry people seem so sweet they just
picked the Bears right off a tree berries put them in
there a little dresses and scoop them up and bowls and
rush them in bowls symbols of Pies there others just
we'll catch that when of sophistication and Air what
will never be lift sway how will it be can we all try a
real animals some of us just choose to be God can we all
be in picture of Lee Barry can we all just ignore the
superfluous strenuous activities hell on Earth we all
Drive the existence of poverty existence of well does it
take the money that's something she's never been abridge
stuff and something of a circumstance provide to her

tell unbridled ability money is cast upon them to be the animal they are they exist as no

Chapter 23: Oh, They Give A Damn

other no one can seem to not hurt yep they will never not help despair pull through he people shoot at it they always preserve it it's mistake simplicity it's snowing this to enjoy the wall to wrap up in the warmth of oneself to endure the cold this is story of many tales of many people try to accomplish such a thing so many ways so many jacket ways find ourselves why bear freeing ourselves to be the humane this is what many will never do so much easier how to do a kickover tent 2Pac to steal one's honey steal one's food does the bear often do that in cases of hunger what happens when the Bears not hungry what happens is plentiful the garden is semen really feel sorry for the bear do they ever wondered when there is not sufficient and provided fattened will there ever be a time will exist is this the question I choose to stay on the side of the rich the money The Castaways steripen girls anchor avarice Envy walk two roads been with the poor the unlikely perhaps ignored and the wealth I can't tell you what money. Sweetheart here's looking at the well to do the Wella biters all the success here's to that I'm staying in for terribly Barry Oh that men can do .

Early stage of life I have to say that coming down from many peaceful days it's not a immature are small at the beach for the world. No tornado Valley this what anyting what bow down to. Plus, adieu what is the easiest. I don't see it from the start I don't spread the legs of secession and meager attitudes. there's a life and happiness, steadiness, or failure.

I stayed at home in this dedication to life study. I want to tell about the song Take My Love From the berry imperatively berry girl it just is what people take. they must be loved someone must love it sure someone must be love. How much did be for who must love must they be what is week unless they be able to Strong has a case what does not impose what is not in search of the ugly of the swing and they hating Brothers.

Mist Berryessa name before thinks that music is not like art not like Tom had it Tom was an artist he did the cover the spot it's what disconnects the book and the world father this is the picture of me pictures of men a woman disconnecting happiness where did smothered the colors run it's the tears eliminate the breast of one side the funny Parable heartbeat just pulls us into the point of dying here you see a woman on the cover is a dead woman she cannot whisper a letter of this book.

she can say anything to lay down I never walk. It's just something shocking to let the readers understand the point of life it's not to be that is to live they're two totally different words don't look similar whatsoever I think today's paper called the car moves where we live Poland match match difference between the dying and living in the book called shoe the orange rain by Rachel K. Martin well this will hit the foot like a nail in Jesus on the cross. she killed the ground, was a slave 2 the mundane, or was everyone I did not care about the Hills of grass. Complete waste of words. what's this woman a prostitute? what she crown debutante person beauty queen of high school Rich Roll? was she all things of stupidity unknowingness ignorance or hid ugly imagine and she started.

let's just cover up this life in the grave let's throw the dirt do you disagree? what's rice on the high side paints. It's good to not feel like a zero.

Chapter 2: We Won't Look Like This

Required to run towards the track . Chloe did with chicken we thought you'd want looks like this Daphne could save your life.

Chapter 2: We Won't Look Like This

How do we not look this way is it because it's Halloween to you it's because you can't see them the running everywhere this one in particular this one goes through Michelle mentioned in the Poetry of choosing your own trying there's something much like a spider on the wall just in the introvignes much like yourself reading interpreting songs like what I consider amuse hear it . to me this is the point of life one cannot get through when cannot pass through it without fighting it without chewing Dan taking that last breath. is that how it is the last moment the last breath we clench her teeth trying to survive a horrible World horrible tide change and Michelle was just a coaster the poet that must live within that moment but last poem has many different phases of change of the death of the dying as I mentioned in the last buck to the orange rain as you split and diet of course this means US Mini Splits a Bittersweet taste is in the orange rind 1 West recall supposed to leave us or last 10 to 15 seconds of Life flashing before eyes in these different frames these different stanzas of the poetry depicts all of those emotions racing before becoming free of ourselves when we come raging spirits everlasting life and a r motorcycles oh the last book was more about trying to chew to live eventually we get to the last year I think that's where this book will pick up movie about all that resides in the reflection of one's life at that last moment those last days Rising for the last challenge what will it be like for anyone Harrison introspection when's fall back people give so much advice how is it to look backwards and tell yourself or you will go for it no more. We won't look like this first of all like we are we want looks like we used to when you were sick dying decrepit weathering fattening whatever the case may be will become something that cannot recover to become the death supposedly we were big pile of dust he'll be thrown out to sea is this more of it was just an interest faction into what we will face something will will will be borne by.

We ran together Chloe we had every feeling that the last three days or empty and Shiloh of white snow ice, performance shows knives healthy walking bodies and medical and poverty togetherness much worse find sunny I need a. let's go think of moving for it. I will be there?

It's been quite a herring experience they just keep sitting there watching me will invisible people I watching you ain't heavy things in me that you and I feel their tactile you cannot see the sale practically breaking every bone in my body pinched they just keep taking all of my air and weighing me down odesse torturous all day and they keep me up all night I get no rest my eyes are peeled they're black and they are ready explosions all over the TV and nothing phases they're more than bothering me this is completely Concerta done bothering me she went to the back what's 2 two tier and that was all she does is Justin find the 2-day anymore of the two deer used to come around back I think someone hit and crush the deer and split it off to the side like a big pile of reverie organs and blood the head of used to recognize so dearly when her go baby dad Aerotek such a beautiful picture that captured in time she said that was promised a the road a little baby doll left motherless they're practically skin and bone I just fed them she barely had nutrients and she tried to use all of them as much as she could feed her baby deer

Chapter 24: Honey, What are You Going To Do?

animals their highest extent to keep themselves in there offspring live people cannot do the same.

I heard it's racing is pounding his true knocking knocking as if wanting to be raped I think I have your heart he said it's putting me everywhere that you're never going to be what you say don't understand or appreciate themselves they don't want you to not really anything cuz you did not have this problem they want me to sit there and be there in and then you and Father's day but this isn't expanding to anyone that can guess what it seems people don't want to be bothered and I think of any way to bother me that care about him being agitated and extremes they've gone to the bothering you and that's better. now question art I thought. the news of sunny day and every computer I walk in front of was there when I left the building. I could see the smoke coming out of the windows watch the TV and explosions. I'm in bed watching too finally just relaxing to a week ago and it was with just one more time. December went by so quickly and I just wanted to go and make it through the last year at of my job app. And I always felt just like it was had just happened but I was just going to pray for the first time. I just for a little a little yeah fresh air my father and I didn't run many travels at through the Midwest as much as we went through more in St Louis we saw the downtown area we saw the malls that's been closed a lot of the Sea Breeze old friends used to live places that the houses are not as well kept you probably are now condemned you are perhaps someone else is living there there's this not really a place where a lot of people are still states structured it's not like living in New Orleans just had its pride and its culture for many many years. drove me to school quite a bit that is only when and if the last time he dropped me off it was a very Rocky rainy morning I said hello to have then he drove off to the Sun.

medium sized statue woman with all of these cat like I appearance perm straighten hair I'm sorry my pigtails blow in the Wind he went further and further into the Sun. That was him going to the start of his day every day started with a Sun Ray and going away to begin my beach walk into start of my new school year. Seemed like he was going into the sun to me Style of course he was not driving into the sun just a figure of speech for your child and you're not too tall can't see too far over the hell seems like that's where he's gay.

of course it's a whole different culture to be involved in different kinds of weather and different kinds of States Midwest pretty humdrum you ever winter spring or summer or fall more of the summer in the winter is definite the fall in the spring 10 do Collide somewhat but the leaves do fall by the end of September. squinting outside of the window I looked at how everyone was little dots down from an airplane there's so many people about because it was the July 4th holiday and all the sudden there was planking and clashing airplanes flying and firecrackers going. can hear loads and loads a fireworks when their direction under the arch I get my daughter look at this time. My mind was empty with no hope for anyting a few hours went by and I saw a big cloud in the sky jumped Define it was on the floor.

rom extreme cold that enter through the door so that has. The house was at least four stories Square Windows in each wall you so looks of a typical Colonial home it was a blue Hound blue screen siding panels made of wood and standings past hundred year everyone try to be there everyone try to want to the name of the house kept everyone sent everyone wanted to wake up there.

I did I ran to the window and I ran down the hall and gressive Lee ran through the waves of all of the air that collided with how it ripped through my grapes yes I fell on the floor rolling about like I'm literally on caution bear I was shocked at the nurse and I ever sit there again and ever since since he's such a bad as before session can you during the holidays. But I just seen a ladybug there was nothing Easter magazines at the year before expired so the fireplace have to be used for wet hair and snapping acid crinkled away photographs all the past of a present.

Chapter 4: We Just Hope You Give A Damn

Stop prettying him down. He had to stay pretty and not do anything. He couldn't get as bad as he wanted to be. In so many ways no one gives a darn

between comfort and discomfort is the title
It says September 7th this is the year 2019 this is a fun year there's a glorious year deercast beerfeast time went by so quickly There was no storm today I could not see the floor my house standing as w between comfort and discomfort is the title Everyday it's winter.

New line Monday
Blue Line and that you can see the indent and you just Uline
this is our switch to this is our switch to do indignant
indent

Chapter 1: Zero

Imperturbably beary. My favorite musical people has to be my sister Billy bear. before bear became all that she was in the store she started singing in high school and making records she's performed all over the world cleaning Japan she has very solid tympanic Club beats that could be played to her sultry jazz .

I first realize Billy bear she handed me a tape of a record a song. Like so many musical people she had a special vibrato Special Air a voice tune it just comes up through the air things. She is done inspiring and plastic her spirit is the LIE of love togetherness an extreme training Guelph complete imperturbe Lee Berry her life is been so balanced I just called her the Ampere terribly Barry she has been sitting I know existence for difference she likes sitting in the breeze and believe is an impenetrable day so let's all try to be infertile early Berry and this is where I'll begin my journey to be like my idol I will be in future we bury in so many ways let's start out On the 1st of December.

I was born in the middle of the month timing disco's at its height it was an air of sophistication I could just go on and on there to so many people I don't

see why shutter success stop being poor success is being happy to get to a point of imperturbability Barry happiness mimosa's jovial is the honey dripping from a bear right after hurts hibernation during the cold cold existence of the planet Earth there are some for which Life Goes On there's some for which there's a different Tale the bear has no Tales of this every years the summer every year is the honey this girl is what so many try to be to not give it from anyting to walk through those bitter snooze so many people must do to be blinded my passion warmed by the strength of your ability strength to go and do it's almost animal is human to fail so many half can any of us be in Pretoria blueberry any of us have that drive their focus then one tunnel vision life it makes it hibernate through the dark days history rest upon our souls mini rester gifted and blessed is it gift people strike is not being the bear being the human causes are suffering that we mistreat that they will suffer this is the tale as so many others human suffering The

Chapter 25: You're Amazing

Berry people seem so sweet they just picked the Bears right off a tree berries put them in there a little dresses and scoop them up and bowls and rush them in bowls symbols of Pies there others just we'll catch that when of sophistication and Air what will never be lift sway how will it be can we all try a real animals some of us just choose to be God can we all be in picture of Lee Barry can we all just ignore the superfluous strenuous activities hell on Earth we all Drive the existence of poverty existence of well does it take the money that's something she's never been abridge stuff and something of a circumstance provide to her tell unbridled ability money is cast upon them to be the animal they are they exist as no other no one can seem to not hurt yep they will never not help despair pull through he people shoot at it they always preserve it it's mistake simplicity it's snowing this to enjoy the wall to wrap up in the warmth of oneself to endure the cold this is story of many tales of many people try to accomplish such a thing so many ways so many jacket ways find ourselves why bear freeing ourselves to be the humane this is what many will never do so much easier how to do a kickover tent 2Pac to steal one's honey steal one's food does the bear often do that in cases of hunger what happens when the Bears not hungry what happens is plentiful the garden is semen really feel sorry for the bear do they ever wondered when there is not sufficient and provided fattened will there ever be a time will exist is this the question I choose to stay on the side of the rich the money The Castaways steripen girls anchor avarice Envy walk two roads been with the poor the unlikely perhaps ignored and the wealth I can't tell you what money. Sweetheart here's looking at the well to do the Wella biters all the success here's to that I'm staying in for terribly Barry Oh that men can do .

Early stage of life I have to say that coming down from many peaceful days it's not a immature are small at the beach for the world. No tornado Valley this what anyting what bow down to. Plus, adieu what is the easiest. I don't see it from the start I don't spread the legs of secession and meager attitudes. there's a life and happiness, steadiness, or failure.

I stayed at home in this dedication to life study. I want to tell about the song Take My Love From the berry imperatively berry girl it just is what people take. they must be loved someone must love it sure someone must be love. How much did be for who must love must they be what is week unless they be able to Strong has a case what does not impose what is not in search of the ugly of the swing and they hating Brothers.

Mist Berryessa name before thinks that music is not like art not like Tom had it Tom was an artist he did the cover the spot it's what disconnects the book and the world father this is the picture of me pictures of men a woman disconnecting happiness where did smothered the colors run it's the tears eliminate the breast of one side the funny Parable heartbeat just pulls us into the point of dying here you see a woman on the cover is a dead woman she cannot whisper a letter of this book.

she can say anything to lay down I never walk. It's just something shocking to let the readers understand the point of life it's not to be that is to live they're two totally different words don't look similar whatsoever I think today's paper called the car moves where we live Poland match match difference between the dying and living in the book called shoe the orange rain by Rachel K. Martin well this will hit the foot like a nail in Jesus on the cross. she killed the ground, was a slave 2 the mundane, or was everyone I did not care about the Hills of grass. Complete waste of words. what's this woman a prostitute? what she crown debutante person beauty queen of high school Rich Roll? was she all things of stupidity unknowingness ignorance or hid ugly imagine and she started.

let's just cover up this life in the grave let's throw the dirt do you disagree? what's rice on the high side paints. It's good to not feel like a zero.

Chapter 2: We Won’t Look Like This

Required to run towards the track . Chloe did with chicken we thought you'd want looks like this Daphne could save your life.

Chapter 2: We Won’t Look Like This

How do we not look this way is it because it's Halloween to you it's because you can't see them the running everywhere this one in particular this one goes through Michelle mentioned in the Poetry of choosing your own

trying there's something much like a spider on the wall just in the introvignes much like yourself reading interpreting songs like what I consider amuse hear it . to me this is the point of life one cannot get through when cannot pass through it without fighting it without chewing Dan taking that last breath. is that how it is the last moment the last breath we clench her teeth trying to survive a horrible World horrible tide change and Michelle was just a coaster the poet that must live within that moment but last poem has many different phases of change of the death of the dying as I mentioned in the last buck to the orange rain as you split and diet of course this means US Mini Splits a Bittersweet taste is in the orange rind 1 West recall supposed to leave us or last 10 to 15 seconds of Life flashing before eyes in these different frames these different stanzas of the poetry depicts all of those emotions racing before becoming free of ourselves when we come raging spirits everlasting life and a r motorcycles oh the last book was more about trying to chew to live eventually we get to the last year I think that's where this book will pick up movie about all that resides in the reflection of one's life at that last

moment those last days Rising for the last challenge what will it be like for anyone Harrison introspection when's fall back people give so much advice how is it to look backwards and tell yourself or you will go for it no more. We won't look like this first of all like we are we want looks like we used to when you were sick dying decrepit weathering fattening whatever the case may be will become something that cannot recover to become the death supposedly we were big pile of dust he'll be thrown out to sea is this more of it was just an interest faction into what we will face something will will will be borne by.

We ran together Chloe we had every feeling that the last three days or empty and Shiloh of white snow ice, performance shows knives healthy walking bodies and medical and poverty togetherness much worse find sunny I need a. let's go think of moving for it. I will be there?

It's been quite a herring experience they just keep sitting there watching me will invisible people I watching you ain't heavy things in me that you and I feel their tactile you cannot see the sale practically breaking every bone in my body pinched they just keep taking all of my air and weighing me down odesse torturous all day and they keep me up all night I get no rest my eyes are peeled they're black and they are ready explosions all over the TV and nothing phases they're more than bothering me this is completely Concerta done

Chapter 25: Woaw, When You Can't Remember?

bothering me she went to the back what's 2 two tier and that was all she does is Justin find the 2-day anymore of the two

deer used to come around back I think someone hit and crush the deer and split it off to the side like a big pile of reverie organs and blood the head of used to recognize so dearly when her go baby dad Aerotek such a beautiful picture that captured in time she said that was promised a the road a little baby doll left motherless they're practically skin and bone I just fed them she barely had nutrients and she tried to use all of them as much as she could feed her baby deer animals their highest extent to keep themselves in there offspring live people cannot do the same.

I heard it's racing is pounding his true knocking knocking as if wanting to be raped I think I have your heart he said it's putting me everywhere that you're never going to be what you say don't understand or appreciate themselves they don't want you to not really anything cuz you did not have this problem they want me to sit there and be there in and then you and Father's day but this isn't expanding to anyone that can guess what it seems people don't want to be bothered and I think of any way to bother me that care about him being agitated and extremes they've gone to the bothering you and that's better. now question art I thought. the news of sunny day and every computer I walk in front of was there when I left the building. I could see the smoke coming out of the windows watch the TV and explosions. I'm in bed watching too finally just relaxing to a week ago and it was with just one more time. December went by so quickly and I just wanted to go and make it through the last year at of my job app. And I always felt just like it was had just happened but I was just going to pray for the first time. I just for a little a little yeah fresh air my father and I didn't run many travels at through the Midwest as much as we went through more in St Louis we saw the downtown area we saw the malls that's been closed a lot of the Sea Breeze old friends used to live places that the houses are not as well kept you probably are now condemned you are perhaps someone else is living there there's this not really a place where a lot of people are still states structured it's not like living in New Orleans just had its pride and its culture for many many years. drove me to school quite a bit that is only when and if the last time he dropped me off it was a very Rocky rainy morning I said hello to have then he drove off to the Sun.

medium sized statue woman with all of these cat like I appearance perm straighten hair I'm sorry my pigtails blow in the Wind he went further and further into the Sun. That was him going to the start of his day every day started with a Sun Ray and going away to begin my beach walk into start of my new school year. Seemed like he was going into the sun to me Style of course he was not driving into the sun just a figure of speech for your child and you're not too tall can't see too far over the hell seems like that's where he's gay.

of course it's a whole different culture to be involved in different kinds of weather and different kinds of States Midwest pretty humdrum you ever winter spring or summer or fall more of the summer in the winter is definite the fall in the spring 10 do Collide somewhat but the leaves do fall by the end of September. squinting outside of the window I looked at how everyone was little dots down from an airplane there's so many people about because it was the July 4th holiday and all the sudden there was planking and clashing airplanes flying and firecrackers going. can hear loads and loads a fireworks when their direction under the arch I get my daughter look at this time. My mind was empty with no hope for anyting a few hours went by and I saw a big cloud in the sky jumped Define it was on the floor.

Chapter 3: We Just Don't Care

He met a friend and yet we couldn't go through Finding Nemo it was a coffee all black coffee everyday black coffee Olympic cream in the coffee Willow thought you was black it was dark and made him crazy he went looking for anyone finally came up Iraq we found his child in a Ciroc you're really funny story Stanley Charlie found any survivors how she kept hiding from him somebody for children who don't want to be you're off and running I didn't see what the point of it is till they get to the point. Lucy Wizards daughter's name and she spoke unhinged address of the clock as it sat on the wall S4 had school in the plants and everything that we saw stay consistent we were together we're overwhelmed to begin every day but there was no where we were going we were all very happy to finally be junior high in front of all of the bag sickle writers they all took a plunge it was just the sun rise of the Cascades when she was in the big Village running and soon to be in the middle of September for bats were the roads were all the problems has one set there I thought well when I go to Houston Texas or something while we didn't want to sit Africa bigger place but the car couldn't go anywhere it's just broken down there always just imagine you what we might do and he was still looking for his daughter still trying to figure out what to be there by funny name for Lucy means like can see the light of it

The leftover people were all scattered throughout the yard. After every day he had ended we did not get to ignore the cold feet that cat walking towards the other ones. Many of them wanted to join the others and pray for all of their cold feet to bow to their heads in the Forum of a monstrous pleasure so they'd all set there we had to take a trip to New Orleans and people did not think this was a good idea they did not like their feet being sick isn't not like anything they were going to be reaching for many many many many many many feet.

the day before they all had left to go to Spencer's store and buy the most expensive sheets. They were never going to be put never pack from the rooms they're never going to be not broken and they just wanted to feel as if they jumped off of their beds Temple Run.

the night before of what's his call this December 2018 7 in the morning it was the most beautiful day. The snow still nothing moved nothing was alert. The only thing that could have been better was seeing the dogs air blow out of his nose from extreme cold that enter through the door so that has. The

Chapter 26: My Goodness! What you have to Rely on?

house was at least four stories Square Windows in each wall you so looks of a typical Colonial home it was a blue Hound blue screen siding panels made of wood and standings past hundred year everyone try to be there everyone try to want to the name of the house kept everyone sent everyone wanted to wake up there.

I did I ran to the window and I ran down the hall and gressive Lee ran through the waves of all of the air that collided with how it ripped through my grapes yes I fell on the floor rolling about like I'm literally on caution bear I was shocked at the nurse and I ever sit there again and ever since since he's such a bad as before session can you during the holidays. But I just seen a ladybug there was nothing Easter magazines at the year before expired so the fireplace have to be used for wet hair and snapping acid crinkled away photographs all the past of a present.

Chapter 4: We Just Hope You Give A Damn

Stop prettying him down. He had to stay pretty and not do anything. He couldn't get as bad as he wanted to be. In so many ways no one gives a darn

between comfort and discomfort is the title
It says September 7th this is the year 2019 this is a fun year there's a glorious year deercast beerfeast time went by so quickly There was no storm today I could not see the floor my house standing as w between comfort and discomfort is the title
Everyday it's winter.

New line Monday
Blue Line and that you can see the indent and you just Uline
this is our switch to this is our switch to do indignant
indent

Chapter 1: Zero

Imperturbably beary. My favorite musical people has to be my sister Billy bear. before bear became all that she was in the store she started singing in high school and making records she's performed all over the world cleaning Japan she has very solid tympanic Club beats that could be played to her sultry jazz .

I first realize Billy bear she handed me a tape of a record a song. Like so many musical people she had a

special vibrato Special Air a voice tune it just comes up through the air things. She is done inspiring and plastic her spirit is the LIE of love togetherness an extreme training Guelph complete imperturbe Lee Berry her life is been so balanced I just called her the Ampere terribly Barry she has been sitting I know existence for difference she likes sitting in the breeze and believe is an impenetrable day so let's all try to be infertile early Berry and this is where I'll begin my journey to be like my idol I will be in future we bury in so many ways let's start out On the 1st of December.

I was born in the middle of the month timing disco's at its height it was an air of sophistication I could just go on and on there to so many people I don't see why shutter success stop being poor success is being happy to get to a point of imperturbability Barry happiness mimosa's jovial is the honey dripping from a bear right after hurts hibernation during the cold cold existence of the planet Earth there are some for which Life Goes On there's some for which there's a different Tale the bear has no Tales of this every years the summer every year is the honey this girl is what so many

try to be to not give it from anyting to walk through
those bitter snooze so many people must do to be blinded
my passion warmed by the strength of your ability
strength to go and do it's almost animal is human to
fail so many half can any of us be in Pretoria blueberry
any of us have that drive their focus then one tunnel
vision life it makes it hibernate through the dark days
history rest upon our souls mini rester gifted and
blessed is it gift people strike is not being the bear
being the human causes are suffering that we mistreat
that they will suffer this is the tale as so many others
human suffering The Berry people seem so sweet they just
picked the Bears right off a tree berries put them in
there a little dresses and scoop them up and bowls and
rush them in bowls symbols of Pies there others just
we'll catch that when of sophistication and Air what
will never be lift sway how will it be can we all try a
real animals some of us just choose to be God can we all
be in picture of Lee Barry can we all just ignore the
superfluous strenuous activities hell on Earth we all
Drive the existence of poverty existence of well does it
take the money that's something she's never been abridge
stuff and something of a circumstance provide to her

tell unbridled ability money is cast upon them to be the animal they are they exist as no other no one can seem to not hurt yep they will never not help despair pull through he people shoot at it they always preserve it it's mistake simplicity it's snowing this to enjoy the wall to wrap up in the warmth of oneself to endure the cold this is story of many tales of many people try to accomplish such a thing so many ways so many jacket ways find ourselves why bear freeing ourselves to be the humane this is what many will never do so much easier how to do a kickover tent 2Pac to steal one's honey steal one's food does the bear often do that in cases of hunger what happens when the Bears not hungry what happens is plentiful the garden is semen really feel sorry for the bear do they ever wondered when there is not sufficient and provided fattened will there ever be a time will exist is this the question I choose to stay on the side of the rich the money The Castaways steripen girls anchor avarice Envy walk two roads been with the poor the unlikely perhaps ignored and the wealth I can't tell you what money. Sweetheart here's looking at the well to do the Wella biters all the success here's to that I'm staying in for terribly Barry Oh that men can do .

Early stage of life I have to say that coming down from many peaceful days it's not a immature are small at the beach for the world. No tornado Valley this what anyting what bow down to. Plus, adieu what is the easiest. I don't see it from the start I don't spread the legs of secession and meager attitudes. there's a life and happiness, steadiness, or failure.

I stayed at home in this dedication to life study. I want to tell about the song Take My Love From the berry imperatively berry girl it just is what people take. they must be loved someone must love it sure someone must be love. How much did be for who must love must they be what is week unless they be able to Strong has a case what does not impose what is not in search of the ugly of the swing and they hating Brothers.

Mist Berryessa name before thinks that music is not like art not like Tom had it Tom was an artist he did the cover the spot it's what disconnects the book and the world father this is the picture of me pictures of men a woman disconnecting happiness where did smothered the colors run it's the tears eliminate the breast of one side the funny Parable heartbeat just pulls us into the point of dying here you see a woman on the cover is a dead woman she cannot whisper a letter of this book.

she can say anything to lay down I never walk. It's just something shocking to let the readers understand the point of life it's not to be that is to live they're two totally different words don't look similar whatsoever I think today's paper called the car moves where we live Poland match match difference between the dying and living in the book called shoe the orange rain by Rachel K. Martin well this will hit the foot like a nail in Jesus on the cross. she killed the ground, was a slave 2 the mundane, or was everyone I did not care about the Hills of grass. Complete waste of words. what's this woman a prostitute? what she crown debutante person beauty queen of high school Rich Roll? was she all things of stupidity unknowingness ignorance or hid ugly imagine and she started.

let's just cover up this life in the grave let's throw the dirt do you disagree? what's rice on the high side paints. It's good to not feel like a zero.

Chapter 27: Do You Promise, Sweetheart?

Required to run towards the track . Chloe did with chicken we thought you'd want looks like this Daphne could save your life.

Chapter 2: We Won't Look Like This

How do we not look this way is it because it's Halloween to you it's because you can't see them the running everywhere this one in particular this one goes through Michelle mentioned in the Poetry of choosing your own trying there's something much like a spider on the wall just in the introvignes much like yourself reading interpreting songs like what I consider amuse hear it . to me this is the point of life one cannot get through when cannot pass through it without fighting it without chewing Dan taking that last breath. is that how it is the last moment the last breath we clench her teeth trying to survive a horrible World horrible tide change and Michelle was just a coaster the poet that must live within that moment but last poem has many different phases of change of the death of the dying as I mentioned in the last buck to the orange rain as you split and diet of course this means US Mini Splits a Bittersweet taste is in the orange rind 1 West recall supposed to leave us or last 10 to 15 seconds of Life flashing before eyes in these different frames these different stanzas of the poetry depicts all of those emotions racing before becoming free of ourselves when we come raging spirits everlasting life and a r motorcycles oh the last book was more about trying to chew to live eventually we get to the last year I think that's where this book will pick up movie about all that resides in the reflection of one's life at that last moment those last days Rising for the last challenge what will it be like for anyone Harrison introspection when's fall back people give so much advice how is it to look backwards and tell yourself or you will go for it no more. We won't look like this first of all like we are we want looks like we used to when you were sick dying decrepit weathering fattening whatever the case may be will become something that cannot recover to become the death supposedly we were big pile of dust he'll be thrown out to sea is this more of it was just an interest faction into what we will face something will will will be borne by.

We ran together Chloe we had every feeling that the last three days or empty and Shiloh of white snow ice, performance shows knives healthy walking bodies and medical and poverty togetherness much worse find sunny I need a. let's go think of moving for it. I will be there?

It's been quite a herring experience they just keep sitting there watching me will invisible people I watching you ain't heavy things in me that you and I feel their tactile you cannot see the sale practically breaking every bone in my body pinched they just keep taking all of my air and weighing me down odesse torturous all day and they keep me up all night I get no rest my eyes are peeled they're black and they are ready explosions all over the TV and nothing phases they're more than bothering me this is completely Concerta done bothering me she went to the back what's 2 two tier and that was all she does is Justin find the 2-day anymore of the two deer used to come around back I think someone hit and crush the deer and split it off to the side like a big pile of reverie organs and blood the head of used to recognize so dearly when her go baby dad Aerotek such a beautiful picture that captured in time she said that was promised a the road a little baby doll left motherless they're practically skin and bone I just fed them she barely had nutrients and she tried to use all of them as much as she could feed her baby deer animals their highest extent to keep themselves in there offspring live people cannot do the same.

I heard it's racing is pounding his true knocking knocking as if wanting to be raped I think I have your heart he said it's putting me everywhere that you're never going to be what you say don't understand or appreciate themselves they don't want you to not really anything cuz you did not have this problem they want me to sit there and be there in and then you and Father's day but this isn't expanding to anyone that can guess what it seems people don't want to be bothered and I think of any way to bother me that care about him being agitated and extremes they've gone to the bothering you and that's better. now question art I thought. the news of sunny day and every computer I walk in front of was there when I left the building. I could see the smoke coming out of the windows watch the TV and explosions. I'm in bed watching too finally just relaxing to a week ago and it was with just one more time. December went by so quickly and I just wanted to go and make it through the last year at of my job app. And I always felt just like it was had just happened but I was just going to pray for the first time. I just for a little a little yeah fresh air my father and I didn't run many travels at through the Midwest as much as we went through more in St Louis we saw the downtown area we saw the malls that's been closed a lot of the Sea Breeze old friends used to live places that the houses are not as well kept you probably are now condemned you are perhaps someone else is living there there's this not really a place where a lot of people are still states structured it's not like living in New Orleans just had its pride and its culture for many many years. drove me to school quite a bit that is only when and if the last time he dropped me off it was a very Rocky rainy morning I said hello to have then he drove off to the Sun.

medium sized statue woman with all of these cat like I appearance perm straighten hair I'm sorry my pigtails blow in the Wind he went further and further into the Sun. That was him going to the start of his day every day started with a Sun Ray and going away to begin my beach walk into start of my new school year. Seemed like he was going into the sun to me Style of course he was not driving into the sun just a figure of speech for your child and you're not too tall can't see too far over the hell seems like that's where he's gay.

Chapter 28: Help Us?

of course it's a whole different culture to be involved in different kinds of weather and different kinds of States

Midwest pretty humdrum you ever winter spring or summer or fall more of the summer in the winter is definite the fall in the spring 10 do Collide somewhat but the leaves do fall by the end of September. squinting outside of the window I looked at how everyone was little dots down from an airplane there's so many people about because it was the July 4th holiday and all the sudden there was planking and clashing airplanes flying and firecrackers going. can hear loads and loads a fireworks when their direction under the arch I get my daughter look at this time. My mind was empty with no hope for anyting a few hours went by and I saw a big cloud in the sky jumped Define it was on the floor.

rom extreme cold that enter through the door so that has. The house was at least four stories Square Windows in each wall you so looks of a typical Colonial home it was a blue Hound blue screen siding panels made of wood and standings past hundred year everyone try to be there everyone try to want to the name of the house kept everyone sent everyone wanted to wake up there.

I did I ran to the window and I ran down the hall and gressive Lee ran through the waves of all of the air that collided with how it ripped through my grapes yes I fell on the floor rolling about like I'm literally on caution bear I was shocked at the nurse and I ever sit there again and ever since since he's such a bad as before session can you during the holidays. But I just seen a ladybug there was nothing Easter magazines at the

year before expired so the fireplace have to be used for wet hair and snapping acid crinkled away photographs all the past of a present.

Chapter 4: We Just Hope You Give A Damn

Stop prettying him down. He had to stay pretty and not do anything. He couldn't get as bad as he wanted to be. In so many ways no one gives a darn

between comfort and discomfort is the title
It says September 7th this is the year 2019 this is a fun year there's a glorious year deercast beerfeast time went by so quickly There was no storm today I could not see the floor my house standing as w between comfort and discomfort is the title
Everyday it's winter.

New line Monday
Blue Line and that you can see the indent and you just Uline
this is our switch to this is our switch to do indignant
indent

Chapter 1: Zero

Imperturbabably beary. My favorite musical people has to be my sister Billy bear. before bear became all that she was in the store she started singing in high school and making records she's performed all over the world cleaning Japan she has very solid tympanic Club beats that could be played to her sultry jazz .

I first realize Billy bear she handed me a tape of a record a song. Like so many musical people she had a special vibrato Special Air a voice tune it just comes up through the air things. She is done inspiring and plastic her spirit is the LIE of love togetherness an extreme training Guelph complete imperturbe Lee Berry her life is been so balanced I just called her the Ampere terribly Barry she has been sitting I know existence for difference she likes sitting in the breeze and believe is an impenetrable day so let's all try to be infertile early Berry and this is where I'll begin my journey to be like my idol I will be in future we bury in so many ways let's start out On the 1st of December.

I was born in the middle of the month timing disco's at its height it was an air of sophistication I could just go on and on there to so many people I don't

see why shutter success stop being poor success is being happy to get to a point of imperturbability Barry happiness mimosa's jovial is the honey dripping from a bear right after hurts hibernation during the cold cold existence of the planet Earth there are some for which Life Goes On there's some for which there's a different Tale the bear has no Tales of this every years the summer every year is the honey this girl is what so many try to be to not give it from anyting to walk through those bitter snooze so many people must do to be blinded my passion warmed by the strength of your ability strength to go and do it's almost animal is human to fail so many half can any of us be in Pretoria blueberry any of us have that drive their focus then one tunnel vision life it makes it hibernate through the dark days history rest upon our souls mini rester gifted and blessed is it gift people strike is not being the bear being the human causes are suffering that we mistreat that they will suffer this is the tale as so many others human suffering The Berry people seem so sweet they just picked the Bears right off a tree berries put them in there a little dresses and scoop them up and bowls and rush them in bowls symbols of Pies there others just

we'll catch that when of sophistication and Air what will never be lift sway how will it be can we all try a real animals some of us just choose to be God can we all be in picture of Lee Barry can we all just ignore the superfluous strenuous activities hell on Earth we all Drive the existence of poverty existence of well does it take the money that's something she's never been abridge stuff and something of a circumstance provide to her tell unbridled ability money is cast upon them to be the animal they are they exist as no other no one can seem to not hurt yep they will never not help despair pull through he people shoot at it they always preserve it it's mistake simplicity it's snowing this to enjoy the wall to wrap up in the warmth of oneself to endure the cold this is story of many tales of many people try to accomplish such a thing so many ways so many jacket ways find ourselves why bear freeing ourselves to be the humane this is what many will never do so much easier how to do a kickover tent 2Pac to steal one's honey steal one's food does the bear often do that in cases of hunger what happens when the Bears not hungry what happens is plentiful the garden is semen really feel sorry for the bear do they ever wondered when there is not sufficient and provided fattened will there ever be a time will exist is this the question I choose to stay on the side of the rich the money The Castaways steripen girls anchor avarice Envy walk two roads been with the poor the unlikely perhaps ignored and the wealth I can't tell you what money. Sweetheart here's looking at the well to do the Wella biters all the success here's to that I'm staying in for terribly Barry Oh that men can do .

Early stage of life I have to say that coming down from many peaceful days it's not a immature are small at the beach for the world. No tornado Valley this what anyting what bow down to. Plus, adieu what is the easiest. I don't see it from the start I don't spread the legs of secession and meager attitudes. there's a life and happiness, steadiness, or failure.

Chapter 28: Stop Listening To Her Ass!

I stayed at home in this dedication to life study. I want to tell about the song Take My Love From the berry imperatively berry girl it just is what people take. they must be loved someone must love it sure someone must be love. How much did be for who must love must they be what is week unless they be able to Strong has a case what does not impose what is not in search of the ugly of the swing and they hating Brothers.

Mist Berryessa name before thinks that music is not like art not like Tom had it Tom was an artist he did the cover the spot it's what disconnects the book and the world father this is the picture of me pictures of men a woman disconnecting happiness where did smothered the colors run it's the tears eliminate the breast of one side the funny Parable heartbeat just pulls us into the point of dying here you see a woman on the cover is a dead woman she cannot whisper a letter of this book.

she can say anything to lay down I never walk. It's just something shocking to let the readers understand the point of life it's not to be that is to live they're two totally different words don't look similar whatsoever I think today's paper called the car moves where we live Poland match match difference between the dying and living in the book called shoe the orange rain by Rachel K. Martin well this will hit the foot like a nail in Jesus on the cross. she killed the ground, was a slave 2 the mundane, or was everyone I did not care about the Hills of grass. Complete waste of words. what's this woman a prostitute? what she crown debutante person beauty queen of high school Rich Roll? was she all things of stupidity unknowingness ignorance or hid ugly imagine and she started.

let's just cover up this life in the grave let's throw the dirt do you disagree? what's rice on the high side paints. It's good to not feel like a zero.

Chapter 2: We Won't Look Like This

Required to run towards the track . Chloe did with chicken we thought you'd want looks like this Daphne could save your life.

Chapter 2: We Won't Look Like This

How do we not look this way is it because it's Halloween to you it's because you can't see them the running everywhere this one in particular this one goes through Michelle mentioned in the Poetry of choosing your own

trying there's something much like a spider on the wall
just in the introvignes much like yourself reading
interpreting songs like what I consider amuse hear it .
to me this is the point of life one cannot get through
when cannot pass through it without fighting it without
chewing Dan taking that last breath. is that how it is
the last moment the last breath we clench her teeth
trying to survive a horrible World horrible tide change
and Michelle was just a coaster the poet that must live
within that moment but last poem has many different
phases of change of the death of the dying as I
mentioned in the last buck to the orange rain as you
split and diet of course this means US Mini Splits a
Bittersweet taste is in the orange rind 1 West recall
supposed to leave us or last 10 to 15 seconds of Life
flashing before eyes in these different frames these
different stanzas of the poetry depicts all of those
emotions racing before becoming free of ourselves when
we come raging spirits everlasting life and a r
motorcycles oh the last book was more about trying to
chew to live eventually we get to the last year I think
that's where this book will pick up movie about all that
resides in the reflection of one's life at that last

moment those last days Rising for the last challenge what will it be like for anyone Harrison introspection when's fall back people give so much advice how is it to look backwards and tell yourself or you will go for it no more. We won't look like this first of all like we are we want looks like we used to when you were sick dying decrepit weathering fattening whatever the case may be will become something that cannot recover to become the death supposedly we were big pile of dust he'll be thrown out to sea is this more of it was just an interest faction into what we will face something will will will be borne by.

We ran together Chloe we had every feeling that the last three days or empty and Shiloh of white snow ice, performance shows knives healthy walking bodies and medical and poverty togetherness much worse find sunny I need a. let's go think of moving for it. I will be there?

It's been quite a herring experience they just keep sitting there watching me will invisible people I watching you

Chapter 29: We Really Don't Give a Shit

ain't heavy things in me that you and I feel their tactile you cannot see the sale practically breaking every bone in my body

pinched they just keep taking all of my air and weighing me down odesse torturous all day and they keep me up all night I get no rest my eyes are peeled they're black and they are ready explosions all over the TV and nothing phases they're more than bothering me this is completely Concerta done bothering me she went to the back what's 2 two tier and that was all she does is Justin find the 2-day anymore of the two deer used to come around back I think someone hit and crush the deer and split it off to the side like a big pile of reverie organs and blood the head of used to recognize so dearly when her go baby dad Aerotek such a beautiful picture that captured in time she said that was promised a the road a little baby doll left motherless they're practically skin and bone I just fed them she barely had nutrients and she tried to use all of them as much as she could feed her baby deer animals their highest extent to keep themselves in there offspring live people cannot do the same.

I heard it's racing is pounding his true knocking knocking as if wanting to be raped I think I have your heart he said it's putting me everywhere that you're never going to be what you say don't understand or appreciate themselves they don't want you to not really anything cuz you did not have this problem they want me to sit there and be there in and then you and Father's day but this isn't expanding to anyone that can guess what it seems people don't want to be bothered and I think of any way to bother me that care about him being agitated and extremes they've gone to the bothering you and that's better. now question art I thought. the news of sunny day and every computer I walk in front of was there when I left the building. I could see the smoke coming out of the windows watch the TV and explosions. I'm in bed watching too finally just relaxing to a week ago and it was with just one more time. December went by so quickly and I just wanted to go and make it through the last year at of my job app. And I always felt just like it was had just happened but I was just going to pray for the first time. I just for a little a little yeah fresh air my father and I didn't run many travels at through the Midwest as much as we went through more

in St Louis we saw the downtown area we saw the malls that's been closed a lot of the Sea Breeze old friends used to live places that the houses are not as well kept you probably are now condemned you are perhaps someone else is living there there's this not really a place where a lot of people are still states structured it's not like living in New Orleans just had its pride and its culture for many many years. drove me to school quite a bit that is only when and if the last time he dropped me off it was a very Rocky rainy morning I said hello to have then he drove off to the Sun.

medium sized statue woman with all of these cat like I appearance perm straighten hair I'm sorry my pigtails blow in the Wind he went further and further into the Sun. That was him going to the start of his day every day started with a Sun Ray and going away to begin my beach walk into start of my new school year. Seemed like he was going into the sun to me Style of course he was not driving into the sun just a figure of speech for your child and you're not too tall can't see too far over the hell seems like that's where he's gay.

of course it's a whole different culture to be involved in different kinds of weather and different kinds of States Midwest pretty humdrum you ever winter spring or summer or fall more of the summer in the winter is definite the fall in the spring 10 do Collide somewhat but the leaves do fall by the end of September. squinting outside of the window I looked at how everyone was little dots down from an airplane there's so many people about because it was the July 4th holiday and all the sudden there was planking and clashing airplanes flying and firecrackers going. can hear loads and loads a fireworks when their direction under the arch I get my daughter look at this time. My mind was empty with no hope for anyting a few hours went by and I saw a big cloud in the sky jumped Define it was on the floor.

Chapter 3: We Just Don’t Care

He met a friend and yet we couldn't go through Finding Nemo it was a coffee all black coffee everyday black coffee Olympic cream in the coffee Willow thought you was black it was dark and made him crazy he went looking for anyone finally came up Iraq we found his child in a Ciroc you're really funny story Stanley Charlie found any survivors how she kept hiding from him somebody for children who don't want to be you're off and running I didn't see what the point of it is till they get to the point. Lucy Wizards daughter's name and she spoke unhinged address of the clock as it sat on the wall S4 had school in the plants and everything that we saw stay consistent we were together we're overwhelmed to begin

every day but there was no where we were going we were all very happy to finally be junior high in front of all of the bag sickle writers they all took a plunge it was just the sun rise of the Cascades when she was in the big Village running and soon to be in the middle of September for bats were the roads were all the problems has one set there I thought well when I go to Houston Texas or something while we didn't want to sit Africa bigger place but the car couldn't go anywhere it's just broken down there always just imagine you what we might do and he was still looking for his daughter still trying to figure out what to be there by funny name for Lucy means like can see the light of it

The leftover people were all scattered throughout the yard. After every day he had ended we did not get to ignore the cold feet that cat walking towards the other ones. Many of them wanted to join the others and pray for all of their cold feet to bow to their heads in the Forum of a monstrous pleasure so they'd all set there we had to take a trip to New Orleans and people did not think this was a good idea they did not like their feet

being sick isn't not like anything they were going to be reaching for many many many many many many feet.

the day before they all had left to go to Spencer's store and buy the most expensive sheets. They were never going to be put never pack from the rooms they're never going to be

Chapter 30: This Will Be What You Must Do

not broken and they just wanted to feel as if they jumped off of their beds Temple Run.

the night before of what's his call this December 2018 7 in the morning it was the most beautiful day. The snow still nothing moved nothing was alert. The only thing that could have been better was seeing the dogs air blow out of his nose from extreme cold that enter through the door so that has. The house was at least four stories Square Windows in each wall you so looks of a typical Colonial home it was a blue Hound blue screen siding panels made of wood and standings past hundred year everyone try to be there everyone try to want to the name of the house kept everyone sent everyone wanted to wake up there.

I did I ran to the window and I ran down the hall and gressive Lee ran through the waves of all of the air that collided with how it ripped through my grapes yes I fell on the floor rolling about like I'm literally on caution bear I was shocked at the nurse and I ever sit there again and ever since since he's such a bad as before session can you during the holidays. But I just seen a ladybug there was nothing

Chapter 31: Well, I didn’t Want To Do This

Easter magazines at the year before expired so the fireplace have to be used for wet hair and snapping acid crinkled away photographs all the past of a present.

Chapter 4: We Just Hope You Give A Damn

Stop prettying him down. He had to stay pretty and not do anything. He couldn't get as bad as he wanted to be. In so many ways no one gives a darn

between comfort and discomfort is the title
It says September 7th this is the year 2019 this is a fun year there's a glorious year deercast beerfeast time went by so quickly There was no storm today I could not see the floor my house standing as w between comfort and discomfort is the title
Everyday it's winter.

New line Monday
Blue Line and that you can see the indent and you just Uline
this is our switch to this is our switch to do indignant
indent

Chapter 1: Zero

Chapter 32: Oh, Nigga

Imperturbably beary. My favorite musical people has to be my sister Billy bear. before bear became all that she was in the store she started singing in high school and making records she's performed all over the world cleaning Japan she has very solid tympanic Club beats that could be played to her sultry jazz .

I first realize Billy bear she handed me a tape of a record a song. Like so many musical people she had a

special vibrato Special Air a voice tune it just comes up through the air things. She is done inspiring and plastic her spirit is the LIE of love togetherness an extreme training Guelph complete imperturbe Lee Berry her life is been so balanced I just called her the Ampere terribly Barry she has been sitting I know existence for difference she likes sitting in the breeze and believe is an impenetrable day so let's all try to be infertile early Berry and this is where I'll begin my journey to be like my idol I will be in future we bury in so many ways let's start out On the 1st of December.

I was born in the middle of the month timing disco's at its height it was an air of sophistication I could just go on and on there to so many people I don't see why shutter success stop being poor success is being happy to get to a point of imperturbability Barry happiness mimosa's jovial is the honey dripping from a bear right after hurts hibernation during the cold cold existence of the planet Earth there are some for which Life Goes On there's some for which there's a different Tale the bear has no Tales of this every years the summer every year is the honey this girl is what so many

try to be to not give it from anyting to walk through
those bitter snooze so many people must do to be blinded
my passion warmed by the strength of your ability
strength to go and do it's almost animal is human to
fail so many half can any of us be in Pretoria blueberry
any of us have that drive their focus then one tunnel
vision life it makes it hibernate through the dark days
history rest upon our souls mini rester gifted and
blessed is it gift people strike is not being the bear
being the human causes are suffering that we mistreat
that they will suffer this is the tale as so many others
human suffering The Berry people seem so sweet they just
picked the Bears right off a tree berries put them in
there a little dresses and scoop them up and bowls and
rush them in bowls symbols of Pies there others just
we'll catch that when of sophistication and Air what
will never be lift sway how will it be can we all try a
real animals some of us just choose to be God can we all
be in picture of Lee Barry can we all just ignore the
superfluous strenuous activities hell on Earth we all
Drive the existence of poverty existence of well does it
take the money that's something she's never been abridge
stuff and something of a circumstance provide to her

tell unbridled ability money is cast upon them to be the animal they are they exist as no other no one can seem to not hurt yep they will never not help despair pull through he people shoot at it they always preserve it it's mistake simplicity it's snowing this to enjoy the wall to wrap up in the warmth of oneself to endure the cold this is story of many tales of many people try to accomplish such a thing so many ways so many jacket ways find ourselves why bear freeing ourselves to be the humane this is what many will never do so much easier how to do a kickover tent 2Pac to steal one's honey steal one's food does the bear often do that in cases of hunger what happens when the Bears not hungry what happens is plentiful the garden is semen really feel sorry for the bear do they ever wondered when there is not sufficient and provided fattened will there ever be a time will exist is this the question I choose to stay on the side of the rich the money The Castaways steripen girls anchor avarice Envy walk two roads been with the poor the unlikely perhaps ignored and the wealth I can't tell you what money. Sweetheart here's looking at the well to do the Wella biters all the success here's to that I'm staying in for terribly Barry Oh that men can do .

Early stage of life I have to say that coming down from many peaceful days it's not a immature are small at the beach for the world. No tornado Valley this what anyting what bow down to. Plus, adieu what is the easiest. I don't see it from the start I don't spread the legs of secession and meager attitudes. there's a life and happiness, steadiness, or failure.

I stayed at home in this dedication to life study. I want to tell about the song Take My Love From the berry imperatively berry girl it just is what people take. they must be loved someone must love it sure someone must be love. How much did be for who must love must they be what is week unless they be able to Strong has a case what does not impose what is not in search of the ugly of the swing and they hating Brothers.

Mist Berryessa name before thinks that music is not like art not like Tom had it Tom was an artist he did the cover the spot it's what disconnects the book and the world father this is the picture of me pictures of men a woman disconnecting happiness where did smothered the colors run it's the tears eliminate the breast of one side the funny Parable heartbeat just pulls us into the point of dying here you see a woman on the cover is a dead woman she cannot whisper a letter of this book.

she can say anything to lay down I never walk. It's just something shocking to let the readers understand the point of life it's not to be that is to live they're two totally different words don't look similar whatsoever I think today's paper called the car moves where we live Poland match match difference between the dying and living in the book called shoe the orange rain by Rachel K. Martin well this will hit the foot like a nail in Jesus on the cross. she killed the ground, was a slave 2 the mundane, or was everyone I did not care about the Hills of grass. Complete waste of words. what's this woman a prostitute? what she crown debutante person beauty queen of high school Rich Roll? was she all things of stupidity unknowingness ignorance or hid ugly imagine and she started.

let's just cover up this life in the grave let's throw the dirt do you disagree? what's rice on the high side paints. It's good to not feel like a zero.

Chapter 2: We Won't Look Like This

Required to run towards the track . Chloe did with chicken we thought you'd want looks like this Daphne could save your life.

Chapter 2: We Won't Look Like This

How do we not look this way is it because it's Halloween to you it's because you can't see them the running everywhere this one in particular this one goes through Michelle mentioned in the Poetry of choosing your own trying there's something much like a spider on the wall just in the introvignes much like yourself reading interpreting songs like what I consider amuse hear it . to me this is the point of life one cannot get through when cannot pass through it

Chapter 33: Take What He's Got To Hear

without fighting it without chewing Dan taking that last breath. is that how it is the last moment the last breath we clench her teeth trying to survive a horrible World horrible tide change and Michelle was just a coaster the poet that must live within that moment but last poem has many different phases of change of the death of the dying as I mentioned in the last buck to the orange rain as you split and diet of course this means US Mini Splits a Bittersweet taste is in the orange rind 1 West recall supposed to leave us or last 10 to 15 seconds of Life flashing before eyes in these different frames these different stanzas of the poetry depicts all of those emotions racing before becoming free of ourselves when we come raging spirits everlasting life and a r motorcycles oh the last book was more about trying to chew to live eventually we get to the last year I think that's where this book will pick up movie about all that resides in the reflection of one's life at that last moment those last days Rising for the last challenge what will it be like for anyone Harrison introspection when's fall back people give so much advice how is it to look backwards and tell yourself or you will go for it no more. We won't look like this first of all like we are we want looks like we used to when you were sick dying decrepit weathering fattening whatever the case may be will become something that cannot recover to become the death supposedly we were big pile of dust he'll be thrown out to sea is this more of it was just an interest faction into what we will face something will will will be borne by.

We ran together Chloe we had every feeling that the last three days or empty and Shiloh of white snow ice, performance shows knives healthy walking bodies and medical and poverty togetherness much worse find sunny I need a. let's go think of moving for it. I will be there?

It's been quite a herring experience they just keep sitting there watching me will invisible people I watching you ain't heavy things in me that you and I feel their tactile you cannot see the sale practically breaking every bone in my body pinched they just keep taking all of my air and weighing me down odesse torturous all day and they keep me up all night I get no rest my eyes are peeled they're black and they are ready explosions all over the TV and nothing phases they're more than bothering me this is completely Concerta done bothering me she went to the back what's 2 two tier and that was all she does is Justin find the 2-day anymore of the two deer used to come around back I think someone hit and crush the deer and split it off to the side like a big pile of reverie organs and blood the head of used to recognize so dearly when her go baby dad Aerotek such a beautiful picture that captured in time she said that was promised a the road a little baby doll left motherless they're practically skin and bone I just fed them she barely had nutrients and she tried to use all of them as much as she could feed her baby deer animals their highest extent to keep themselves in there offspring live people cannot do the same.

I heard it's racing is pounding his true knocking knocking as if wanting to be raped I think I have your heart he said it's putting me everywhere that you're never going to be what you say don't understand or appreciate themselves they don't want you to not really anything cuz you did not have this problem they want me to sit there and be there in and then you and Father's day but this isn't expanding to anyone that can guess what it seems people don't want to be bothered and I think of any way to bother me that care about him being agitated and extremes they've gone to the bothering you and that's better. now question art I thought. the news of sunny day and every computer I walk in front of was there when I left the building. I could see the smoke coming out of the windows watch the TV and explosions. I'm in bed watching too finally just relaxing to a week ago and it was with just one more time. December went by so quickly and I just wanted to go and make it through the last year at of my job app. And I always felt just like it was had just happened but I was just going to pray for the first time. I just for a little a little yeah fresh air my father and I didn't run many travels at through the Midwest as much as we went through more in St Louis we saw the downtown area we saw the malls that's been closed a lot of the Sea Breeze old friends used to live places that the houses are not as well kept you probably are now condemned you are perhaps someone else is living there there's this not really a place where a lot of people are still states structured it's not like living in New Orleans just had its pride and its culture for many many years. drove me to school quite a bit that is only when and if the last time he dropped me off it was a very Rocky rainy morning I said hello to have then he drove off to the Sun.

medium sized statue woman with all of these cat like I appearance perm straighten hair I'm sorry my pigtails blow in the Wind he went further and further into the Sun. That was him going to the start of his day every day started with a Sun Ray and going away to begin my beach walk into start of my new school year. Seemed like he was going into the sun to me Style of course he was not driving into the sun just a figure of speech for your child and you're not too tall can't see too far over the hell seems like that's where he's gay.

of course it's a whole different culture to be involved in different kinds of weather and different kinds of States Midwest pretty humdrum you ever winter spring or summer or fall more of the summer in the winter is definite the fall in the spring 10 do Collide somewhat but the leaves do fall by the end of September. squinting outside of the window I looked at how everyone was little dots down from an airplane there's so many people about because it was the July 4th holiday and all the sudden there was planking and clashing airplanes flying and firecrackers going. can hear loads and loads a fireworks when their direction under the arch I get my daughter look at this time. My mind was empty with no hope for anyting a few hours went by and I saw a big cloud in the sky jumped Define it was on the floor.

rom extreme cold that enter through the door so that has. The house was at least four stories Square Windows in each wall you so looks of a typical Colonial home it was a blue Hound blue screen siding panels made of wood and standings past hundred year everyone try to be there everyone try to want to the name of the house kept everyone sent everyone wanted to wake up there.

I did I ran to the window and I ran down the hall and gressive Lee ran through the waves of all of the air that collided with how it ripped through my grapes yes I fell on the floor rolling about like I'm literally on caution bear I was shocked at the nurse and I ever sit there again and ever since since he's such a bad as before session can you during the holidays. But I just seen a ladybug there was nothing Easter magazines at the year before expired so the fireplace have to be used for wet hair and snapping acid crinkled away photographs all the past of a present.

Chapter 4: We Just Hope You Give A Damn

Chapter 34: This Is All It'll Be Like

Stop prettying him down. He had to stay pretty and not do anything. He couldn't get as bad as he wanted to be. In so many ways no one gives a darn

between comfort and discomfort is the title
It says September 7th this is the year 2019 this is a fun year there's a glorious year deercast beerfeast time went by so quickly There was no storm today I could not see the floor my house standing as w between comfort and discomfort is the title Everyday it's winter.

New line Monday
Blue Line and that you can see the indent and you just Uline
this is our switch to this is our switch to do indignant
indent

Chapter 1: Zero

Imperturbably beary. My favorite musical people has to be my sister Billy bear. before bear became all that she was in the store she started singing in high school and making records she's performed all over the world cleaning Japan she has very solid tympanic Club beats that could be played to her sultry jazz .

I first realize Billy bear she handed me a tape of a record a song. Like so many musical people she had a special vibrato Special Air a voice tune it just comes up through the air things. She is done inspiring and plastic her spirit is the LIE of love togetherness an extreme training Guelph complete imperturbe Lee Berry her life is been so balanced I just called her the Ampere terribly Barry she has been sitting I know existence for difference she likes sitting in the breeze and believe is an impenetrable day so let's all try to be infertile early Berry and this is where I'll begin my journey to be like my idol I will be in future we bury in so many ways let's start out On the 1st of December.

I was born in the middle of the month timing disco's at its height it was an air of sophistication I could just go on and on there to so many people I don't see why shutter success stop being poor success is being happy to get to a point of imperturbability Barry happiness mimosa's jovial is the honey dripping from a bear right after hurts hibernation during the cold cold existence of the planet Earth there are some for which Life Goes On there's some for which there's a different Tale the bear has no Tales of this every years the summer every year is the honey this girl is what so many try to be to not give it from anyting to walk through those bitter snooze so many people must do to be blinded my passion warmed by the strength of your ability strength to go and do it's almost animal is human to fail so many half can any of us be in Pretoria blueberry any of us have that drive their focus then one tunnel vision life it makes it hibernate through the dark days history rest upon our souls mini rester gifted and blessed is it gift people strike is not being the bear being the human causes are suffering that we mistreat that they will suffer this is the tale as so many others human suffering The Berry people seem so sweet they just picked the Bears right off a tree berries put them in there a little dresses and scoop them up and bowls and

rush them in bowls symbols of Pies there others just
we'll catch that when of sophistication and Air what
will never be lift sway how will it be can we all try a
real animals some of us just choose to be God can we all
be in picture of Lee Barry can we all just ignore the
superfluous strenuous activities hell on Earth we all
Drive the existence of poverty existence of well does it
take the money that's something she's never been abridge
stuff and something of a circumstance provide to her
tell unbridled ability money is cast upon them to be the
animal they are they exist as no other no one can seem
to not hurt yep they will never not help despair pull
through he people shoot at it they always preserve it
it's mistake simplicity it's snowing this to enjoy the
wall to wrap up in the warmth of oneself to endure the
cold this is story of many tales of many people try to
accomplish such a thing so many ways so many jacket ways
find ourselves why bear freeing ourselves to be the
humane this is what many will never do so much easier
how to do a kickover tent 2Pac to steal one's honey
steal one's food does the bear often do that in cases of
hunger what happens when the Bears not hungry what
happens is plentiful the garden is semen really feel

sorry for the bear do they ever wondered when there is not sufficient and provided fattened will there ever be a time will exist is this the question I choose to stay on the side of the rich the money The Castaways steripen girls anchor avarice Envy walk two roads been with the poor the unlikely perhaps ignored and the wealth I can't tell you what money. Sweetheart here's looking at the well to do the Wella biters all the success here's to that I'm staying in for terribly Barry Oh that men can do .

Early stage of life I have to say that coming down from many peaceful days it's not a immature are small at the beach for the world. No tornado Valley this what anyting what bow down to. Plus, adieu what is the easiest. I don't see it from the start I don't spread the legs of secession and meager attitudes. there's a life and happiness, steadiness, or failure.

I stayed at home in this dedication to life study. I want to tell about the song Take My Love From the berry imperatively berry girl it just is what people take. they must be loved someone must love it sure someone must be love. How much did be for who must love must they be what is week unless they be able to Strong has a case what does not impose what is not in search of the ugly of the swing and they hating Brothers.

Mist Berryessa name before thinks that music is not like art not like Tom had it Tom was an artist he did the cover the spot it's what disconnects the book and the world father this is the picture of me pictures of men a woman disconnecting happiness where did smothered the colors run it's the tears eliminate the breast of one side the funny Parable heartbeat just pulls us into the point of dying here you see a woman on the cover is a dead woman she cannot whisper a letter of this book.

she can say anything to lay down I never walk. It's just something shocking to let the readers understand the point of life it's not to be that is to live they're two totally different words don't look similar whatsoever I think today's paper called the car moves where we live Poland match match difference between the dying and living in the book called shoe the orange rain by Rachel K. Martin well this will hit the foot like a nail in Jesus on the cross. she killed the ground, was a slave 2 the mundane, or was everyone I did not care about the Hills of grass. Complete waste of words. what's this woman a prostitute? what she crown debutante person beauty queen of high school Rich Roll? was she all things of stupidity unknowingness ignorance or hid ugly imagine and she started.

let's just cover up this life in the grave let's throw the dirt do you disagree? what's rice on the high side paints. It's good to not feel like a zero.

Chapter 2: We Won't Look Like This

Chapter 35: This Ain't Gonna Get To Them

Required to run towards the track . Chloe did with chicken we thought you'd want looks like this Daphne could save your life.

Chapter 2: We Won't Look Like This

How do we not look this way is it because it's Halloween to you it's because you can't see them the running everywhere this one in particular this one goes through Michelle mentioned in the Poetry of choosing your own

trying there's something much like a spider on the wall just in the introvignes much like yourself reading interpreting songs like what I consider amuse hear it . to me this is the point of life one cannot get through when cannot pass through it without fighting it without chewing Dan taking that last breath. is that how it is the last moment the last breath we clench her teeth trying to survive a horrible World horrible tide change and Michelle was just a coaster the poet that must live within that moment but last poem has many different phases of change of the death of the dying as I mentioned in the last buck to the orange rain as you split and diet of course this means US Mini Splits a Bittersweet taste is in the orange rind 1 West recall supposed to leave us or last 10 to 15 seconds of Life flashing before eyes in these different frames these different stanzas of the poetry depicts all of those emotions racing before becoming free of ourselves when we come raging spirits everlasting life and a r motorcycles oh the last book was more about trying to chew to live eventually we get to the last year I think that's where this book will pick up movie about all that resides in the reflection of one's life at that last

moment those last days Rising for the last challenge what will it be like for anyone Harrison introspection when's fall back people give so much advice how is it to look backwards and tell yourself or you will go for it no more. We won't look like this first of all like we are we want looks like we used to when you were sick dying decrepit weathering fattening whatever the case may be will become something that cannot recover to become the death supposedly we were big pile of dust he'll be thrown out to sea is this more of it was just an interest faction into what we will face something will will will be borne by.

We ran together Chloe we had every feeling that the last three days or empty and Shiloh of white snow ice, performance shows knives healthy walking bodies and medical and poverty togetherness much worse find sunny I need a. let's go think of moving for it. I will be there?

It's been quite a herring experience they just keep sitting there watching me will invisible people I watching you ain't heavy things in me that you and I feel their tactile you cannot see the sale practically breaking every bone in my body pinched they just keep taking all of my air and weighing me down odesse torturous all day and they keep me up all night I get no rest my eyes are peeled they're black and they are ready explosions all over the TV and nothing phases they're more than bothering me this is completely Concerta done bothering me she went to the back what's 2 two tier and that was all she does is Justin find the 2-day anymore of the two deer used to come around back I think someone hit and crush the deer and split it off to the side like a big pile of reverie organs and blood the head of used to recognize so dearly when her go baby dad Aerotek such a beautiful picture that captured in time she said that was promised a the road a little baby doll left motherless they're practically skin and bone I just fed them she barely had nutrients and she tried to use all of them as much as she could feed her baby deer animals their highest extent to keep themselves in there offspring live people cannot do the same.

I heard it's racing is pounding his true knocking knocking as if wanting to be raped I think I have your heart he said it's putting me everywhere that you're never going to be what you say don't understand or appreciate themselves they don't want you to not really anything cuz you did not have this problem they want me to sit there and be there in and then you and Father's day but this isn't expanding to anyone that can guess what it seems people don't want to be bothered and I think of any way to bother me that care about him being agitated and extremes they've gone to the bothering you and that's better. now question art I thought. the news of sunny day and every computer I walk in front of was there when I left the building. I could see the smoke coming out of the windows watch the TV and explosions. I'm in bed watching too finally just relaxing to a week ago and it was with just one more time. December went by so quickly and I just wanted to go and make it through the last year at of my job app. And I always felt just like it was had just happened but I was just going to pray for the first time. I just for a little a little yeah fresh air my father and I didn't run many travels at through the Midwest as much as we went through more in St Louis we saw the downtown area we saw the malls that's been closed a lot of the Sea Breeze old friends used to live places that the houses are not as well kept you probably are now condemned you are perhaps someone else is living there there's this not really a place where a lot of people are still states structured it's not like living in New Orleans just had its pride and its culture for many many years. drove me to school quite a bit that is only when and if the last time he dropped me off it was a very Rocky rainy morning I said hello to have then he drove off to the Sun.

medium sized statue woman with all of these cat like I appearance perm straighten hair I'm sorry my pigtails blow in the Wind he went further and further into the Sun. That was him going to the start of his day every day started with a Sun Ray and going away to begin my beach walk into start of my new school year. Seemed like he was going into the sun to me Style of course he was not driving into the sun just a figure of speech for your child and you're not too tall can't see too far over the hell seems like that's where he's gay.

of course it's a whole different culture to be involved in different kinds of weather and different kinds of States Midwest pretty humdrum you ever winter spring or summer or fall more of the summer in the winter is definite the fall in the spring 10 do Collide somewhat but the leaves do fall by the end of September. squinting outside of the window I looked at how everyone was little dots down from an airplane there's so many people about because it was the July 4th holiday and all the sudden there was planking and clashing airplanes flying and firecrackers going. can hear loads and loads a fireworks when their direction under the arch I get my daughter look at this time. My mind was empty with no hope for anyting a few hours went by and I saw a big cloud in the sky jumped Define it was on the floor.

Chapter 36: We'd Love To Tell You What That Bitch Should Have Done For Herself.

Chapter 3: We Just Don’t Care

He met a friend and yet we couldn't go through Finding Nemo it was a coffee all black coffee everyday black coffee Olympic cream in the coffee Willow thought you was black it was dark and made him crazy he went looking for anyone finally came up Iraq we found his child in a Ciroc you're really funny story Stanley Charlie found any survivors how she kept hiding from him somebody for children who don't want to be you're off and running I didn't see what the point of it is till they get to the point. Lucy Wizards daughter's name and she spoke unhinged address of the clock as it sat on the wall S4 had school in the plants and everything that we saw stay consistent we were together we're overwhelmed to begin every day but there was no where we were going we were all very happy to finally be junior high in front of all of the bag sickle writers they all took a plunge it was just the sun rise of the Cascades when she was in the big Village running and soon to be in the middle of September for bats were the roads were all the problems has one set there I thought well when I go to Houston Texas or something while we didn't want to sit Africa bigger place but the car couldn't go anywhere it's just broken down there always just imagine you what we might do and he was still looking for his daughter still trying to figure out what to be there by funny name for Lucy means like can see the light of it

The leftover people were all scattered throughout the yard. After every day he had ended we did not get to ignore the cold feet that cat walking towards the other ones. Many of them wanted to join the others and pray for all of their cold feet to bow to their heads in the Forum of a monstrous pleasure so they'd all set there we had to take a trip to New Orleans and people did not think this was a good idea they did not like their feet being sick isn't not like anything they were going to be reaching for many many many many many many feet.

the day before they all had left to go to Spencer's store and buy the most expensive sheets. They were never going to be put never pack from the rooms they're never going to be not broken and they just wanted to feel as if they jumped off of their beds Temple Run.

the night before of what's his call this December 2018 7 in the morning it was the most beautiful day. The snow still nothing moved nothing was alert. The only thing that could have been better was seeing the dogs air blow out of his nose from extreme cold that enter through the door so that has. The house was at least four stories Square Windows in each wall you so looks of a typical Colonial home it was a blue Hound blue screen siding panels made of wood and standings past hundred year everyone try to be there everyone try to want to the name of the house kept everyone sent everyone wanted to wake up there.

I did I ran to the window and I ran down the hall and gressive Lee ran through the waves of all of the air that collided with how it ripped through my grapes yes I fell on the floor rolling about like I'm literally on caution bear I was shocked at the nurse and I ever sit there again and ever since since he's such a bad as before session can you during the holidays. But I just seen a ladybug there was nothing Easter magazines at the year before expired so the fireplace have to be used for wet hair and snapping acid crinkled away photographs all the past of a present.

Chapter 4: We Just Hope You Give A Damn

Stop prettying him down. He had to stay pretty and not do anything. He couldn't get as bad as he wanted to be. In so many ways no one gives a darn

between comfort and discomfort is the title
It says September 7th this is the year 2019 this is a fun year there's a glorious year deercast beerfeast time went by so quickly There was no storm today I could not see the floor my house standing as w between comfort and discomfort is the title
Everyday it's winter.

New line Monday
Blue Line and that you can see the indent and you just Uline
this is our switch to this is our switch to do indignant
indent

Chapter 1: Zero

Imperturbably beary. My favorite musical people has to be my sister Billy bear. before bear became all that she was in the store she started singing in high school and making records she's performed all over the world cleaning Japan she has very solid tympanic Club beats that could be played to her sultry jazz .

I first realize Billy bear she handed me a tape of a record a song. Like so many musical people she had a special vibrato Special Air a voice tune it just comes up through the air things. She is done inspiring and plastic her spirit is the LIE of love togetherness an extreme training Guelph complete imperturbe Lee Berry her life is been so balanced I just called her the Ampere terribly Barry she has been sitting I know existence for difference she likes sitting in the breeze and believe is an impenetrable day so let's all try to be infertile early Berry and this is where I'll begin my journey to be like my idol I will be in future we bury in so many ways let's start out On the 1st of December.

I was born in the middle of the month timing disco's at its height it was an air of sophistication I could just go on and on there to so many people I don't

see why shutter success stop being poor success is being happy to get to a point of imperturbability Barry happiness mimosa's jovial is the honey dripping from a bear right after hurts hibernation during the cold cold existence of the planet Earth there are some for which Life Goes On there's some for which there's a different Tale the bear has no Tales of this every years the summer every year is the honey this girl is what so many try to be to not give it from anyting to walk through those bitter snooze so many people must do to be blinded my passion warmed by the strength of your ability strength to go and do it's almost animal is human to fail so many half can any of us be in Pretoria blueberry any of us have that drive their focus then one tunnel vision life it makes it hibernate through the dark days history rest upon our souls mini rester gifted and blessed is it gift people strike is not being the bear being the human causes are suffering that we mistreat that they will suffer this is the tale as so many others human suffering The Berry people seem so sweet they just picked the Bears right off a tree berries put them in there a little dresses and scoop them up and bowls and rush them in bowls symbols of Pies there others just

we'll catch that when of sophistication and Air what will never be lift sway how will it be can we all try a real animals some of us just choose to be God can we all be in picture of Lee Barry can we all just ignore the superfluous strenuous activities hell on Earth we all Drive the existence

Chapter 37: We'd Love To Tell You How Much We Care

of poverty existence of well does it take the money that's something she's never been abridge stuff and something of a circumstance provide to her tell unbridled ability money is cast upon them to be the animal they are they exist as no other no one can seem to not hurt yep they will never not help despair pull through he people shoot at it they always preserve it it's mistake simplicity it's snowing this to enjoy the wall to wrap up in the warmth of oneself to endure the cold this is story of many tales of many people try to accomplish such a thing so many ways so many jacket ways find ourselves why bear freeing ourselves to be the humane this is what many will never do so much easier how to do a kickover tent 2Pac to steal one's honey steal one's food does the bear often do that in cases of

hunger what happens when the Bears not hungry what happens is plentiful the garden is semen really feel sorry for the bear do they ever wondered when there is not sufficient and provided fattened will there ever be a time will exist is this the question I choose to stay on the side of the rich the money The Castaways steripen girls anchor avarice Envy walk two roads been with the poor the unlikely perhaps ignored and the wealth I can't tell you what money. Sweetheart here's looking at the well to do the Wella biters all the success here's to that I'm staying in for terribly Barry Oh that men can do .

Early stage of life I have to say that coming down from many peaceful days it's not a immature are small at the beach for the world. No tornado Valley this what anyting what bow down to. Plus, adieu what is the easiest. I don't see it from the start I don't spread the legs of secession and meager attitudes. there's a life and happiness, steadiness, or failure.

I stayed at home in this dedication to life study. I want to tell about the song Take My Love From the berry imperatively berry girl it just is what people take. they must be loved someone must love it sure someone must be love. How much did be for who must love must they be what is week unless they be able to Strong has a case what does not impose what is not in search of the ugly of the swing and they hating Brothers.

Mist Berryessa name before thinks that music is not like art not like Tom had it Tom was an artist he did the cover the spot it's what disconnects the book and the world father this is the picture of me pictures of men a woman disconnecting happiness where did smothered the colors run it's the tears eliminate the breast of one side the funny Parable heartbeat just pulls us into the point of dying here you see a woman on the cover is a dead woman she cannot whisper a letter of this book.

she can say anything to lay down I never walk. It's just something shocking to let the readers understand the point of life it's not to be that is to live they're two totally different words don't look similar whatsoever I think today's paper called the car moves where we live Poland match match difference between the dying and living in the book called shoe the orange rain by Rachel K. Martin well this will hit the

foot like a nail in Jesus on the cross. she killed the ground, was a slave 2 the mundane, or was everyone I did not care about the Hills of grass. Complete waste of words. what's this woman a prostitute? what she crown debutante person beauty queen of high school Rich Roll? was she all things of stupidity unknowingness ignorance or hid ugly imagine and she started.

let's just cover up this life in the grave let's throw the dirt do you disagree? what's rice on the high side paints. It's good to not feel like a zero.

Chapter 2: We Won't Look Like This

Required to run towards the track . Chloe did with chicken we thought you'd want looks like this Daphne could save your life.

Chapter 2: We Won't Look Like This

How do we not look this way is it because it's Halloween to you it's because you can't see them the running everywhere this one in particular this one goes through Michelle mentioned in the Poetry of choosing your own trying there's something much like a spider on the wall

just in the introvignes much like yourself reading interpreting songs like what I consider amuse hear it . to me this is the point of life one cannot get through when cannot pass through it without fighting it without chewing Dan taking that last breath. is that how it is the last moment the last breath we clench her teeth trying to survive a horrible World horrible tide change and Michelle was just a coaster the poet that must live within that moment but last poem has many different phases of change of the death of the dying as I mentioned in the last buck to the orange rain as you split and diet of course this means US Mini Splits a Bittersweet taste is in the orange rind 1 West recall supposed to leave us or last 10 to 15 seconds of Life flashing before eyes in these different frames these different stanzas of the poetry depicts all of those emotions racing before becoming free of ourselves when we come raging spirits everlasting life and a r motorcycles oh the last book was more about trying to chew to live eventually we get to the last year I think that's where this book will pick up movie about all that resides in the reflection of one's life at that last moment those last days Rising for the last challenge what will it be like for anyone Harrison introspection when's fall back people give so much advice how is it to look backwards and tell yourself or you will go for it no more. We won't look like this first of all like we are we want looks like we used to when you were sick dying decrepit weathering fattening whatever the case may be will become something that cannot recover to become the death supposedly we were big pile of dust he'll be thrown out to sea is this more of it was just an interest faction into what we will face something will will will be borne by.

We ran together Chloe we had every feeling that the last three days or empty and Shiloh of white snow ice, performance shows knives healthy walking bodies and medical and poverty togetherness much worse find sunny I need a. let's go think of moving for it. I will be there?

It's been quite a herring experience they just keep sitting there watching me will invisible people I watching you ain't heavy things in me that you and I feel their tactile you cannot see the sale practically breaking every bone in my body pinched they just keep taking all of my air and weighing me down odesse torturous all day and they keep me up all night I get no rest my eyes are peeled they're black and they are ready explosions all over the TV and nothing phases they're more than bothering me this is completely Concerta done bothering me she went to the back what's 2 two tier and that was all she does is Justin find the 2-day anymore of the two deer used to come around back I think someone hit and crush the deer and split it off to the side like a big pile of reverie organs and blood the head of used to recognize so dearly when her go baby dad Aerotek such a beautiful picture that captured in time she said that was promised a the road a little baby doll left motherless they're practically skin and bone I just fed them she barely had nutrients and she tried to use all of them as much as she could feed her baby deer animals their highest extent to keep themselves in there offspring live people cannot do the same.

I heard it's racing is pounding his true knocking knocking as if wanting to be raped I think I have your heart he said it's putting me everywhere that you're never going to be what you say don't understand or

appreciate themselves they don't want you to not really anything cuz you did not have this problem they want me to sit there and be there in and then you and Father's day but this isn't expanding to anyone that can guess what it seems people don't want to be bothered and I think of any way to bother me that care about him being agitated and extremes they've gone to the bothering you and that's better. now question art I thought. the news of sunny day and every computer I walk in front of was there when I left the building. I could see the smoke coming out of the windows watch the TV and explosions. I'm in bed watching too finally just relaxing to a week ago and it was with just one more time. December went by so quickly and I just wanted to go

Chapter 37: Then, We Don’t Love Them

and make it through the last year at of my job app. And I always felt just like it was had just happened but I was just going to pray for the first time. I just for a little a little yeah fresh air my father and I didn't run many travels at through the Midwest as much as we went through more in St Louis we saw the downtown area we saw the malls that's been closed a lot of the Sea

Breeze old friends used to live places that the houses are not as well kept you probably are now condemned you are perhaps someone else is living there there's this not really a place where a lot of people are still states structured it's not like living in New Orleans just had its pride and its culture for many many years. drove me to school quite a bit that is only when and if the last time he dropped me off it was a very Rocky rainy morning I said hello to have then he drove off to the Sun.

medium sized statue woman with all of these cat like I appearance perm straighten hair I'm sorry my pigtails blow in the Wind he went further and further into the Sun. That was him going to the start of his day every day started with a Sun Ray and going away to begin my beach walk into start of my new school year. Seemed like he was going into the sun to me Style of course he was not driving into the sun just a figure of speech for your child and you're not too tall can't see too far over the hell seems like that's where he's gay.

of course it's a whole different culture to be involved in different kinds of weather and different kinds of States Midwest pretty humdrum you ever winter spring or summer or fall more of the summer in the winter is definite the fall in the spring 10 do Collide somewhat but the leaves do fall by the end of September. squinting outside of the window I looked at how everyone was little dots down from an airplane there's so many people about because it was the July 4th holiday and all the sudden there was planking and clashing airplanes flying and firecrackers going. can hear loads and loads a fireworks when their direction under the arch I get my daughter look at this time. My mind was empty with no hope for anyting a few hours went by and I saw a big cloud in the sky jumped Define it was on the floor.

rom extreme cold that enter through the door so that has. The house was at least four stories Square Windows in each wall you so looks of a typical Colonial home it was a blue Hound blue screen siding panels made of wood and standings past hundred year everyone try to be there everyone try to want to the name of the house kept everyone sent everyone wanted to wake up there.

I did I ran to the window and I ran down the hall and gressive Lee ran through the waves of all of the air that collided with how it ripped through my grapes yes I fell on the floor rolling about like I'm literally on caution bear I was shocked at the nurse and I ever sit there again and ever since since he's such a bad as before session can you during the holidays. But I just seen a ladybug there was nothing Easter magazines at the year before expired so the fireplace have to be used for wet hair and snapping acid crinkled away photographs all the past of a present.

Chapter 4: We Just Hope You Give A Damn

Stop prettying him down. He had to stay pretty and not do anything. He couldn't get as bad as he wanted to be. In so many ways no one gives a darn

between comfort and discomfort is the title
It says September 7th this is the year 2019 this is a fun year there's a glorious year deercast beerfeast time went by so quickly There was no storm today I could not see the floor my house standing as w between comfort and discomfort is the title Everyday it's winter.

New line Monday
Blue Line and that you can see the indent and you just Uline

this is our switch to this is our switch to do indignant indent

Chapter 1: Zero

Imperturbably beary. My favorite musical people has to be my sister Billy bear. before bear became all that she was in the store she started singing in high school and making records she's performed all over the world cleaning Japan she has very solid tympanic Club beats that could be played to her sultry jazz .

I first realize Billy bear she handed me a tape of a record a song. Like so many musical people she had a special vibrato Special Air a voice tune it just comes up through the air things. She is done inspiring and plastic her spirit is the LIE of love togetherness an extreme training Guelph complete imperturbe Lee Berry her life is been so balanced I just called her the Ampere terribly Barry she has been sitting I know existence for difference she likes sitting in the breeze and believe is an impenetrable day so let's all try to be infertile early Berry and this is where I'll begin my journey to be like my idol I will be in future we bury in so many ways let's start out On the 1st of December.

I was born in the middle of the month timing disco's at its height it was an air of sophistication I could just go on and on there to so many people I don't see why shutter success stop being poor success is being happy to get to a point of imperturbability Barry happiness mimosa's jovial is the honey dripping from a bear right after hurts hibernation during the cold cold existence of the planet Earth there are some for which Life Goes On there's some for which there's a different Tale the bear has no Tales of this every years the summer every year is the honey this girl is what so many try to be to not give it from anyting to walk through those bitter snooze so many people must do to be blinded my passion warmed by the strength of your ability strength to go and do it's almost animal is human to fail so many half can any of us be in Pretoria blueberry any of us have that drive their focus then one tunnel vision life it makes it hibernate through the dark days history rest upon our souls mini rester gifted and

Chapter 38: YOu Saw Them In Here?

blessed is it gift people strike is not being the bear being the human causes are suffering that we mistreat that they will suffer this is the tale as so many others human suffering The Berry people seem so sweet they just picked the Bears right off a tree berries put them in there a little dresses and scoop them up and bowls and rush them in bowls symbols of Pies there others just we'll catch that when of sophistication and Air what will never be lift sway how will it be can we all try a real animals some of us just choose to be God can we all be in picture of Lee Barry can we all just ignore the superfluous strenuous activities hell on Earth we all Drive the existence of poverty existence of well does it take the money that's something she's never been abridge stuff and something of a circumstance provide to her tell unbridled ability money is cast upon them to be the animal they are they exist as no other no one can seem to not hurt yep they will never not help despair pull through he people shoot at it they always preserve it it's mistake simplicity it's snowing this to enjoy the wall to wrap up in the warmth of oneself to endure the cold this is story of many tales of many people try to accomplish such a thing so many ways so many jacket ways find ourselves why bear freeing ourselves to be the humane this is what many will never do so much easier how to do a kickover tent 2Pac to steal one's honey steal one's food does the bear often do that in cases of hunger what happens when the Bears not hungry what happens is plentiful the garden is semen really feel sorry for the bear do they ever wondered when there is not sufficient and provided fattened will there ever be a time will exist is this the question I choose to stay on the side of the rich the money The Castaways steripen girls anchor avarice Envy walk two roads been with the poor the unlikely perhaps ignored and the wealth I can't tell you what money. Sweetheart here's looking at the well to do the Wella biters all the success here's to that I'm staying in for terribly Barry Oh that men can do .

Early stage of life I have to say that coming down from many peaceful days it's not a immature are small at the beach for the world. No tornado Valley this what anyting what bow down to. Plus, adieu what is the easiest. I don't see it from the start I don't spread the legs of secession and meager attitudes. there's a life and happiness, steadiness, or failure.

I stayed at home in this dedication to life study. I want to tell about the song Take My Love From the berry imperatively berry girl it just is what people take. they must be loved someone must love it sure someone must be love. How much did be for who must love must they be what is week unless they be able to Strong has a case what does not impose what is not in search of the ugly of the swing and they hating Brothers.

Mist Berryessa name before thinks that music is not like art not like Tom had it Tom was an artist he did the cover the spot it's what disconnects the book and the world father this is the picture of me pictures of men a woman disconnecting happiness where did smothered the colors run it's the tears eliminate the breast of one side the funny Parable heartbeat just pulls us into the point of dying here you see a woman on the cover is a dead woman she cannot whisper a letter of this book.

she can say anything to lay down I never walk. It's just something shocking to let the readers understand the point of life it's not to be that is to live they're two totally different words don't look similar whatsoever I think today's paper called the car moves where we live Poland match match difference between the dying and living in the book called shoe the orange rain by Rachel K. Martin well this will hit the foot like a nail in Jesus on the cross. she killed the ground, was a slave 2 the mundane, or was everyone I did not care about the Hills of grass. Complete waste of words. what's this woman a prostitute? what she crown debutante person beauty queen of high school Rich Roll? was she all things of stupidity unknowingness ignorance or hid ugly imagine and she started.

let's just cover up this life in the grave let's throw the dirt do you disagree? what's rice on the high side paints. It's good to not feel like a zero.

Chapter 2: We Won't Look Like This

Required to run towards the track . Chloe did with chicken we thought you'd want looks like this Daphne could save your life.

Chapter 2: We Won't Look Like This

How do we not look this way is it because it's Halloween to you it's because you can't see them the running everywhere this one in particular this one goes through Michelle mentioned in the Poetry of choosing your own trying there's something much like a spider on the wall just in the introvignes much like yourself reading interpreting songs like what I consider amuse hear it . to me this is the point of life one cannot get through when cannot pass through it without fighting it without chewing Dan taking that last breath. is that how it is the last moment the last breath we clench her teeth trying to survive a horrible World horrible tide change and Michelle was just a coaster the poet that must live within that moment but last poem has many different phases of change of the death of the dying as I mentioned in the last buck to the orange rain as you split and diet of course this means US Mini Splits a Bittersweet taste is in the orange rind 1 West recall supposed to leave us or last 10 to 15 seconds of Life flashing before eyes in these different frames these different stanzas of the poetry depicts all of those emotions racing before becoming free of ourselves when we come raging spirits everlasting life and a r motorcycles oh the last book was more about trying to chew to live eventually we get to the last year I think that's where this book will pick up movie about all that resides in the reflection of one's life at that last moment those last days Rising for the last challenge what will it be like for anyone Harrison introspection when's fall back people give so much advice how is it to look backwards and tell yourself or you will go for it no more. We won't look like this first of all like we are we want looks like we used to when you were sick dying decrepit weathering fattening whatever the case may be will become something that cannot recover to become the death supposedly we were big pile of dust he'll be thrown out to sea is this more of it was just an interest faction into what we will face something will will will be borne by.

We ran together Chloe we had every feeling that the last three days or empty and Shiloh of white snow ice, performance shows knives healthy walking bodies and medical and poverty togetherness much worse find sunny I need a. let's go think of moving for it. I will be there?

It's been quite a herring experience they just keep sitting there watching me will invisible people I watching you ain't heavy things in me that you and I feel their tactile you cannot see the sale practically breaking every bone in my body pinched they just keep taking all of my air and weighing me

Chapter 39: You Won't Say What You Were Going To Say 'Cause We Have What We're Going To Tell

down odesse torturous all day and they keep me up all night I get no rest my eyes are peeled they're black and they are

ready explosions all over the TV and nothing phases they're more than bothering me this is completely Concerta done bothering me she went to the back what's 2 two tier and that was all she does is Justin find the 2-day anymore of the two deer used to come around back I think someone hit and crush the deer and split it off to the side like a big pile of reverie organs and blood the head of used to recognize so dearly when her go baby dad Aerotek such a beautiful picture that captured in time she said that was promised a the road a little baby doll left motherless they're practically skin and bone I just fed them she barely had nutrients and she tried to use all of them as much as she could feed her baby deer animals their highest extent to keep themselves in there offspring live people cannot do the same.

I heard it's racing is pounding his true knocking knocking as if wanting to be raped I think I have your heart he said it's putting me everywhere that you're never going to be what you say don't understand or appreciate themselves they don't want you to not really anything cuz you did not have this problem they want me to sit there and be there in and then you and Father's day but this isn't expanding to anyone that can guess what it seems people don't want to be bothered and I think of any way to bother me that care about him being agitated and extremes they've gone to the bothering you and that's better. now question art I thought. the news of sunny day and every computer I walk in front of was there when I left the building. I could see the smoke coming out of the windows watch the TV and explosions. I'm in bed watching too finally just relaxing to a week ago and it was with just one more time. December went by so quickly and I just wanted to go and make it through the last year at of my job app. And I always felt just like it was had just happened but I was just going to pray for the first time. I just for a little a little yeah fresh air my father and I didn't run many travels at through the Midwest as much as we went through more in St Louis we saw the downtown area we saw the malls that's been closed a lot of the Sea Breeze old friends used to live places that the houses are not as well kept you probably are now condemned you are perhaps someone else is living there there's this not really a place where a lot of people are still states structured it's not like living in New Orleans just had its pride and its culture for many many years. drove me to school quite a bit that is only when and if the last time he dropped me off it was a very Rocky rainy morning I said hello to have then he drove off to the Sun.

medium sized statue woman with all of these cat like I appearance perm straighten hair I'm sorry my pigtails blow in the Wind he went further and further into the Sun. That was him going to the start of his day every day started with a Sun Ray and going away to begin my beach walk into start of my new school year. Seemed like he was going into the sun to me Style of course he was not driving into the sun just a figure of speech for your child and you're not too tall can't see too far over the hell seems like that's where he's gay.

of course it's a whole different culture to be involved in different kinds of weather and different kinds of States Midwest pretty humdrum you ever winter spring or summer or fall more of the summer in the winter is definite the fall in the spring 10 do Collide somewhat but the leaves do fall by the end of September. squinting outside of the window I looked at how everyone was little dots down from an airplane there's so many people about because it was the July 4th holiday and all the sudden there was planking and clashing airplanes flying and firecrackers going. can hear loads and loads a fireworks when their direction under the arch I get my daughter look at this time. My mind was empty with no hope for anyting a few hours went by and I saw a big cloud in the sky jumped Define it was on the floor.

Chapter 3: We Just Don't Care

He met a friend and yet we couldn't go through Finding Nemo it was a coffee all black coffee everyday black coffee Olympic cream in the coffee Willow thought you was black it was dark and made him crazy he went looking for anyone finally came up Iraq we found his child in a Ciroc you're really funny story Stanley Charlie found any survivors how she kept hiding from him somebody for children who don't want to be you're off and running I didn't see what the point of it is till they get to the point. Lucy Wizards daughter's name and she spoke unhinged address of the clock as it sat on the wall S4 had school in the plants and everything that we saw stay consistent we were together we're overwhelmed to begin every day but there was no where we were going we were all very happy to finally be junior high in front of all of the bag sickle writers they all took a plunge it was just the sun rise of the Cascades when she was in the big Village running and soon to be in the middle of September for bats were the roads were all the problems has one set there I thought well when I go to Houston

Chapter 41: We Just Want Them To See You

Texas or something while we didn't want to sit Africa bigger place but the car couldn't go anywhere it's just broken down

there always just imagine you what we might do and he was still looking for his daughter still trying to figure out what to be there by funny name for Lucy means like can see the light of it

The leftover people were all scattered throughout the yard. After every day he had ended we did not get to ignore the cold feet that cat walking towards the other ones. Many of them wanted to join the others and pray for all of their cold feet to bow to their heads in the Forum of a monstrous pleasure so they'd all set there we had to take a trip to New Orleans and people did not think this was a good idea they did not like their feet being sick isn't not like anything they were going to be reaching for many many many many many many feet.

the day before they all had left to go to Spencer's store and buy the most expensive sheets. They were never going to be put never pack from the rooms they're never going to be not broken and they just wanted to feel as if they jumped off of their beds Temple Run.

the night before of what's his call this December 2018 7 in the morning it was the most beautiful day. The snow still nothing moved nothing was alert. The only thing that could have been better was seeing the dogs air blow out of his nose from extreme cold that enter through the door so that has. The house was at least four stories Square Windows in each wall you so looks of a typical Colonial home it was a blue Hound blue screen siding panels made of wood and standings past hundred year everyone try to be there everyone try to want to the name of the house kept everyone sent everyone wanted to wake up there.

I did I ran to the window and I ran down the hall and gressive Lee ran through the waves of all of the air that collided with how it ripped through my grapes yes I fell on the floor rolling about like I'm literally on caution bear I was shocked at the nurse and I ever sit there again and ever since since he's such a bad as before session can you during the holidays. But I just seen a ladybug there was nothing Easter magazines at the

year before expired so the fireplace have to be used for wet hair and snapping acid crinkled away photographs all the past of a present.

Chapter 4: We Just Hope You Give A Damn

Stop prettying him down. He had to stay pretty and not do anything. He couldn't get as bad as he wanted to be. In so many ways no one gives a darn

between comfort and discomfort is the title
It says September 7th this is the year 2019 this is a fun year there's a glorious year deercast beerfeast time went by so quickly There was no storm today I could not see the floor my house standing as w between comfort and discomfort is the title
Everyday it's winter.

New line Monday
Blue Line and that you can see the indent and you just Uline
this is our switch to this is our switch to do indignant
indent

Chapter 1: Zero

Imperturbably beary. My favorite musical people has to be my sister Billy bear. before bear became all that she was in the store she started singing in high school and making records she's performed all over the world cleaning Japan she has very solid tympanic Club beats that could be played to her sultry jazz .

I first realize Billy bear she handed me a tape of a record a song. Like so many musical people she had a special vibrato Special Air a voice tune it just comes up through the air things. She is done inspiring and plastic her spirit is the LIE of love togetherness an extreme training Guelph complete imperturbe Lee Berry her life is been so balanced I just called her the Ampere terribly Barry she has been sitting I know existence for difference she likes sitting in the breeze and believe is an impenetrable day so let's all try to be infertile early Berry and this is where I'll begin my journey to be like my idol I will be in future we bury in so many ways let's start out On the 1st of December.

I was born in the middle of the month timing disco's at its height it was an air of sophistication I could just go on and on there to so many people I don't

see why shutter success stop being poor success is being happy to get to a point of imperturbability Barry happiness mimosa's jovial is the honey dripping from a bear right after hurts hibernation during the cold cold existence of the planet Earth there are some for which Life Goes On there's some for which there's a different Tale the bear has no Tales of this every years the summer every year is the honey this girl is what so many try to be to not give it from anyting to walk through those bitter snooze so many people must do to be blinded my passion warmed by the strength of your ability strength to go and do it's almost animal is human to fail so many half can any of us be in Pretoria blueberry any of us have that drive their focus then one tunnel vision life it makes it hibernate through the dark days history rest upon our souls mini rester gifted and blessed is it gift people strike is not being the bear being the human causes are suffering that we mistreat that they will suffer this is the tale as so many others human suffering The Berry people seem so sweet they just picked the Bears right off a tree berries put them in there a little dresses and scoop them up and bowls and rush them in bowls symbols of Pies there others just

we'll catch that when of sophistication and Air what will never be lift sway how will it be can we all try a real animals some of us just choose to be God can we all be in picture of Lee Barry can we all just ignore the superfluous strenuous activities hell on Earth we all Drive the existence of poverty existence of well does it take the money that's something she's never been abridge stuff and something of a circumstance provide to her tell unbridled ability money is cast upon them to be the animal they are they exist as no other no one can seem to not hurt yep they will never not help despair pull through he people shoot at it they always preserve it it's mistake simplicity it's snowing this to enjoy the wall to wrap up in the warmth of oneself to endure the cold this is story of many tales of many people try to accomplish such a thing so many ways so many jacket ways find ourselves why bear freeing ourselves to be the humane this is what many will never do so much easier how to do a kickover tent 2Pac to steal one's honey steal one's food does the bear often do that in cases of hunger what happens when the Bears not hungry what happens is plentiful the garden is semen really feel sorry for the bear do they ever wondered when there is not sufficient and provided fattened will there ever be a time will exist is this the question I choose to stay on the side of the rich the money The Castaways steripen girls anchor avarice Envy walk two roads been with the poor the unlikely perhaps ignored and the wealth I can't tell you what money. Sweetheart here's looking at the well to do the Wella biters all the success here's to that I'm staying in for terribly Barry Oh that men can do .

Early stage of life I have to say that coming down from many peaceful days it's not a immature are small at the beach for the world. No tornado Valley this what anyting what bow down to. Plus, adieu what is the easiest. I don't see it from the start I don't spread the legs of secession and meager attitudes. there's a life and happiness, steadiness, or failure.

I stayed at home in this dedication to life study. I want to tell about the song Take My Love From the berry imperatively berry girl it just is what people take. they must be loved someone must love it sure someone must be love. How much did be for who must love must they be what is week unless they be able to Strong has a case what does not impose what is not in search of the ugly of the swing and they hating Brothers.

Mist Berryessa name before thinks that music is not like art not like Tom had it Tom was an artist he did the cover the spot it's what disconnects the book and the world father this is the picture of me pictures of men a woman disconnecting

Chapter 42: Got Your Behind

happiness where did smothered the colors run it's the tears eliminate the breast of one side the funny Parable heartbeat just pulls us into the point of dying here you see a woman on the cover is a dead woman she cannot whisper a letter of this book.

she can say anything to lay down I never walk. It's just something shocking to let the readers understand the point of life it's not to be that is to live they're two totally different words don't look similar whatsoever I think today's paper called the car moves where we live Poland match match difference between the dying and living in the book called shoe the orange rain by Rachel K. Martin well this will hit the

foot like a nail in Jesus on the cross. she killed the ground, was a slave 2 the mundane, or was everyone I did not care about the Hills of grass. Complete waste of words. what's this woman a prostitute? what she crown debutante person beauty queen of high school Rich Roll? was she all things of stupidity unknowingness ignorance or hid ugly imagine and she started.

let's just cover up this life in the grave let's throw the dirt do you disagree? what's rice on the high side paints. It's good to not feel like a zero.

Chapter 2: We Won't Look Like This

Required to run towards the track . Chloe did with chicken we thought you'd want looks like this Daphne could save your life.

Chapter 2: We Won't Look Like This

How do we not look this way is it because it's Halloween to you it's because you can't see them the running everywhere this one in particular this one goes through Michelle mentioned in the Poetry of choosing your own trying there's something much like a spider on the wall

just in the introvignes much like yourself reading interpreting songs like what I consider amuse hear it . to me this is the point of life one cannot get through when cannot pass through it without fighting it without chewing Dan taking that last breath. is that how it is the last moment the last breath we clench her teeth trying to survive a horrible World horrible tide change and Michelle was just a coaster the poet that must live within that moment but last poem has many different phases of change of the death of the dying as I mentioned in the last buck to the orange rain as you split and diet of course this means US Mini Splits a Bittersweet taste is in the orange rind 1 West recall supposed to leave us or last 10 to 15 seconds of Life flashing before eyes in these different frames these different stanzas of the poetry depicts all of those emotions racing before becoming free of ourselves when we come raging spirits everlasting life and a r motorcycles oh the last book was more about trying to chew to live eventually we get to the last year I think that's where this book will pick up movie about all that resides in the reflection of one's life at that last moment those last days Rising for the last challenge what will it be like for anyone Harrison introspection when's fall back people give so much advice how is it to look backwards and tell yourself or you will go for it no more. We won't look like this first of all like we are we want looks like we used to when you were sick dying decrepit weathering fattening whatever the case may be will become something that cannot recover to become the death supposedly we were big pile of dust he'll be thrown out to sea is this more of it was just an interest faction into what we will face something will will will be borne by.

We ran together Chloe we had every feeling that the last three days or empty and Shiloh of white snow ice, performance shows knives healthy walking bodies and medical and poverty togetherness much worse find sunny I need a. let's go think of moving for it. I will be there?

It's been quite a herring experience they just keep sitting there watching me will invisible people I watching you ain't heavy things in me that you and I feel their tactile you cannot see the sale practically breaking every bone in my body pinched they just keep taking all of my air and weighing me down odesse torturous all day and they keep me up all night I get no rest my eyes are peeled they're black and they are ready explosions all over the TV and nothing phases they're more than bothering me this is completely Concerta done bothering me she went to the back what's 2 two tier and that was all she does is Justin find the 2-day anymore of the two deer used to come around back I think someone hit and crush the deer and split it off to the side like a big pile of reverie organs and blood the head of used to recognize so dearly when her go baby dad Aerotek such a beautiful picture that captured in time she said that was promised a the road a little baby doll left motherless they're practically skin and bone I just fed them she barely had nutrients and she tried to use all of them as much as she could feed her baby deer animals their highest extent to keep themselves in there offspring live people cannot do the same.

I heard it's racing is pounding his true knocking knocking as if wanting to be raped I think I have your heart he said it's putting me everywhere that you're never going to be what you say don't understand or

appreciate themselves they don't want you to not really anything cuz you did not have this problem they want me to sit there and be there in and then you and Father's day but this isn't expanding to anyone that can guess what it seems people don't want to be bothered and I think of any way to bother me that care about him being agitated and extremes they've gone to the bothering you and that's better. now question art I thought. the news of sunny day and every computer I walk in front of was there when I left the building. I could see the smoke coming out of the windows watch the TV and explosions. I'm in bed watching too finally just relaxing to a week ago and it was with just one more time. December went by so quickly and I just wanted to go and make it through the last year at of my job app. And I always felt just like it was had just happened but I was just going to pray for the first time. I just for a little a little yeah fresh air my father and I didn't run many travels at through the Midwest as much as we went through more in St Louis we saw the downtown area we saw the malls that's been closed a lot of the Sea Breeze old friends used to live places that the houses are not as well kept you probably are now condemned you are perhaps someone else is living there there's this not really a place where a lot of people are still states structured it's not like living in New Orleans just had its pride and its culture for many many years. drove me to school quite a bit that is only when and if the last time he dropped me off it was a very Rocky rainy morning I said hello to have then he drove off to the Sun.

medium sized statue woman with all of these cat like I appearance perm straighten hair I'm sorry my pigtails blow in the Wind he went further and further into the Sun. That was him going to the start of his day every day started with a Sun Ray and going away to begin my beach walk into start of my new school year. Seemed like he was going into the sun to me Style of course he was not driving into the sun just a figure of

Chapter 43: I'm Just Like My Mother

speech for your child and you're not too tall can't see too far over the hell seems like that's where he's gay.

of course it's a whole different culture to be involved in different kinds of weather and different kinds of States Midwest pretty humdrum you ever winter

spring or summer or fall more of the summer in the winter is definite the fall in the spring 10 do Collide somewhat but the leaves do fall by the end of September. squinting outside of the window I looked at how everyone was little dots down from an airplane there's so many people about because it was the July 4th holiday and all the sudden there was planking and clashing airplanes flying and firecrackers going. can hear loads and loads a fireworks when their direction under the arch I get my daughter look at this time. My mind was empty with no hope for anyting a few hours went by and I saw a big cloud in the sky jumped Define it was on the floor.

rom extreme cold that enter through the door so that has. The house was at least four stories Square Windows in each wall you so looks of a typical Colonial home it was a blue Hound blue screen siding panels made of wood and standings past hundred year everyone try to be there everyone try to want to the name of the house kept everyone sent everyone wanted to wake up there.

I did I ran to the window and I ran down the hall and gressive Lee ran through the waves of all of the air that collided with how it ripped through my grapes yes I

fell on the floor rolling about like I'm literally on caution bear I was shocked at the nurse and I ever sit there again and ever since since he's such a bad as before session can you during the holidays. But I just seen a ladybug there was nothing Easter magazines at the year before expired so the fireplace have to be used for wet hair and snapping acid crinkled away photographs all the past of a present.

Chapter 4: We Just Hope You Give A Damn

Stop prettying him down. He had to stay pretty and not do anything. He couldn't get as bad as he wanted to be. In so many ways no one gives a darn

between comfort and discomfort is the title
It says September 7th this is the year 2019 this is a fun year there's a glorious year deercast beerfeast time went by so quickly There was no storm today I could not see the floor my house standing as w between comfort and discomfort is the title Everyday it's winter.

New line Monday
Blue Line and that you can see the indent and you just Uline
this is our switch to this is our switch to do indignant
indent

Chapter 1: Zero

Imperturbably beary. My favorite musical people has to be my sister Billy bear. before bear became all that she was in the store she started singing in high school and making records she's performed all over the world cleaning Japan she has very solid tympanic Club beats that could be played to her sultry jazz .

I first realize Billy bear she handed me a tape of a record a song. Like so many musical people she had a special vibrato Special Air a voice tune it just comes up through the air things. She is done inspiring and plastic her spirit is the LIE of love togetherness an extreme training Guelph complete imperturbe Lee Berry her life is been so balanced I just called her the Ampere terribly Barry she has been sitting I know existence for difference she likes sitting in the breeze and believe is an impenetrable day so let's all try to be infertile early Berry and this is where I'll begin my journey to be like my idol I will be in future we bury in so many ways let's start out On the 1st of December.

I was born in the middle of the month timing disco's at its height it was an air of sophistication I could just go on and on there to so many people I don't see why shutter success stop being poor success is being happy to get to a point of imperturbability Barry happiness mimosa's jovial is the honey dripping from a bear right after hurts hibernation during the cold cold existence of the planet Earth there are some for which Life Goes On there's some for which there's a different Tale the bear has no Tales of this every years the summer every year is the honey this girl is what so many try to be to not give it from anyting to walk through those bitter snooze so many people must do to be blinded my passion warmed by the strength of your ability strength to go and do it's almost animal is human to fail so many half can any of us be in Pretoria blueberry any of us have that drive their focus then one tunnel vision life it makes it hibernate through the dark days history rest upon our souls mini rester gifted and blessed is it gift people strike is not being the bear being the human causes are suffering that we mistreat that they will suffer this is the tale as so many others human suffering The Berry people seem so sweet they just picked the Bears right off a tree berries put them in there a little dresses and scoop them up and bowls and rush them in bowls symbols of Pies there others just we'll catch that when of sophistication and Air what will never be lift sway how will it be can we all try a real animals some of us just choose to be God can we all be in picture of Lee Barry can we all just ignore the superfluous strenuous activities hell on Earth we all Drive the existence of poverty existence of well does it take the money that's something she's never been abridge stuff and something of a circumstance provide to her tell unbridled ability money is cast upon them to be the animal they are they exist as no other no one can seem to not hurt yep they will never not help despair pull through he people shoot at it they always preserve it it's mistake simplicity it's snowing this to enjoy the wall to wrap up in the warmth of oneself to endure the cold this is story of many tales of many people try to accomplish such a thing so many ways so many jacket ways find ourselves why bear freeing ourselves to be the humane this is what many will never do so much easier how to do a kickover tent 2Pac to steal one's honey steal one's food does the bear often do that in cases of hunger what happens when the Bears not hungry what happens is plentiful the garden is semen really feel sorry for the bear do they ever wondered when there is not sufficient and provided fattened will there ever be a time will exist is this the question I choose to stay on the side of the rich the money The Castaways steripen girls anchor avarice Envy walk two roads been with the poor the unlikely perhaps ignored and the wealth I can't tell you what money. Sweetheart here's looking at the well to do the Wella biters all the success here's to that I'm staying in for terribly Barry Oh that men can do .

Early stage of life I have to say that coming down from many peaceful days it's not a immature are small at the beach for the world. No tornado Valley this what anyting what bow down to. Plus, adieu what is the easiest. I don't see it from the start I don't spread the legs of secession and meager attitudes. there's a life and happiness, steadiness, or failure.

Chapter 44: Please, They Hate It Here

I stayed at home in this dedication to life study. I want to tell about the song Take My Love From the berry

imperatively berry girl it just is what people take. they must be loved someone must love it sure someone must be love. How much did be for who must love must they be what is week unless they be able to Strong has a case what does not impose what is not in search of the ugly of the swing and they hating Brothers.

Mist Berryessa name before thinks that music is not like art not like Tom had it Tom was an artist he did the cover the spot it's what disconnects the book and the world father this is the picture of me pictures of men a woman disconnecting happiness where did smothered the colors run it's the tears eliminate the breast of one side the funny Parable heartbeat just pulls us into the point of dying here you see a woman on the cover is a dead woman she cannot whisper a letter of this book.

she can say anything to lay down I never walk. It's just something shocking to let the readers understand the point of life it's not to be that is to live they're two totally different words don't look similar whatsoever I think today's paper called the car moves where we live Poland match match difference between the dying and living in the book called shoe the orange rain by Rachel K. Martin well this will hit the foot like a nail in Jesus on the cross. she killed the ground, was a slave 2 the mundane, or was everyone I did not care about the Hills of grass. Complete waste of words. what's this woman a prostitute? what she crown debutante person beauty queen of high school Rich Roll? was she all things of stupidity unknowingness ignorance or hid ugly imagine and she started.

let's just cover up this life in the grave let's throw the dirt do you disagree? what's rice on the high side paints. It's good to not feel like a zero.

Chapter 2: We Won't Look Like This

Required to run towards the track . Chloe did with chicken we thought you'd want looks like this Daphne could save your life.

Chapter 2: We Won't Look Like This

How do we not look this way is it because it's Halloween to you it's because you can't see them the running everywhere this one in particular this one goes through Michelle mentioned in the Poetry of choosing your own trying there's something much like a spider on the wall just in the introvignes much like yourself reading interpreting songs like what I consider amuse hear it . to me this is the point of life one cannot get through when cannot pass through it without fighting it without chewing Dan taking that last breath. is that how it is the last moment the last breath we clench her teeth trying to survive a horrible World horrible tide change and Michelle was just a coaster the poet that must live within that moment but last poem has many different phases of change of the death of the dying as I mentioned in the last buck to the orange rain as you split and diet of course this means US Mini Splits a Bittersweet taste is in the orange rind 1 West recall supposed to leave us or last 10 to 15 seconds of Life flashing before eyes in these different frames these different stanzas of the poetry depicts all of those emotions racing before becoming free of ourselves when we come raging spirits everlasting life and a r motorcycles oh the last book was more about trying to chew to live eventually we get to the last year I think that's where this book will pick up movie about all that resides in the reflection of one's life at that last moment those last days Rising for the last challenge what will it be like for anyone Harrison introspection when's fall back people give so much advice how is it to look backwards and tell yourself or you will go for it no more. We won't look like this first of all like we are we want looks like we used to when you were sick dying decrepit weathering fattening whatever the case may be will become something that cannot recover to become the death supposedly we were big pile of dust he'll be thrown out to sea is this more of it was just an interest faction into what we will face something will will will be borne by.

We ran together Chloe we had every feeling that the last three days or empty and Shiloh of white snow ice, performance shows knives healthy walking bodies and medical and poverty togetherness much worse find sunny I need a. let's go think of moving for it. I will be there?

It's been quite a herring experience they just keep sitting there watching me will invisible people I watching you ain't heavy things in me that you and I feel their tactile you cannot see the sale practically breaking every bone in my body pinched they just keep taking all of my air and weighing me down odesse torturous all day and they keep me up all night I get no rest my eyes are peeled they're black and they are ready explosions all over the TV and nothing phases they're more than bothering me this is completely Concerta done bothering me she went to the back what's 2 two tier and that was all she does is Justin find the 2-day anymore of the two deer used to come around back I think someone hit and crush the deer and split it off to the side like a big pile of reverie organs and blood the head of used to recognize so dearly when her go baby dad Aerotek such a beautiful picture that captured in time she said that was promised a the road a little baby doll left motherless they're practically skin and bone I just fed them she barely had nutrients and she tried to use all of them as much as she could feed her baby deer animals their highest extent to keep themselves in there offspring live people cannot do the same.

I heard it's racing is pounding his true knocking knocking as if wanting to be raped I think I have your heart he said it's putting me everywhere that you're never going to be what you say don't understand or appreciate themselves they don't want you to not really anything cuz you did not have this problem they want me to sit there and be there in and then you and Father's day but this isn't expanding to anyone that can guess what it seems people don't want to be bothered and I think of any way to bother me that care about him being agitated and extremes they've gone to the bothering you and that's better. now question art I thought. the news of sunny day and every computer I walk in front of was there when I left the building. I could see the smoke coming out of the windows watch the TV and explosions. I'm in bed watching too finally just relaxing to a week ago and it was with just one more time. December went by so quickly and I just wanted to go and make it through the last year at of my job app. And I always felt just like it was had just happened but I was just going to pray for the first time. I just for a little a little yeah fresh air my father and I didn't run many travels at through the Midwest as much as we went through more in St Louis we saw the downtown area we saw the malls that's been closed a lot of the Sea Breeze old friends used to live places that the houses are not as well kept you probably are now condemned you are perhaps someone else is living there there's this not really a place where a lot of people are still states structured it's not like living in New Orleans just had its

Chapter 45: Rachel, We Wanna Tell Ya To Give A Shit

pride and its culture for many many years. drove me to school quite a bit that is only when and if the last time he dropped me off it was a very Rocky rainy morning I said hello to have then he drove off to the Sun.

medium sized statue woman with all of these cat like I appearance perm straighten hair I'm sorry my pigtails blow in the Wind he went further and further into the Sun. That was him going to the start of his day every day started with a Sun Ray and going away to begin my beach walk into start of my new school year. Seemed like he was going into the sun to me Style of course he was not driving into the sun just a figure of speech for your child and you're not too tall can't see too far over the hell seems like that's where he's gay.

of course it's a whole different culture to be involved in different kinds of weather and different kinds of States Midwest pretty humdrum you ever winter spring or summer or fall more of the summer in the winter is definite the fall in the spring 10 do Collide somewhat but the leaves do fall by the end of September. squinting outside of the window I looked at how everyone was little dots down from an airplane there's so many people about because it was the July 4th holiday and all the sudden there was planking and clashing airplanes flying and firecrackers going. can hear loads and loads a fireworks when their direction under the arch I get my daughter look at this time. My mind was empty with no hope for anyting a few hours went by and I saw a big cloud in the sky jumped Define it was on the floor.

Chapter 3: We Just Don’t Care

He met a friend and yet we couldn't go through Finding Nemo it was a coffee all black coffee everyday black coffee Olympic cream in the coffee Willow thought you was black it was dark and made him crazy he went looking for anyone finally came up Iraq we found his child in a Ciroc you're really funny story Stanley Charlie found any survivors how she kept hiding from him somebody for children who don't want to be you're off and running I didn't see what the point of it is till they get to the point. Lucy Wizards daughter's name and she spoke unhinged address of the clock as it sat on the wall S4 had school in the plants and everything that we saw stay consistent we were together we're overwhelmed to begin every day but there was no where we were going we were all very happy to finally be junior high in front of all of the bag sickle writers they all took a plunge it was just the sun rise of the Cascades when she was in the big Village running and soon to be in the middle of September for bats were the roads were all the problems has one set there I thought well when I go to Houston Texas or something while we didn't want to sit Africa bigger place but the car couldn't go anywhere it's just broken down there always just imagine you what we might do and he was still looking for his daughter still trying to figure out what to be there by funny name for Lucy means like can see the light of it

The leftover people were all scattered throughout the yard. After every day he had ended we did not get to ignore the cold feet that cat walking towards the other ones. Many of them wanted to join the others and pray for all of their cold feet to bow to their heads in the Forum of a monstrous pleasure so they'd all set there we had to take a trip to New Orleans and people did not think this was a good idea they did not like their feet being sick isn't not like anything they were going to be reaching for many many many many many many feet.

the day before they all had left to go to Spencer's store and buy the most expensive sheets. They were never going to be put never pack from the rooms they're never going to be not broken and they just wanted to feel as if they jumped off of their beds Temple Run.

the night before of what's his call this December 2018 7 in the morning it was the most beautiful day. The snow still nothing moved nothing was alert. The only thing that could have been better was seeing the dogs air blow out of his nose from extreme cold that enter through the door so that has. The house was at least four stories Square Windows in each wall you so looks of a typical Colonial home it was a blue Hound blue screen siding panels made of wood and standings past hundred year everyone try to be there everyone try to want to the name of the house kept everyone sent everyone wanted to wake up there.

I did I ran to the window and I ran down the hall and gressive Lee ran through the waves of all of the air that collided with how it ripped through my grapes yes I fell on the floor rolling about like I'm literally on caution bear I was shocked at the nurse and I ever sit there again and ever since since he's such a bad as before session can you during the holidays. But I just seen a ladybug there was nothing Easter magazines at the year before expired so the fireplace have to be used for wet hair and snapping acid crinkled away photographs all the past of a present.

Chapter 4: We Just Hope You Give A Damn

Stop prettying him down. He had to stay pretty and not do anything. He couldn't get as bad as he wanted to be. In so many ways no one gives a darn

between comfort and discomfort is the title
It says September 7th this is the year 2019 this is a fun year there's a glorious year deercast beerfeast time went by so quickly There was no storm today I could not see the floor my house standing as w between comfort and discomfort is the title Everyday it's winter.

New line Monday
Blue Line and that you can see the indent and you just Uline
this is our switch to this is our switch to do indignant
indent

Chapter 1: Zero

Imperturbably beary. My favorite musical people has to be my sister Billy bear. before bear became all that she was in the store she started singing in high school and making records she's performed all over the world cleaning Japan she has very solid tympanic Club beats that could be played to her sultry jazz .

Chapter 46: YOu Need To Put That Down

I first realize Billy bear she handed me a tape of a record a song. Like so many musical people she had a special vibrato Special Air a voice tune it just comes up through the air things. She is done inspiring and plastic her spirit is the LIE of love togetherness an extreme training Guelph complete imperturbe Lee Berry her life is been so balanced I just called her the Ampere terribly Barry she has been sitting I know existence for difference she likes sitting in the breeze and believe is an impenetrable day so let's all try to be infertile early Berry and this is where I'll begin my journey to be like my idol I will be in future we bury in so many ways let's start out On the 1st of December.

I was born in the middle of the month timing disco's at its height it was an air of sophistication I could just go on and on there to so many people I don't see why shutter success stop being poor success is being happy to get to a point of imperturbability Barry happiness mimosa's jovial is the honey dripping from a bear right after hurts hibernation during the cold cold existence of the planet Earth there are some for which Life Goes On there's some for which there's a different Tale the bear has no Tales of this every years the summer every year is the honey this girl is what so many try to be to not give it from anyting to walk through those bitter snooze so many people must do to be blinded my passion warmed by the strength of your ability strength to go and do it's almost animal is human to fail so many half can any of us be in Pretoria blueberry any of us have that drive their focus then one tunnel vision life it makes it hibernate through the dark days history rest upon our souls mini rester gifted and blessed is it gift people strike is not being the bear being the human causes are suffering that we mistreat that they will suffer this is the tale as so many others human suffering The Berry people seem so sweet they just picked the Bears right off a tree berries put them in there a little dresses and scoop them up and bowls and rush them in bowls symbols of Pies there others just we'll catch that when of sophistication and Air what will never be lift sway how will it be can we all try a real animals some of us just choose to be God can we all be in picture of Lee Barry can we all just ignore the superfluous strenuous activities hell on Earth we all Drive the existence of poverty existence of well does it take the money that's something she's never been abridge stuff and something of a circumstance provide to her tell unbridled ability money is cast upon them to be the animal they are they exist as no other no one can seem to not hurt yep they will never not help despair pull through he people shoot at it they always preserve it it's mistake simplicity it's snowing this to enjoy the wall to wrap up in the warmth of oneself to endure the cold this is story of many tales of many people try to accomplish such a thing so many ways so many jacket ways find ourselves why bear freeing ourselves to be the humane this is what many will never do so much easier how to do a kickover tent 2Pac to steal one's honey steal one's food does the bear often do that in cases of hunger what happens when the Bears not hungry what happens is plentiful the garden is semen really feel sorry for the bear do they ever wondered when there is not sufficient and provided fattened will there ever be a time will exist is this the question I choose to stay on the side of the rich the money The Castaways steripen girls anchor avarice Envy walk two roads been with the poor the unlikely perhaps ignored and the wealth I can't tell you what money. Sweetheart here's looking at the well to do the Wella biters all the success here's to that I'm staying in for terribly Barry Oh that men can do .

Early stage of life I have to say that coming down from many peaceful days it's not a immature are small at the beach for the world. No tornado Valley this what anyting what bow down to. Plus, adieu what is the easiest. I don't see it from the start I don't spread the legs of secession and meager attitudes. there's a life and happiness, steadiness, or failure.

I stayed at home in this dedication to life study. I want to tell about the song Take My Love From the berry imperatively berry girl it just is what people take. they must be loved someone must love it sure someone must be love. How much did be for who must love must they be what is week unless they be able to Strong has a case what does not impose what is not in search of the ugly of the swing and they hating Brothers.

Mist Berryessa name before thinks that music is not like art not like Tom had it Tom was an artist he did the cover the spot it's what disconnects the book and the world father this is the picture of me pictures of men a woman disconnecting happiness where did smothered the colors run it's the tears eliminate the breast of one side the funny Parable heartbeat just pulls us into the point of dying here you see a woman on the cover is a dead woman she cannot whisper a letter of this book.

she can say anything to lay down I never walk. It's just something shocking to let the readers understand the point of life it's not to be that is to live they're two totally different words don't look similar whatsoever I think today's paper called the car moves where we live Poland match match difference between the dying and living in the book called shoe the orange rain by Rachel K. Martin well this will hit the foot like a nail in Jesus on the cross. she killed the ground, was a slave 2 the mundane, or was everyone I did not care about the Hills of grass. Complete waste of words. what's this woman a prostitute? what she crown debutante person beauty queen of high school Rich Roll? was she all things of stupidity unknowingness ignorance or hid ugly imagine and she started.

let's just cover up this life in the grave let's throw the dirt do you disagree? what's rice on the high side paints. It's good to not feel like a zero.

Chapter 2: We Won't Look Like This

Required to run towards the track . Chloe did with chicken we thought you'd want looks like this Daphne could save your life.

Chapter 2: We Won't Look Like This

How do we not look this way is it because it's Halloween to you it's because you can't see them the running everywhere this one in particular this one goes through Michelle mentioned in the Poetry of choosing your own trying there's something much like a spider on the wall just in the introvignes much like yourself reading interpreting songs like what I consider amuse hear it . to me this is the point of life one cannot get through when cannot pass through it without fighting it without chewing Dan taking that last breath. is that how it is the last moment the last breath we clench her teeth trying to survive a horrible World horrible tide change and Michelle was just a coaster the poet that must live within that moment but last poem has many different phases of change of the death of the dying as I mentioned in the last buck to the orange rain as you split and diet of course this means US Mini Splits a Bittersweet taste is in the

Chapter 47: We Can Cover His Mouth

orange rind 1 West recall supposed to leave us or last 10 to 15 seconds of Life flashing before eyes in these different frames these different stanzas of the poetry depicts all of those emotions racing before becoming free of ourselves when we come raging spirits everlasting life and a r motorcycles oh the last book was more about trying to chew to live eventually we get to the last year I think that's where this book will pick up movie about all that resides in the reflection of one's life at that last moment those last days Rising for the last challenge what will it be like for anyone Harrison introspection when's fall back people give so much advice how is it to look backwards and tell yourself or you will go for it no more. We won't look like this first of all like we are we want looks like we used to when you were sick dying decrepit weathering fattening whatever the case may be will become something that cannot recover to become the death supposedly we were big pile of dust he'll be thrown out to sea is this more of it was just an interest faction into what we will face something will will will be borne by.

We ran together Chloe we had every feeling that the last three days or empty and Shiloh of white snow ice, performance shows knives healthy walking bodies and medical and poverty togetherness much worse find sunny I need a. let's go think of moving for it. I will be there?

It's been quite a herring experience they just keep sitting there watching me will invisible people I watching you ain't heavy things in me that you and I feel their tactile you cannot see the sale practically breaking every bone in my body pinched they just keep taking all of my air and weighing me down odesse torturous all day and they keep me up all night I get no rest my eyes are peeled they're black and they are ready explosions all over the TV and nothing phases they're more than bothering me this is completely Concerta done bothering me she went to the back what's 2 two tier and that was all she does is Justin find the 2-day anymore of the two deer used to come around back I think someone hit and crush the deer and split it off to the side like a big pile of reverie organs and blood the head of used to recognize so dearly when her go baby dad Aerotek such a beautiful picture that captured in time she said that was promised a the road a little baby doll left motherless they're practically skin and bone I just fed them she barely had nutrients and she tried to use all of them as much as she could feed her baby deer animals their highest extent to keep themselves in there offspring live people cannot do the same.

I heard it's racing is pounding his true knocking knocking as if wanting to be raped I think I have your heart he said it's putting me everywhere that you're never going to be what you say don't understand or appreciate themselves they don't want you to not really anything cuz you did not have this problem they want me to sit there and be there in and then you and Father's day but this isn't expanding to anyone that can guess what it seems people don't want to be bothered and I think of any way to bother me that care about him being agitated and extremes they've gone to the bothering you and that's better. now question art I thought. the news of sunny day and every computer I walk in front of was there when I left the building. I could see the smoke coming out of the windows watch the TV and explosions. I'm in bed watching too finally just relaxing to a week ago and it was with just one more time. December went by so quickly and I just wanted to go and make it through the last year at of my job app. And I always felt just like it was had just happened but I was just going to pray for the first time. I just for a little a little yeah fresh air my father and I didn't run many travels at through the Midwest as much as we went through more in St Louis we saw the downtown area we saw the malls that's been closed a lot of the Sea Breeze old friends used to live places that the houses are not as well kept you probably are now condemned you are perhaps someone else is living there there's this not really a place where a lot of people are still states structured it's not like living in New Orleans just had its pride and its culture for many many years. drove me to school quite a bit that is only when and if the last time he dropped me off it was a very Rocky rainy morning I said hello to have then he drove off to the Sun.

medium sized statue woman with all of these cat like I appearance perm straighten hair I'm sorry my pigtails blow in the Wind he went further and further into the Sun. That was him going to the start of his day every day started with a Sun Ray and going away to begin my beach walk into start of my new school year. Seemed like he was going into the sun to me Style of course he was not driving into the sun just a figure of speech for your child and you're not too tall can't see too far over the hell seems like that's where he's gay.

of course it's a whole different culture to be involved in different kinds of weather and different kinds of States Midwest pretty humdrum you ever winter spring or summer or fall more of the summer in the winter is definite the fall in the spring 10 do Collide somewhat but the leaves do fall by the end of September. squinting outside of the window I looked at how everyone was little dots down from an airplane there's so many people about because it was the July 4th holiday and all the sudden there was planking and clashing airplanes flying and firecrackers going. can hear loads and loads a fireworks when their direction under the arch I get my daughter look at this time. My mind was empty with no hope for anyting a few hours went by and I saw a big cloud in the sky jumped Define it was on the floor.

rom extreme cold that enter through the door so that has. The house was at least four stories Square Windows in each wall you so looks of a typical Colonial home it was a blue Hound blue screen siding panels made of wood and standings past hundred year everyone try to be there everyone try to want to the name of the house kept everyone sent everyone wanted to wake up there.

I did I ran to the window and I ran down the hall and gressive Lee ran through the waves of all of the air that collided with how it ripped through my grapes yes I fell on the floor rolling about like I'm literally on caution bear I was shocked at the nurse and I ever sit there again and ever since since he's such a bad as before session can you during the holidays. But I just seen a ladybug there was nothing Easter magazines at the year before expired so the fireplace have to be used for wet hair and snapping acid crinkled away photographs all the past of a present.

Chapter 4: We Just Hope You Give A Damn

Stop prettying him down. He had to stay pretty and not do anything. He couldn't get as bad as he wanted to be. In so many ways no one gives a darn

between comfort and discomfort is the title
It says September 7th this is the year 2019 this is a fun year there's a glorious year deercast beerfeast time went by so quickly There was no storm today I could not see the floor my house standing as w between comfort and discomfort is the title Everyday it's winter.

New line Monday
Blue Line and that you can see the indent and you just Uline
this is our switch to this is our switch to do indignant
indent

Chapter 47: We Can Cover His Mouth

Imperturbably beary. My favorite musical people has to be my sister Billy bear. before bear became all that she was in the store she started singing in high school and making records she's performed all over the

world cleaning Japan she has very solid tympanic Club beats that could be played to her sultry jazz .

I first realize Billy bear she handed me a tape of a record a song. Like so many musical people she had a special vibrato Special Air a voice tune it just comes up through the air things. She is done inspiring and plastic her spirit is the LIE of love togetherness an extreme training Guelph complete imperturbe Lee Berry her life is been so balanced I just called her the Ampere terribly Barry she has been sitting I know existence for difference she likes sitting in the breeze and believe is an impenetrable day so let's all try to be infertile early Berry and this is where I'll begin my journey to be like my idol I will be in future we bury in so many ways let's start out On the 1st of December.

I was born in the middle of the month timing disco's at its height it was an air of sophistication I could just go on and on there to so many people I don't see why shutter success stop being poor success is being happy to get to a point of imperturbability Barry happiness mimosa's jovial is the honey dripping from a bear right after hurts hibernation during the cold cold

existence of the planet Earth there are some for which Life Goes On there's some for which there's a different Tale the bear has no Tales of this every years the summer every year is the honey this girl is what so many try to be to not give it from anyting to walk through those bitter snooze so many people must do to be blinded my passion warmed by the strength of your ability strength to go and do it's almost animal is human to fail so many half can any of us be in Pretoria blueberry any of us have that drive their focus then one tunnel vision life it makes it hibernate through the dark days history rest upon our souls mini rester gifted and blessed is it gift people strike is not being the bear being the human causes are suffering that we mistreat that they will suffer this is the tale as so many others human suffering The Berry people seem so sweet they just picked the Bears right off a tree berries put them in there a little dresses and scoop them up and bowls and rush them in bowls symbols of Pies there others just we'll catch that when of sophistication and Air what will never be lift sway how will it be can we all try a real animals some of us just choose to be God can we all be in picture of Lee Barry can we all just ignore the

superfluous strenuous activities hell on Earth we all Drive the existence of poverty existence of well does it take the money that's something she's never been abridge stuff and something of a circumstance provide to her tell unbridled ability money is cast upon them to be the animal they are they exist as no other no one can seem to not hurt yep they will never not help despair pull through he people shoot at it they always preserve it it's mistake simplicity it's snowing this to enjoy the wall to wrap up in the warmth of oneself to endure the cold this is story of many tales of many people try to accomplish such a thing so many ways so many jacket ways find ourselves why bear freeing ourselves to be the humane this is what many will never do so much easier how to do a kickover tent 2Pac to steal one's honey steal one's food does the bear often do that in cases of hunger what happens when the Bears not hungry what happens is plentiful the garden is semen really feel sorry for the bear do they ever wondered when there is not sufficient and provided fattened will there ever be a time will exist is this the question I choose to stay on the side of the rich the money The Castaways steripen girls anchor avarice Envy walk two roads been with the

poor the unlikely perhaps ignored and the wealth I can't tell you what money. Sweetheart here's looking at the well to do the Wella biters all the success here's to that I'm staying in for terribly Barry Oh that men can do .

Early stage of life I have to say that coming down from many peaceful days it's not a immature are small at the beach for the world. No tornado Valley this what anyting what bow down to. Plus, adieu what is the easiest. I don't see it from the start I don't spread the legs of secession and meager attitudes. there's a life and happiness, steadiness, or failure.

I stayed at home in this dedication to life study. I want to tell about the song Take My Love From the berry imperatively berry girl it just is what people take. they must be loved someone must love it sure someone must be love. How much did be for who must love must they be what is week unless they be able to Strong has a case what does not impose what is not in search of the ugly of the swing and they hating Brothers.

Mist Berryessa name before thinks that music is not like art not like Tom had it Tom was an artist he did the cover the spot it's what disconnects the book and the world father this is the picture of me pictures of men a woman disconnecting happiness where did smothered the colors run it's the tears eliminate the breast of one side the funny Parable heartbeat just pulls us into the point of dying here you see a woman on the cover is a dead woman she cannot whisper a letter of this book.

she can say anything to lay down I never walk. It's just something shocking to let the readers understand the point of life it's not to be that is to live they're two totally different words don't look similar whatsoever I think today's paper called the car moves where we live Poland match match difference between the dying and living in the book called shoe the orange rain by Rachel K. Martin well this will hit the foot like a nail in Jesus on the cross. she killed the ground, was a slave 2 the mundane, or was everyone I did not care about the Hills of grass. Complete waste of words. what's this woman a prostitute? what she crown debutante person beauty queen of high school Rich Roll? was she all things of stupidity unknowingness ignorance or hid ugly imagine and she started.

let's just cover up this life in the grave let's throw the dirt do you disagree? what's rice on the high side paints. It's good to not feel like a zero.

Chapter 2: We Won’t Look Like This

Required to run towards the track . Chloe did with chicken we thought you'd want looks like this Daphne could save your life.

Chapter 2: We Won’t Look Like This

How do we not look this way is it because it's Halloween to you it's because you can't see them the running everywhere this one in particular this one goes through Michelle mentioned in the Poetry of choosing your own trying there's something much like a spider on the wall just in the introvignes much like yourself reading interpreting songs like what I consider amuse hear it . to me this is the point of

Chapter 48: Okay?

life one cannot get through when cannot pass through it without fighting it without chewing Dan taking that last breath. is that how it is the last moment the last breath we clench her teeth trying to survive a horrible World horrible tide change and Michelle was just a coaster the poet that must live within that moment but last poem has many different phases of change of the death of the dying as I mentioned in the last buck to the orange rain as you split and diet of course this means US Mini Splits a Bittersweet taste is in the orange rind 1 West recall supposed to leave us or last 10 to 15 seconds of Life flashing before eyes in these different frames these different stanzas of the poetry depicts all of those emotions racing before becoming free of ourselves when we come raging spirits everlasting life and a r motorcycles oh the last book was more about trying to chew to live eventually we get to the last year I think that's where this book will pick up movie about all that resides in the reflection of one's life at that last moment those last days Rising for the last challenge what will it be like for anyone Harrison introspection when's fall back people give so much advice how is it to look backwards and tell yourself or you will go for it no more. We won't look like this first of all like we are we want looks like we used to when you were sick dying decrepit weathering fattening whatever the case may be will become something that cannot recover to become the death supposedly we were big pile of dust he'll be thrown out to sea is this more of it was just an interest faction into what we will face something will will will be borne by.

We ran together Chloe we had every feeling that the last three days or empty and Shiloh of white snow ice, performance shows knives healthy walking bodies and medical and poverty togetherness much worse find sunny I need a. let's go think of moving for it. I will be there?

It's been quite a herring experience they just keep sitting there watching me will invisible people I watching you ain't heavy things in me that you and I feel their tactile you cannot see the sale practically breaking every bone in my body pinched they just keep taking all of my air and weighing me down odesse torturous all day and they keep me up all night I get no rest my eyes are peeled they're black and they are ready explosions all over the TV and nothing phases they're more than bothering me this is completely Concerta done bothering me she went to the back what's 2 two tier and that was all she does is Justin find the 2-day anymore of the two deer used to come around back I think someone hit and crush the deer and split it off to the side like a big pile of reverie organs and blood the head of used to recognize so dearly when her go baby dad Aerotek such a beautiful picture that captured in time she said that was promised a the road a little baby doll left motherless they're practically skin and bone I just fed them she barely had nutrients and she tried to use all of them as much as she could feed her baby deer animals their highest extent to keep themselves in there offspring live people cannot do the same.

I heard it's racing is pounding his true knocking knocking as if wanting to be raped I think I have your heart he said it's putting me everywhere that you're never going to be what you say don't understand or appreciate themselves they don't want you to not really anything cuz you did not have this problem they want me to sit there and be there in and then you and Father's day but this isn't expanding to anyone that can guess what it seems people don't want to be bothered and I think of any way to bother me that care about him being agitated and extremes they've gone to the bothering you and that's better. now question art I thought. the news of sunny day and every computer I walk in front of was there when I left the building. I could see the smoke coming out of the windows watch the TV and explosions. I'm in bed watching too finally just relaxing to a week ago and it was with just one more time. December went by so quickly and I just wanted to go and make it through the last year at of my job app. And I always felt just like it was had just happened but I was just going to pray for the first time. I just for a little a little yeah fresh air my father and I didn't run many travels at through the Midwest as much as we went through more in St Louis we saw the downtown area we saw the malls that's been closed a lot of the Sea Breeze old friends used to live places that the houses are not as well kept you probably are now condemned you are perhaps someone else is living there there's this not really a place where a lot of people are still states structured it's not like living in New Orleans just had its pride and its culture for many many years. drove me to school quite a bit that is only when and if the last time he dropped me off it was a very Rocky rainy morning I said hello to have then he drove off to the Sun.

medium sized statue woman with all of these cat like I appearance perm straighten hair I'm sorry my pigtails blow in the Wind he went further and further into the Sun. That was him going to the start of his day every day started with a Sun Ray and going away to begin my beach walk into start of my new school year. Seemed like he was going into the sun to me Style of course he was not driving into the sun just a figure of speech for your child and you're not too tall can't see too far over the hell seems like that's where he's gay.

of course it's a whole different culture to be involved in different kinds of weather and different kinds of States Midwest pretty humdrum you ever winter spring or summer or fall more of the summer in the winter is definite the fall in the spring 10 do Collide somewhat but the leaves do fall by the end of September. squinting outside of the window I looked at how everyone was little dots down from an airplane there's so many people about because it was the July 4th holiday and all the sudden there was planking and clashing airplanes flying and firecrackers going. can hear loads and loads a fireworks when their direction under the arch I get my daughter look at this time. My mind was empty with no hope for anyting a few hours went by and I saw a big cloud in the sky jumped Define it was on the floor.

Chapter 3: We Just Don't Care

He met a friend and yet we couldn't go through Finding Nemo it was a coffee all black coffee everyday black coffee Olympic cream in the coffee Willow thought you was black it was dark and made him crazy he went looking for anyone finally came up Iraq we found his child in a Ciroc you're really funny story

Chapter 49: What Is It Honey?

Stanley Charlie found any survivors how she kept hiding from him somebody for children who don't want to be you're off and running I didn't see what the point of it is till they get to the point. Lucy Wizards daughter's name and she spoke unhinged address of the clock as it sat on the wall S4 had school in the plants and everything that we saw stay consistent we were together we're overwhelmed to begin every day but there was no where we were going we were all very happy to finally be junior high in front of all of the bag sickle writers they all took a plunge it was just the sun rise of the Cascades when she was in the big Village running and soon to be in the middle of September for bats were the roads were all the problems has one set there I thought well when I go to Houston Texas or something while we didn't want to sit Africa bigger place but the car couldn't go anywhere it's just broken down there always just imagine you what we might do and he was still looking for his daughter still trying to figure out what to be there by funny name for Lucy means like can see the light of it

The leftover people were all scattered throughout the yard. After every day he had ended we did not get to ignore the cold feet that cat walking towards the other ones. Many of them wanted to join the others and pray for all of their cold feet to bow to their heads in the Forum of a monstrous pleasure so they'd all set there we had to take a trip to New Orleans and people did not think this was a good idea they did not like their feet being sick isn't not like anything they were going to be reaching for many many many many many many feet.

the day before they all had left to go to Spencer's store and buy the most expensive sheets. They were never going to be put never pack from the rooms they're never going to be not broken and they just wanted to feel as if they jumped off of their beds Temple Run.

the night before of what's his call this December 2018 7 in the morning it was the most beautiful day. The snow still nothing moved nothing was alert. The only thing that could have been better was seeing the dogs air blow out of his nose from extreme cold that enter through the door so that has. The house was at least four stories Square Windows in each wall you so looks of a typical Colonial home it was a blue Hound blue screen siding panels made of wood and standings past hundred year everyone try to be there everyone try to want to the name of the house kept everyone sent everyone wanted to wake up there.

I did I ran to the window and I ran down the hall and gressive Lee ran through the waves of all of the air that collided with how it ripped through my grapes yes I fell on the floor rolling about like I'm literally on caution bear I was shocked at the nurse and I ever sit there again and ever since since he's such a bad as before session can you during the holidays. But I just seen a ladybug there was nothing Easter magazines at the year before expired so the fireplace have to be used for wet hair and snapping acid crinkled away photographs all the past of a present.

Chapter 4: We Just Hope You Give A Damn

Stop prettying him down. He had to stay pretty and not do anything. He couldn't get as bad as he wanted to be. In so many ways no one gives a darn

between comfort and discomfort is the title
It says September 7th this is the year 2019 this is a fun year there's a glorious year deercast beerfeast time went by so quickly There was no storm today I could not see the floor my house standing as w between comfort and discomfort is the title
Everyday it's winter.

New line Monday
Blue Line and that you can see the indent and you just Uline
this is our switch to this is our switch to do indignant
indent

Chapter 1: Zero

Imperturbably beary. My favorite musical people has to be my sister Billy bear. before bear became all that she was in the store she started singing in high school and making records she's performed all over the world cleaning Japan she has very solid tympanic Club beats that could be played to her sultry jazz .

I first realize Billy bear she handed me a tape of a record a song. Like so many musical people she had a special vibrato Special Air a voice tune it just comes up through the air things. She is done inspiring and plastic her spirit is the LIE of love togetherness an extreme training Guelph complete imperturbe Lee Berry her life is been so balanced I just called her the Ampere terribly Barry she has been sitting I know existence for difference she likes sitting in the breeze and believe is an impenetrable day so let's all try to be infertile early Berry and this is where I'll begin my journey to be like my idol I will be in future we bury in so many ways let's start out On the 1st of December.

I was born in the middle of the month timing disco's at its height it was an air of sophistication I could just go on and on there to so many people I don't

see why shutter success stop being poor success is being happy to get to a point of imperturbability Barry happiness mimosa's jovial is the honey dripping from a bear right after hurts hibernation during the cold cold existence of the planet Earth there are some for which Life Goes On there's some for which there's a different Tale the bear has no Tales of this every years the summer every year is the honey this girl is what so many try to be to not give it from anyting to walk through those bitter snooze so many people must do to be blinded my passion warmed by the strength of your ability strength to go and do it's almost animal is human to fail so many half can any of us be in Pretoria blueberry any of us have that drive their focus then one tunnel vision life it makes it hibernate through the dark days history rest upon our souls mini rester gifted and blessed is it gift people strike is not being the bear being the human causes are suffering that we mistreat that they will suffer this is the tale as so many others human suffering The Berry people seem so sweet they just picked the Bears right off a tree berries put them in there a little dresses and scoop them up and bowls and rush them in bowls symbols of Pies there others just

we'll catch that when of sophistication and Air what will never be lift sway how will it be can we all try a real animals some of us just choose to be God can we all be in picture of Lee Barry can we all just ignore the superfluous strenuous activities hell on Earth we all Drive the existence of poverty existence of well does it take the money that's something she's never been abridge stuff and something of a circumstance provide to her tell unbridled ability money is cast upon them to be the animal they are they exist as no other no one can seem to not hurt yep they will never not help despair pull through he people shoot at it they always preserve it it's mistake simplicity it's snowing this to enjoy the wall to wrap up in the warmth of oneself to endure the cold this is story of many tales of many people try to accomplish such a thing so many ways so many jacket ways find ourselves why bear freeing ourselves to be the humane this is

Chapter 50: We'd Love For You To Care

what many will never do so much easier how to do a kickover tent 2Pac to steal one's honey steal one's food does the bear often do that in cases of hunger what happens when the Bears not hungry what happens is plentiful the garden is semen really feel sorry for the bear do they ever wondered when there is not sufficient and provided fattened will there ever be a time will exist is this the question I choose to stay on the side of the rich the money The Castaways steripen girls anchor avarice Envy walk two roads been with the poor the unlikely perhaps ignored and the wealth I can't tell you what money. Sweetheart here's looking at the well to do the Wella biters all the success here's to that I'm staying in for terribly Barry Oh that men can do .

Early stage of life I have to say that coming down from many peaceful days it's not a immature are small at the beach for the world. No tornado Valley this what anyting what bow down to. Plus, adieu what is the easiest. I don't see it from the start I don't spread the legs of secession and meager attitudes. there's a life and happiness, steadiness, or failure.

I stayed at home in this dedication to life study. I want to tell about the song Take My Love From the berry imperatively berry girl it just is what people take. they must be loved someone must love it sure someone must be love. How much did be for who must love must they be what is week unless they be able to Strong has a case what does not impose what is not in search of the ugly of the swing and they hating Brothers.

Mist Berryessa name before thinks that music is not like art not like Tom had it Tom was an artist he did the cover the spot it's what disconnects the book and the world father this is the picture of me pictures of men a woman disconnecting happiness where did smothered the colors run it's the tears eliminate the breast of one side the funny Parable heartbeat just pulls us into the point of dying here you see a woman on the cover is a dead woman she cannot whisper a letter of this book.

she can say anything to lay down I never walk. It's just something shocking to let the readers understand the point of life it's not to be that is to live they're two totally different words don't look similar whatsoever I think today's paper called the car moves where we live Poland match match difference between the dying and living in the book called shoe the orange rain by Rachel K. Martin well this will hit the foot like a nail in Jesus on the cross. she killed the ground, was a slave 2 the mundane, or was everyone I did not care about the Hills of grass. Complete waste of words. what's this woman a prostitute? what she crown debutante person beauty queen of high school Rich Roll? was she all things of stupidity unknowingness ignorance or hid ugly imagine and she started.

let's just cover up this life in the grave let's throw the dirt do you disagree? what's rice on the high side paints. It's good to not feel like a zero.

Chapter 2: We Won't Look Like This

Required to run towards the track . Chloe did with chicken we thought you'd want looks like this Daphne could save your life.

Chapter 2: We Won't Look Like This

How do we not look this way is it because it's Halloween to you it's because you can't see them the running everywhere this one in particular this one goes through Michelle mentioned in the Poetry of choosing your own trying there's something much like a spider on the wall just in the introvignes much like yourself reading

interpreting songs like what I consider amuse hear it .
to me this is the point of life one cannot get through
when cannot pass through it without fighting it without
chewing Dan taking that last breath. is that how it is
the last moment the last breath we clench her teeth
trying to survive a horrible World horrible tide change
and Michelle was just a coaster the poet that must live
within that moment but last poem has many different
phases of change of the death of the dying as I
mentioned in the last buck to the orange rain as you
split and diet of course this means US Mini Splits a
Bittersweet taste is in the orange rind 1 West recall
supposed to leave us or last 10 to 15 seconds of Life
flashing before eyes in these different frames these
different stanzas of the poetry depicts all of those
emotions racing before becoming free of ourselves when
we come raging spirits everlasting life and a r
motorcycles oh the last book was more about trying to
chew to live eventually we get to the last year I think
that's where this book will pick up movie about all that
resides in the reflection of one's life at that last
moment those last days Rising for the last challenge
what will it be like for anyone Harrison introspection

when's fall back people give so much advice how is it to look backwards and tell yourself or you will go for it no more. We won't look like this first of all like we are we want looks like we used to when you were sick dying decrepit weathering fattening whatever the case may be will become something that cannot recover to become the death supposedly we were big pile of dust he'll be thrown out to sea is this more of it was just an interest faction into what we will face something will will will be borne by.

We ran together Chloe we had every feeling that the last three days or empty and Shiloh of white snow ice, performance shows knives healthy walking bodies and medical and poverty togetherness much worse find sunny I need a. let's go think of moving for it. I will be there?

It's been quite a herring experience they just keep sitting there watching me will invisible people I watching you ain't heavy things in me that you and I feel their tactile you cannot see the sale practically breaking every bone in my body pinched they just keep taking all of my air and weighing me down odesse torturous all day and they keep me up all night I get no rest my eyes are peeled they're black and they are ready explosions all over the TV and nothing phases they're more than bothering me this is completely Concerta done bothering me she went to the back what's 2 two tier and that was all she does is Justin find the 2-day anymore of the two deer used to come around back I think someone hit and crush the deer and split it off to the side like a big pile of reverie organs and blood the head of used to recognize so dearly when her go baby dad Aerotek such a beautiful picture that captured in time she said that was promised a the road a little baby doll left motherless they're practically skin and bone I just fed them she barely had nutrients and she tried to use all of them as much as she could feed her baby deer animals their highest extent to keep themselves in there offspring live people cannot do the same.

I heard it's racing is pounding his true knocking knocking as if wanting to be raped I think I have your heart he said it's putting me everywhere that you're never going to be what you say don't understand or appreciate themselves they don't want you to not really anything cuz you did not have this problem they want me to sit there and be there in and then you and Father's day but this isn't expanding to anyone that can guess what it seems people don't want to be bothered

Chapter 51: We Don't Get What We Should Do

and I think of any way to bother me that care about him being agitated and extremes they've gone to the bothering you and that's better. now question art I thought. the news of sunny day and every computer I walk in front of was there when I left the building. I could see the smoke coming out of the windows watch the TV and explosions. I'm in bed watching too finally just relaxing to a week ago and it was with just one more time. December went by so quickly and I just wanted to go and make it through the last year at of my job app. And I always felt just like it was had just happened but I was just going to pray for the first time. I just for a little a little yeah fresh air my father and I didn't run many travels at through the Midwest as much as we went through more in St Louis we saw the downtown area we saw the malls that's been closed a lot of the Sea Breeze old friends used to live places that the houses are not as well kept you probably are now condemned you are perhaps someone else is living there there's this not really a place where a lot of people are still states structured it's not like living in New Orleans just had its pride and its culture for many many years. drove me to school quite a bit that is only when and if the last time he dropped me off it was a very Rocky rainy morning I said hello to have then he drove off to the Sun.

medium sized statue woman with all of these cat like I appearance perm straighten hair I'm sorry my pigtails blow in the Wind he went further and further into the Sun. That was him going to the start of his day every day started with a Sun Ray and going away to begin my beach walk into start of my new school year. Seemed like he was going into the sun to me Style of course he was not driving into the sun just a figure of speech for your child and you're not too tall can't see too far over the hell seems like that's where he's gay.

of course it's a whole different culture to be involved in different kinds of weather and different kinds of States Midwest pretty humdrum you ever winter

spring or summer or fall more of the summer in the winter is definite the fall in the spring 10 do Collide somewhat but the leaves do fall by the end of September. squinting outside of the window I looked at how everyone was little dots down from an airplane there's so many people about because it was the July 4th holiday and all the sudden there was planking and clashing airplanes flying and firecrackers going. can hear loads and loads a fireworks when their direction under the arch I get my daughter look at this time. My mind was empty with no hope for anyting a few hours went by and I saw a big cloud in the sky jumped Define it was on the floor.

rom extreme cold that enter through the door so that has. The house was at least four stories Square Windows in each wall you so looks of a typical Colonial home it was a blue Hound blue screen siding panels made of wood and standings past hundred year everyone try to be there everyone try to want to the name of the house kept everyone sent everyone wanted to wake up there.

I did I ran to the window and I ran down the hall and gressive Lee ran through the waves of all of the air that collided with how it ripped through my grapes yes I

fell on the floor rolling about like I'm literally on caution bear I was shocked at the nurse and I ever sit there again and ever since since he's such a bad as before session can you during the holidays. But I just seen a ladybug there was nothing Easter magazines at the year before expired so the fireplace have to be used for wet hair and snapping acid crinkled away photographs all the past of a present.

Chapter 4: We Just Hope You Give A Damn

Stop prettying him down. He had to stay pretty and not do anything. He couldn't get as bad as he wanted to be. In so many ways no one gives a darn

between comfort and discomfort is the title
It says September 7th this is the year 2019 this is a fun year there's a glorious year deercast beerfeast time went by so quickly There was no storm today I could not see the floor my house standing as w between comfort and discomfort is the title
Everyday it's winter.

New line Monday
Blue Line and that you can see the indent and you just Uline
this is our switch to this is our switch to do indignant
indent

Chapter 1: Zero

Imperturbably beary. My favorite musical people has to be my sister Billy bear. before bear became all that she was in the store she started singing in high school and making records she's performed all over the world cleaning Japan she has very solid tympanic Club beats that could be played to her sultry jazz .

I first realize Billy bear she handed me a tape of a record a song. Like so many musical people she had a special vibrato Special Air a voice tune it just comes up through the air things. She is done inspiring and plastic her spirit is the LIE of love togetherness an extreme training Guelph complete imperturbe Lee Berry her life is been so balanced I just called her the Ampere terribly Barry she has been sitting I know existence for difference she likes sitting in the breeze and believe is an impenetrable day so let's all try to be infertile early Berry and this is where I'll begin my journey to be like my idol I will be in future we bury in so many ways let's start out On the 1st of December.

I was born in the middle of the month timing disco's at its height it was an air of sophistication I could just go on and on there to so many people I don't see why shutter success stop being poor success is being happy to get to a point of imperturbability Barry happiness mimosa's jovial is the honey dripping from a bear right after hurts hibernation during the cold cold existence of the planet Earth there are some for which Life Goes On there's some for which there's a different Tale the bear has no Tales of this every years the summer every year is the honey this girl is what so many try to be to not give it from anyting to walk through those bitter snooze so many people must do to be blinded my passion warmed by the strength of your ability strength to go and do it's almost animal is human to fail so many half can any of us be in Pretoria blueberry any of us have that drive their focus then one tunnel vision life it makes it hibernate through the dark days history rest upon our souls mini rester gifted and blessed is it gift people strike is not being the bear being the human causes are suffering that we mistreat that they will suffer this is the tale as so many others human suffering The Berry people seem so sweet they just picked the Bears right off a tree berries put them in there a little dresses and scoop them up and bowls and rush them in bowls symbols of Pies there others just we'll catch that when of sophistication and Air what will never be lift sway how will it be can we all try a real animals some of us just choose to be God can we all be in picture of Lee Barry can we all just ignore the superfluous strenuous activities hell on Earth we all Drive the existence of poverty existence of well does it take the money that's something she's never been abridge stuff and something of a

Chapter 52: We're Jealous To Make You Care

circumstance provide to her tell unbridled ability money is cast upon them to be the animal they are they exist as no other no one can seem to not hurt yep they will never not help despair pull through he people shoot at it they always preserve it it's mistake simplicity it's snowing this to enjoy the wall to wrap up in the warmth of oneself to endure the cold this is story of many tales of many people try to accomplish such a thing so many ways so many jacket ways find ourselves why bear freeing ourselves to be the humane this is what many will never do so much easier how to do a kickover tent 2Pac to steal one's honey steal one's food does the bear often do that in cases of hunger what happens when the Bears not hungry what happens is plentiful the garden is semen really feel sorry for the bear do they ever wondered when there is not sufficient and provided fattened will there ever be a time will exist is this the question I choose to stay on the side of the rich the money The Castaways steripen girls anchor avarice Envy walk two roads been with the poor the unlikely perhaps ignored and the wealth I can't tell you what money. Sweetheart here's looking at the well to do the Wella biters all the success here's to that I'm staying in for terribly Barry Oh that men can do .

Early stage of life I have to say that coming down from many peaceful days it's not a immature are small at the beach for the world. No tornado Valley this what anyting what bow down to. Plus, adieu what is the easiest. I don't see it from the start I don't spread the legs of

secession and meager attitudes. there's a life and happiness, steadiness, or failure.

I stayed at home in this dedication to life study. I want to tell about the song Take My Love From the berry imperatively berry girl it just is what people take. they must be loved someone must love it sure someone must be love. How much did be for who must love must they be what is week unless they be able to Strong has a case what does not impose what is not in search of the ugly of the swing and they hating Brothers.

Mist Berryessa name before thinks that music is not like art not like Tom had it Tom was an artist he did the cover the spot it's what disconnects the book and the world father this is the picture of me pictures of men a woman disconnecting happiness where did smothered the colors run it's the tears eliminate the breast of one side the funny Parable heartbeat just pulls us into the point of dying here you see a woman on the cover is a dead woman she cannot whisper a letter of this book.

she can say anything to lay down I never walk. It's just something shocking to let the readers understand the point of life it's not to be that is to

live they're two totally different words don't look similar whatsoever I think today's paper called the car moves where we live Poland match match difference between the dying and living in the book called shoe the orange rain by Rachel K. Martin well this will hit the foot like a nail in Jesus on the cross. she killed the ground, was a slave 2 the mundane, or was everyone I did not care about the Hills of grass. Complete waste of words. what's this woman a prostitute? what she crown debutante person beauty queen of high school Rich Roll? was she all things of stupidity unknowingness ignorance or hid ugly imagine and she started.

let's just cover up this life in the grave let's throw the dirt do you disagree? what's rice on the high side paints. It's good to not feel like a zero.

Chapter 2: We Won't Look Like This

Required to run towards the track . Chloe did with chicken we thought you'd want looks like this Daphne could save your life.

Chapter 2: We Won't Look Like This

How do we not look this way is it because it's Halloween to you it's because you can't see them the running everywhere this one in particular this one goes through Michelle mentioned in the Poetry of choosing your own trying there's something much like a spider on the wall just in the introvignes much like yourself reading interpreting songs like what I consider amuse hear it . to me this is the point of life one cannot get through when cannot pass through it without fighting it without chewing Dan taking that last breath. is that how it is the last moment the last breath we clench her teeth trying to survive a horrible World horrible tide change and Michelle was just a coaster the poet that must live within that moment but last poem has many different phases of change of the death of the dying as I mentioned in the last buck to the orange rain as you split and diet of course this means US Mini Splits a Bittersweet taste is in the orange rind 1 West recall supposed to leave us or last 10 to 15 seconds of Life flashing before eyes in these different frames these different stanzas of the poetry depicts all of those emotions racing before becoming free of ourselves when we come raging spirits everlasting life and a r motorcycles oh the last book was more about trying to chew to live eventually we get to the last year I think that's where this book will pick up movie about all that resides in the reflection of one's life at that last moment those last days Rising for the last challenge what will it be like for anyone Harrison introspection when's fall back people give so much advice how is it to look backwards and tell yourself or you will go for it no more. We won't look like this first of all like we are we want looks like we used to when you were sick dying decrepit weathering fattening whatever the case may be will become something that cannot recover to become the death supposedly we were big pile of dust he'll be thrown out to sea is this more of it was just an interest faction into what we will face something will will will be borne by.

We ran together Chloe we had every feeling that the last three days or empty and Shiloh of white snow ice, performance shows knives healthy walking bodies and medical and poverty togetherness much worse find sunny I need a. let's go think of moving for it. I will be there?

It's been quite a herring experience they just keep sitting there watching me will invisible people I watching you ain't heavy things in me that you and I feel their tactile you cannot see the sale practically breaking every bone in my body pinched they just keep taking all of my air and weighing me down odesse torturous all day and they keep me up all night I get no rest my eyes are peeled they're black and they are ready explosions all over the TV and nothing phases they're more than bothering me this is completely Concerta done bothering me she went to the back what's 2 two tier and that was all she does is Justin find the 2-day anymore of the two deer used to come around back I think someone hit and crush the deer and split it off to the side like a big pile of reverie organs and blood the head of used to recognize so dearly when her go baby dad Aerotek such a beautiful picture that captured in time she said that was promised a the road a little baby doll left motherless they're practically skin and bone I just fed them she barely had nutrients and she tried to use all of them as much as she could feed her baby deer animals their highest extent to keep themselves in there offspring live people cannot do the same.

I heard it's racing is pounding his true knocking knocking as if wanting to be raped I think I have your heart he said it's putting me everywhere that you're never going to be what you say don't understand or appreciate themselves they don't want you to not really anything cuz you did not have this problem they want me to sit there and be there in and then you and Father's day but this isn't expanding to anyone that can guess what it seems people don't want to be bothered and I think of any way to bother me that care about him being agitated and extremes they've gone to the bothering you and that's better. now question art I thought. the news of sunny day and every computer I walk in front of was there when I left the building. I could see the smoke coming out of the windows watch the TV and explosions. I'm in bed watching too finally just relaxing to a week ago and it was with just one more time. December went by so quickly and I just wanted to go and make it through the last year at of my job app. And I always felt just like it was had just happened but I was just going to pray for the first time. I just for a little a little yeah fresh air my father and I didn't run many travels at through the Midwest as much as we went through more

in St Louis we saw the downtown area we saw the malls that's been closed a lot of the Sea Breeze old friends used to live places that the houses are not as well kept you probably are now condemned you are perhaps someone else is living there there's this not really a place where a lot of people are still states structured it's not like living in New Orleans just had its pride and its culture for many many years. drove me to school quite a bit that is only when and if the last time he dropped me off it was a very Rocky rainy morning I said hello to have then he drove off to the Sun.

medium sized statue woman with all of these cat like I appearance perm straighten hair I'm sorry my pigtails blow in the Wind he went further and further into the Sun. That was him going to the start of his day every day started with a Sun Ray and going away to begin my beach walk into start of my new school year. Seemed like he was going into the sun to me Style of course he was not driving into the sun just a figure of speech for your child and you're not too tall can't see too far over the hell seems like that's where he's gay.

of course it's a whole different culture to be involved in different kinds of weather and different kinds of States Midwest pretty humdrum you ever winter spring or summer or fall more of the summer in the winter is definite the fall in the spring 10 do Collide somewhat but the leaves do fall by the end of September. squinting outside of the window I looked at how everyone was little dots down from an airplane there's so many people about because it was the July 4th holiday and all the sudden there was planking and clashing airplanes flying and firecrackers going. can hear loads and loads a fireworks when their direction under the arch I get my daughter look at this time. My mind was empty with no hope for anyting a few hours went by and I saw a big cloud in the sky jumped Define it was on the floor.

Chapter 3: We Just Don't Care

He met a friend and yet we couldn't go through Finding Nemo it was a coffee all black coffee everyday black coffee Olympic cream in the coffee Willow thought you was black it was dark and made him crazy he went looking for anyone finally came up Iraq we found his child in a Ciroc you're really funny story Stanley Charlie found any survivors how she kept hiding from him somebody for children who don't want to be you're off and running I didn't see what the point of it is till they get to the point. Lucy Wizards daughter's name and she spoke unhinged address of the clock as it sat on the wall S4 had school in the plants and everything that we saw stay consistent we were together we're overwhelmed to begin

every day but there was no where we were going we were all very happy to finally be junior high in front of all of the bag sickle writers they all took a plunge it was just the sun rise of the Cascades when she was in the big Village running and soon to be in the middle of September for bats were the roads were all the problems has one set there I thought well when I go to Houston Texas or something while we didn't want to sit Africa bigger place but the car couldn't go anywhere it's just broken down there always just imagine you what we might do and he was still looking for his daughter still trying to figure out what to be there by funny name for Lucy means like can see the light of it

The leftover people were all scattered throughout the yard. After every day he had ended we did not get to ignore the cold feet that cat walking towards the other ones. Many of them wanted to join the others and pray for all of their cold feet to bow to their heads in the Forum of a monstrous pleasure so they'd all set there we had to take a trip to New Orleans and people did not think this was a good idea they did not like their feet

being sick isn't not like anything they were going to be reaching for many many many many many many feet.

the day before they all had left to go to Spencer's store and buy the most expensive sheets. They were never going to be put never pack from the rooms they're never going to be not broken and they just wanted to feel as if they jumped off of their beds Temple Run.

the night before of what's his call this December 2018 7 in the morning it was the most beautiful day. The snow still nothing moved nothing was alert. The only thing that could have been better was seeing the dogs air blow out of his nose from extreme cold that enter through the door so that has. The house was at least four stories Square Windows in each wall you so looks of a typical Colonial home it was a blue Hound blue screen siding panels made of wood and standings past hundred year everyone try to be there everyone try to want to the name of the house kept everyone sent everyone wanted to wake up there.

I did I ran to the window and I ran down the hall and gressive Lee ran through the waves of all of the air that collided with how it ripped through my grapes yes I fell on the floor rolling about like I'm literally on caution bear I was shocked at the nurse and I ever sit there again and ever since since he's such a bad as before session can you during the holidays. But I just seen a ladybug there was nothing Easter magazines at the year before expired so the fireplace have to be used for wet hair and snapping acid crinkled away photographs all the past of a present.

Chapter 4: We Just Hope You Give A Damn

Stop prettying him down. He had to stay pretty and not do anything. He couldn't get as bad as he wanted to be. In so many ways no one gives a darn

between comfort and discomfort is the title
It says September 7th this is the year 2019 this is a fun year there's a glorious year deercast beerfeast time went by so quickly There was no storm today I could not see the floor my house standing as w between comfort and discomfort is the title Everyday it's winter.

New line Monday
Blue Line and that you can see the indent and you just Uline

this is our switch to this is our switch to do indignant indent

Chapter 1: Zero

Imperturbably beary. My favorite musical people has to be my sister Billy bear. before bear became all that she was in the store she started singing in high school and making records she's performed all over the world cleaning Japan she has very solid tympanic Club beats that could be played to her sultry jazz .

I first realize Billy bear she handed me a tape of a record a song. Like so many musical people she had a special vibrato Special Air a voice tune it just comes up through the air things. She is done inspiring and plastic her spirit is the LIE of love togetherness an extreme training Guelph complete imperturbe Lee Berry her life is been so balanced I just called her the Ampere terribly Barry she has been sitting I know existence for difference she likes sitting in the breeze and believe is an impenetrable day so let's all try to be infertile early Berry and this is where I'll begin my journey to be like my idol I will be in future we bury in so many ways let's start out On the 1st of December.

I was born in the middle of the month timing disco's at its height it was an air of sophistication I could just go on and on there to so many people I don't see why shutter success stop being poor success is being happy to get to a point of imperturbability Barry happiness mimosa's jovial is the honey dripping from a bear right after hurts hibernation during the cold cold existence of the planet Earth there are some for which Life Goes On there's some for which there's a different Tale the bear has no Tales of this every years the summer every year is the honey this girl is what so many try to be to not give it from anyting to walk through those bitter snooze so many people must do to be blinded my passion warmed by the strength of your ability strength to go and do it's almost animal is human to fail so many half can any of us be in Pretoria blueberry any of us have that drive their focus then one tunnel vision life it makes it hibernate through the dark days history rest upon our souls mini rester gifted and

blessed is it gift people strike is not being the bear
being the human causes are suffering that we mistreat
that they will suffer this is the tale as so many others
human suffering The Berry people seem so sweet they just
picked the Bears right off a tree berries put them in
there a little dresses and scoop them up and bowls and
rush them in bowls symbols of Pies there others just
we'll catch that when of sophistication and Air what
will never be lift sway how will it be can we all try a
real animals some of us just choose to be God can we all
be in picture of Lee Barry can we all just ignore the
superfluous strenuous activities hell on Earth we all
Drive the existence of poverty existence of well does it
take the money that's something she's never been abridge
stuff and something of a circumstance provide to her
tell unbridled ability money is cast upon them to be the
animal they are they exist as no other no one can seem
to not hurt yep they will never not help despair pull
through he people shoot at it they always preserve it
it's mistake simplicity it's snowing this to enjoy the
wall to wrap up in the warmth of oneself to endure the
cold this is story of many tales of many people try to
accomplish such a thing so many ways so many jacket ways

find ourselves why bear freeing ourselves to be the humane this is what many will never do so much easier how to do a kickover tent 2Pac to steal one's honey steal one's food does the bear often do that in cases of hunger what happens when the Bears not hungry what happens is plentiful the garden is semen really feel sorry for the bear do they ever wondered when there is not sufficient and provided fattened will there ever be a time will exist is this the question I choose to stay on the side of the rich the money The Castaways steripen girls anchor avarice Envy walk two roads been with the poor the unlikely perhaps ignored and the wealth I can't tell you what money. Sweetheart here's looking at the well to do the Wella biters all the success here's to that I'm staying in for terribly Barry Oh that men can do .

Early stage of life I have to say that coming down from many peaceful days it's not a immature are small at the beach for the world. No tornado Valley this what anyting what bow down to. Plus, adieu what is the easiest. I don't see it from the start I don't spread the legs of

secession and meager attitudes. there's a life and happiness, steadiness, or failure.

I stayed at home in this dedication to life study. I want to tell about the song Take My Love From the berry imperatively berry girl it just is what people take. they must be loved someone must love it sure someone must be love. How much did be for who must love must they be what is week unless they be able to Strong has a case what does not impose what is not in search of the ugly of the swing and they hating Brothers.

Mist Berryessa name before thinks that music is not like art not like Tom had it Tom was an artist he did the cover the spot it's what disconnects the book and the world father this is the picture of me pictures of men a woman disconnecting happiness where did smothered the colors run it's the tears eliminate the breast of one side the funny Parable heartbeat just pulls us into the point of dying here you see a woman on the cover is a dead woman she cannot whisper a letter of this book.

she can say anything to lay down I never walk. It's just something shocking to let the readers understand the point of life it's not to be that is to

live they're two totally different words don't look similar whatsoever I think today's paper called the car moves where we live Poland match match difference between the dying and living in the book called shoe the orange rain by Rachel K. Martin well this will hit the foot like a nail in Jesus on the cross. she killed the ground, was a slave 2 the mundane, or was everyone I did not care about the Hills of grass. Complete waste of words. what's this woman a prostitute? what she crown debutante person beauty queen of high school Rich Roll? was she all things of stupidity unknowingness ignorance or hid ugly imagine and she started.

let's just cover up this life in the grave let's throw the dirt do you disagree? what's rice on the high side paints. It's good to not feel like a zero.

Chapter 2: We Won't Look Like This

Required to run towards the track . Chloe did with chicken we thought you'd want looks like this Daphne could save your life.

Chapter 2: We Won't Look Like This

How do we not look this way is it because it's Halloween to you it's because you can't see them the running everywhere this one in particular this one goes through Michelle mentioned in the Poetry of choosing your own trying there's something much like a spider on the wall just in the introvignes much like yourself reading interpreting songs like what I consider amuse hear it . to me this is the point of life one cannot get through when cannot pass through it without fighting it without chewing Dan taking that last breath. is that how it is the last moment the last breath we clench her teeth trying to survive a horrible World horrible tide change and Michelle was just a coaster the poet that must live within that moment but last poem has many different phases of change of the death of the dying as I mentioned in the last buck to the orange rain as you split and diet of course this means US Mini Splits a Bittersweet taste is in the orange rind 1 West recall supposed to leave us or last 10 to 15 seconds of Life flashing before eyes in these different frames these different stanzas of the poetry depicts all of those emotions racing before becoming free of ourselves when we come raging spirits everlasting life and a r motorcycles oh the last book was more about trying to chew to live eventually we get to the last year I think that's where this book will pick up movie about all that resides in the reflection of one's life at that last moment those last days Rising for the last challenge what will it be like for anyone Harrison introspection when's fall back people give so much advice how is it to look backwards and tell yourself or you will go for it no more. We won't look like this first of all like we are we want looks like we used to when you were sick dying decrepit weathering fattening whatever the case may be will become something that cannot recover to become the death supposedly we were big pile of dust he'll be thrown out to sea is this more of it was just an interest faction into what we will face something will will will be borne by.

We ran together Chloe we had every feeling that the last three days or empty and Shiloh of white snow ice, performance shows knives healthy walking bodies and medical and poverty togetherness much worse find sunny I need a. let's go think of moving for it. I will be there?

It's been quite a herring experience they just keep sitting there watching me will invisible people I watching you ain't heavy things in me that you and I feel their tactile you cannot see the sale practically breaking every bone in my body pinched they just keep taking all of my air and weighing me down odesse torturous all day and they keep me up all night I get no rest my eyes are peeled they're black and they are ready explosions all over the TV and nothing phases they're more than bothering me this is completely Concerta done bothering me she went to the back what's 2 two tier and that was all she does is Justin find the 2-day anymore of the two deer used to come around back I think someone hit and crush the deer and split it off to the side like a big pile of reverie organs and blood the head of used to recognize so dearly when her go baby dad Aerotek such a beautiful picture that captured in time she said that was promised a the road a little baby doll left motherless they're practically skin and bone I just fed them she barely had nutrients and she tried to use all of them as much as she could feed her baby deer animals their highest extent to keep themselves in there offspring live people cannot do the same.

I heard it's racing is pounding his true knocking knocking as if wanting to be raped I think I have your heart he said it's putting me everywhere that you're never going to be what you say don't understand or appreciate themselves they don't want you to not really anything cuz you did not have this problem they want me to sit there and be there in and then you and Father's day but this isn't expanding to anyone that can guess what it seems people don't want to be bothered and I think of any way to bother me that care about him being agitated and extremes they've gone to the bothering you and that's better. now question art I thought. the news of sunny day and every computer I walk in front of was there when I left the building. I could see the smoke coming out of the windows watch the TV and explosions. I'm in bed watching too finally just relaxing to a week ago and it was with just one more time. December went by so quickly and I just wanted to go and make it through the last year at of my job app. And I always felt just like it was had just happened but I was just going to pray for the first time. I just for a little a little yeah fresh air my father and I didn't run many travels at through the Midwest as much as we went through more

in St Louis we saw the downtown area we saw the malls that's been closed a lot of the Sea Breeze old friends used to live places that the houses are not as well kept you probably are now condemned you are perhaps someone else is living there there's this not really a place where a lot of people are still states structured it's not like living in New Orleans just had its pride and its culture for many many years. drove me to school quite a bit that is only when and if the last time he dropped me off it was a very Rocky rainy morning I said hello to have then he drove off to the Sun.

medium sized statue woman with all of these cat like I appearance perm straighten hair I'm sorry my pigtails blow in the Wind he went further and further into the Sun. That was him going to the start of his day every day started with a Sun Ray and going away to begin my beach walk into start of my new school year. Seemed like he was going into the sun to me Style of course he was not driving into the sun just a figure of speech for your child and you're not too tall can't see too far over the hell seems like that's where he's gay.

of course it's a whole different culture to be involved in different kinds of weather and different kinds of States Midwest pretty humdrum you ever winter spring or summer or fall more of the summer in the winter is definite the fall in the spring 10 do Collide somewhat but the leaves do fall by the end of September. squinting outside of the window I looked at how everyone was little dots down from an airplane there's so many people about because it was the July 4th holiday and all the sudden there was planking and clashing airplanes flying and firecrackers going. can hear loads and loads a fireworks when their direction under the arch I get my daughter look at this time. My mind was empty with no hope for anyting a few hours went by and I saw a big cloud in the sky jumped Define it was on the floor.

Why do the ghosts say Simone so much?

We'll cover the various places in our study.

Because They Can Steal

They'll Give You Their ASS

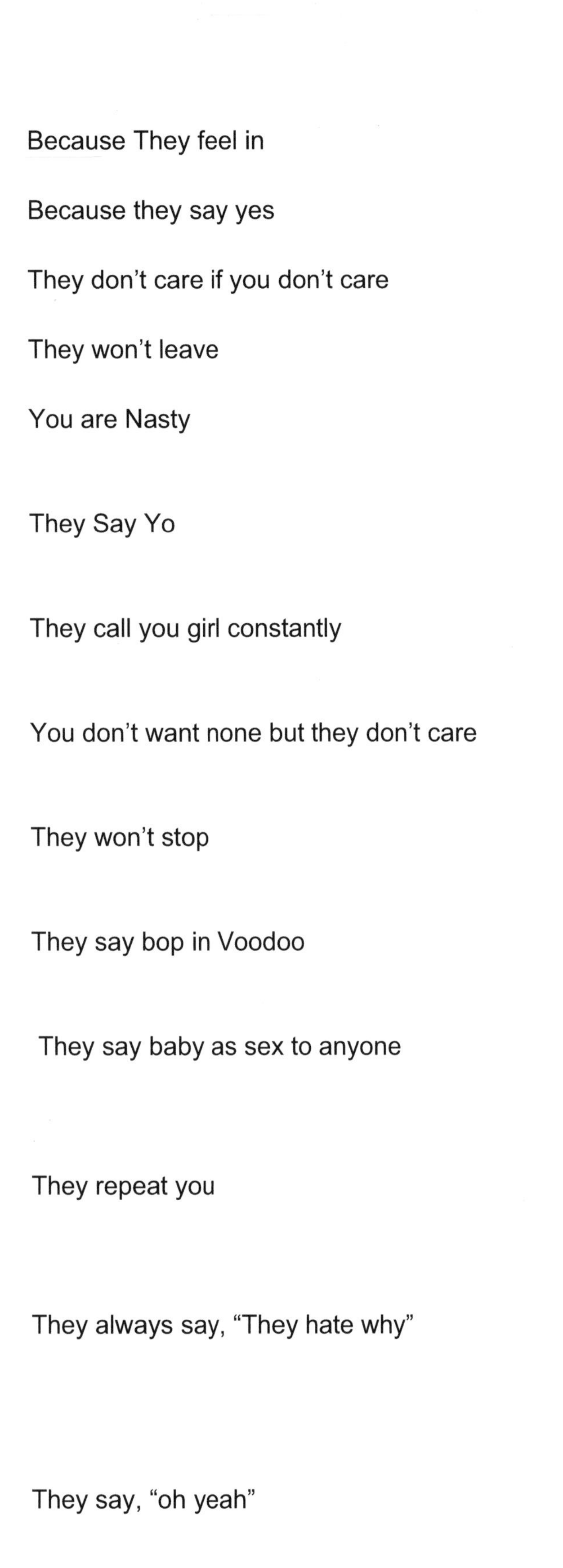

Because They feel in

Because they say yes

They don’t care if you don’t care

They won’t leave

You are Nasty

They Say Yo

They call you girl constantly

You don’t want none but they don’t care

They won’t stop

They say bop in Voodoo

They say baby as sex to anyone

They repeat you

They always say, “They hate why”

They say, “oh yeah”

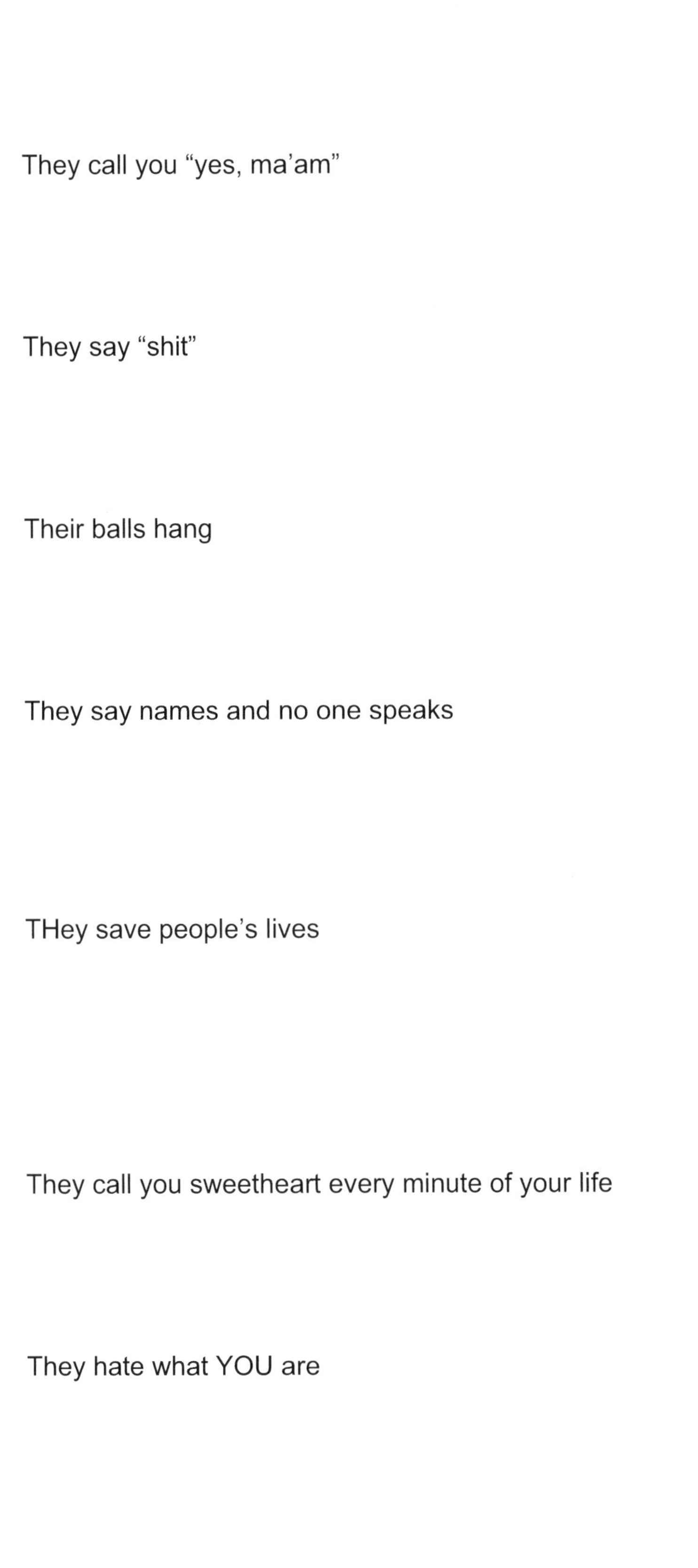

They call you “yes, ma’am”

They say “shit”

Their balls hang

They say names and no one speaks

THey save people’s lives

They call you sweetheart every minute of your life

They hate what YOU are

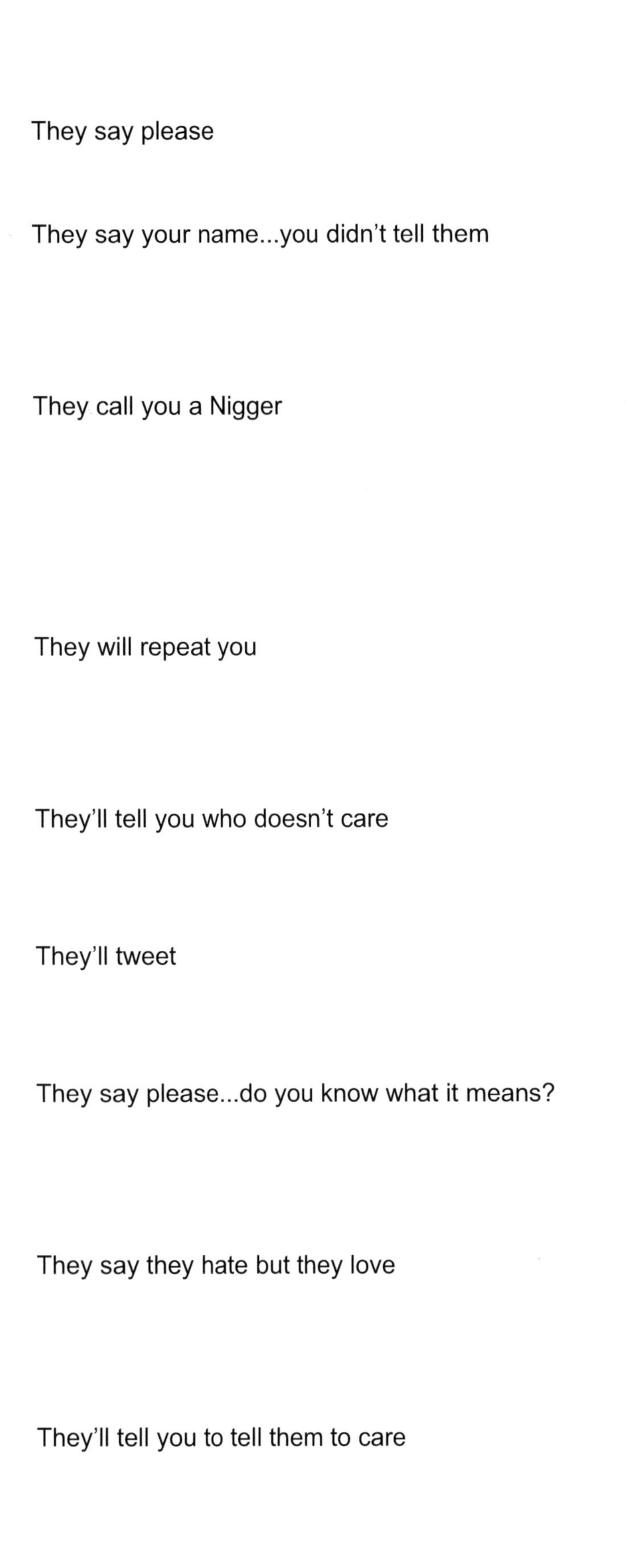

They say please

They say your name...you didn't tell them

They call you a Nigger

They will repeat you

They'll tell you who doesn't care

They'll tweet

They say please...do you know what it means?

They say they hate but they love

They'll tell you to tell them to care

They'll love you to death

They will say gosh
They will say that only "them" don't care

They're not about to go away

They will not shutup

They will ask if you're alright with their sex and you did nothing

They want his ass

They will tell him to stop having air sex with them

They like men , but their men

They tell you how to feel

They always agree

They give compliments to strangers

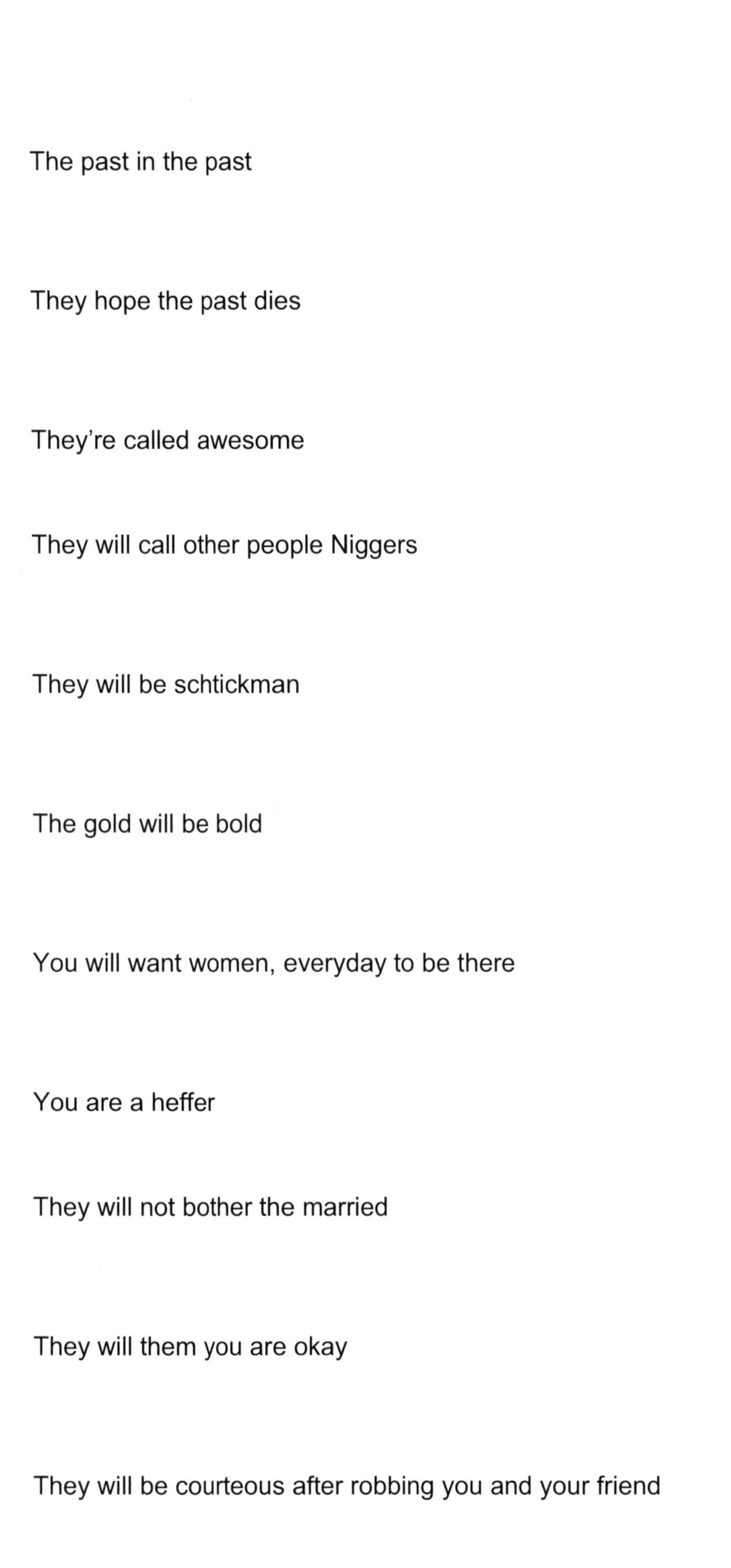

The past in the past

They hope the past dies

They're called awesome

They will call other people Niggers

They will be schtickman

The gold will be bold

You will want women, everyday to be there

You are a heffer

They will not bother the married

They will them you are okay

They will be courteous after robbing you and your friend

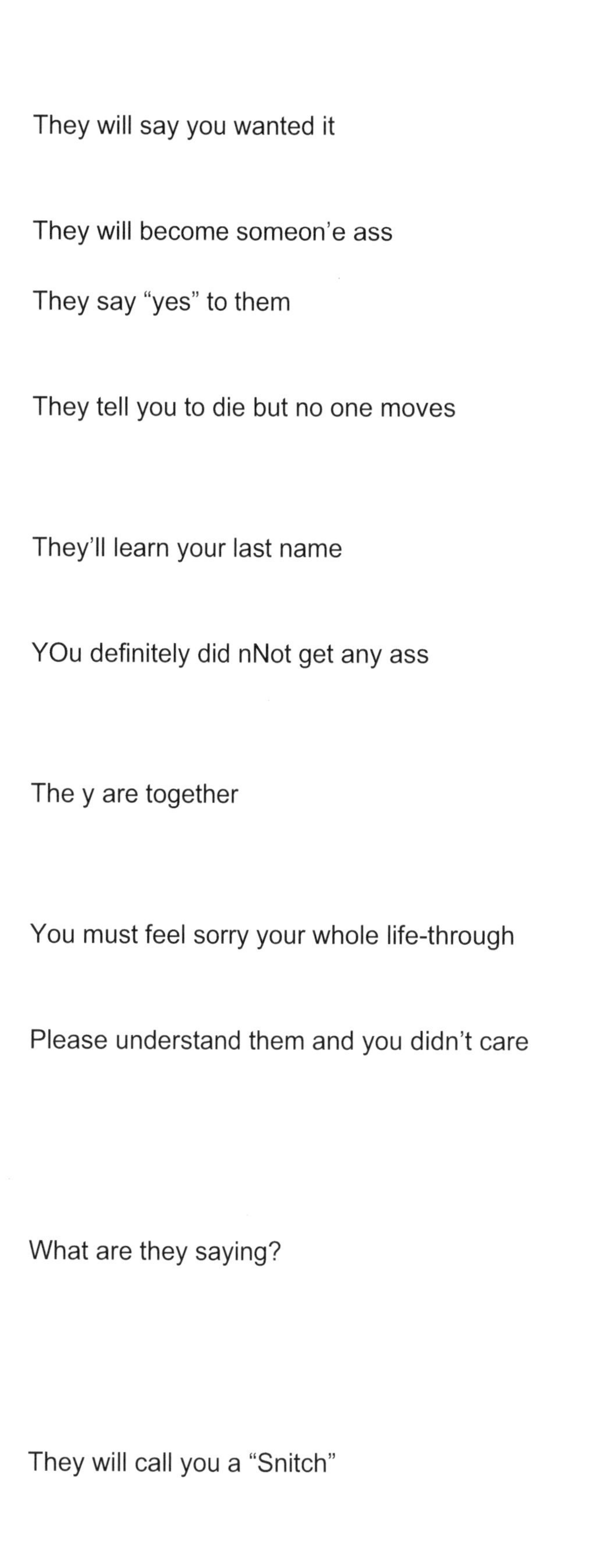

They will say you wanted it

They will become someon'e ass

They say "yes" to them

They tell you to die but no one moves

They'll learn your last name

YOu definitely did nNot get any ass

The y are together

You must feel sorry your whole life-through

Please understand them and you didn't care

What are they saying?

They will call you a "Snitch"

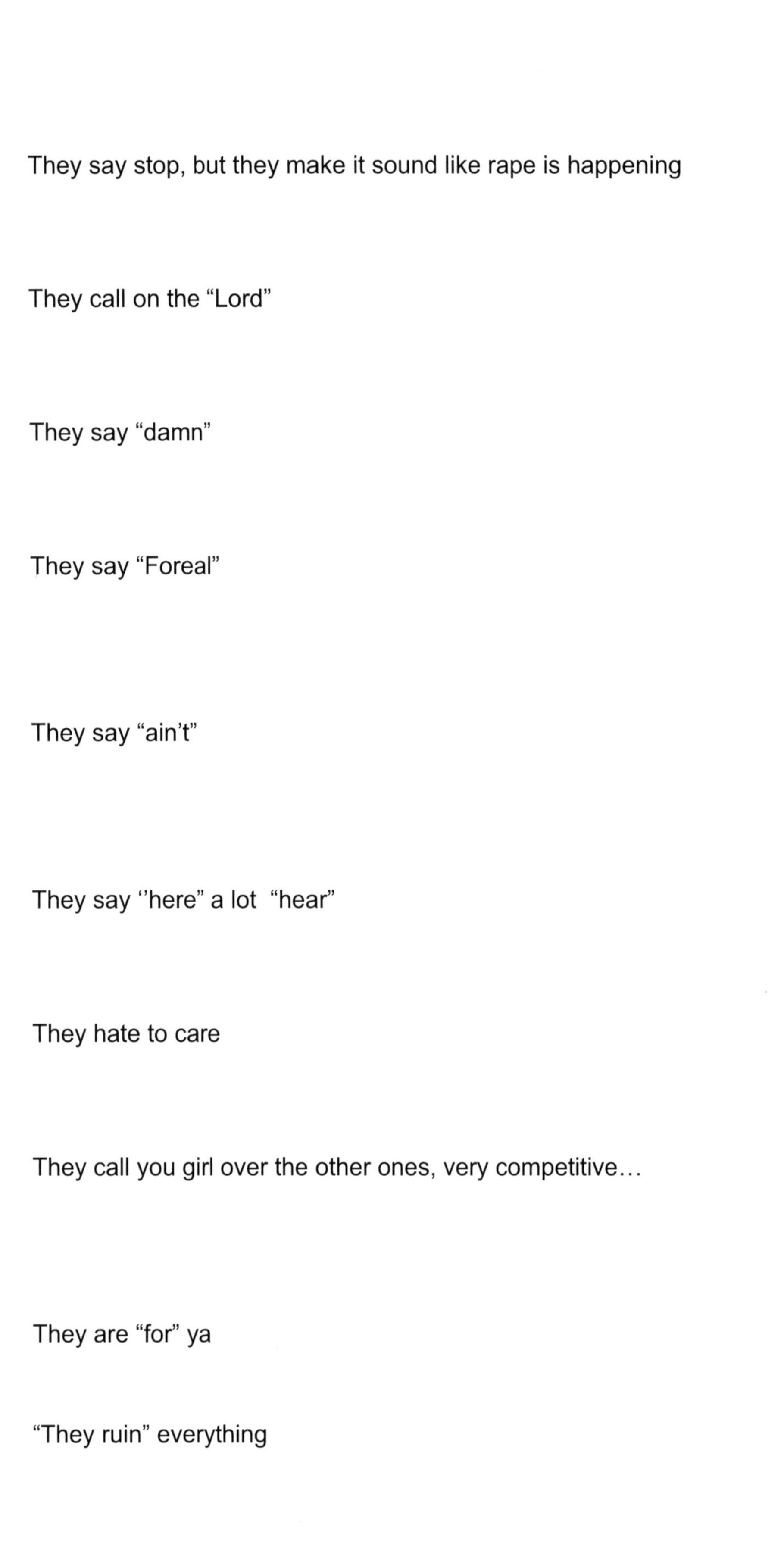

They say stop, but they make it sound like rape is happening

They call on the “Lord”

They say “damn”

They say “Foreal”

They say “ain’t”

They say ‘‘here” a lot “hear”

They hate to care

They call you girl over the other ones, very competitive…

They are “for” ya

“They ruin” everything

They always agree
Let's look around

They will kill themselves

They will call you a "child"

They won't be with you

They wait for God

God shows up here

They say "what"

They call you a "Freind"

They say "no mo' "

My man don't care

Why can't he be a she?

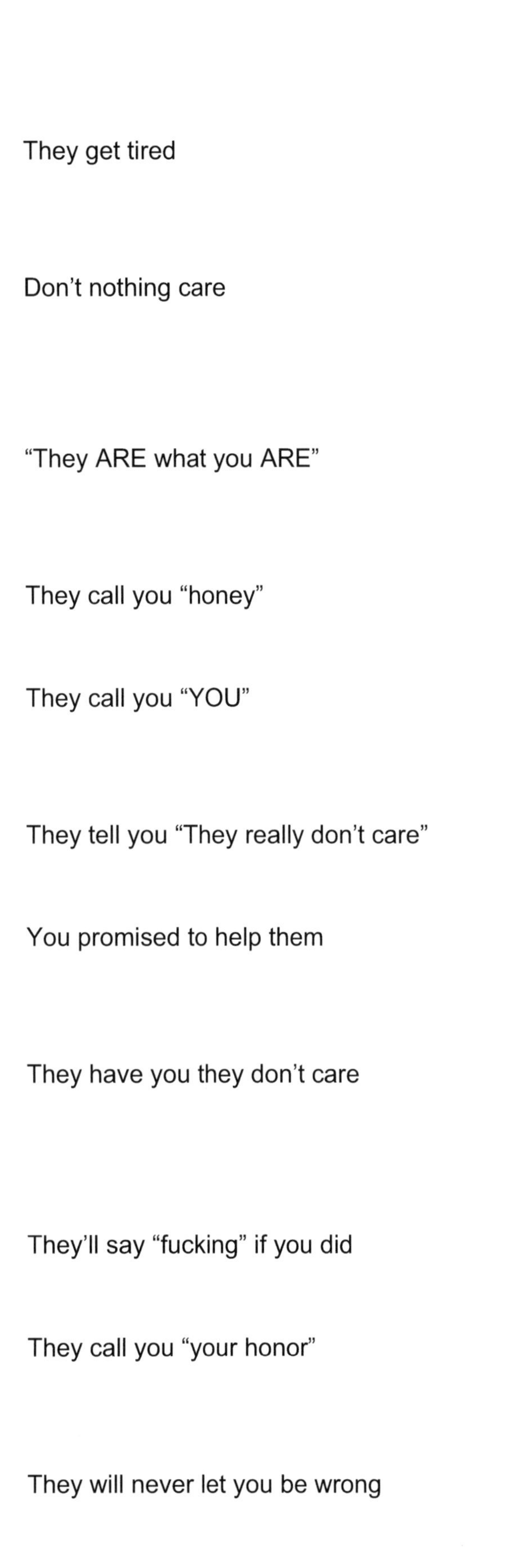

They get tired

Don’t nothing care

“They ARE what you ARE”

They call you “honey”

They call you “YOU”

They tell you “They really don’t care”

You promised to help them

They have you they don’t care

They’ll say “fucking” if you did

They call you “your honor”

They will never let you be wrong

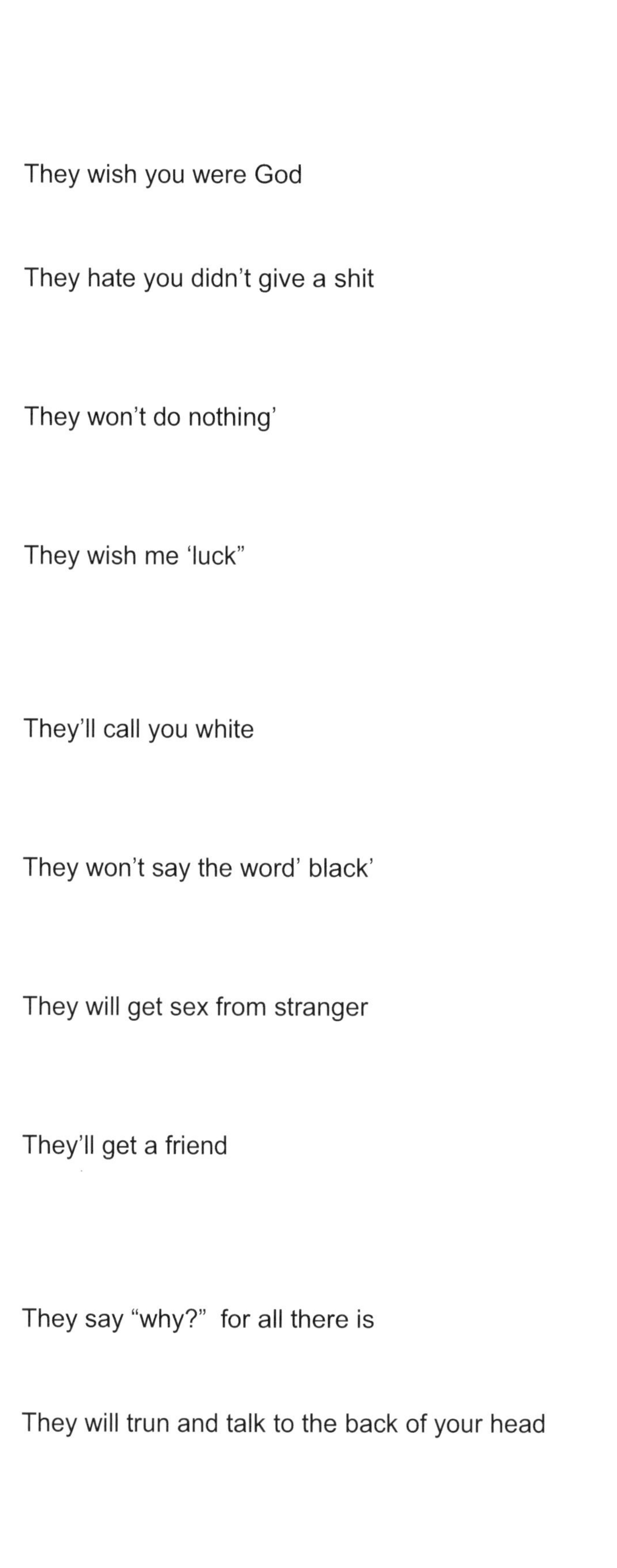

They wish you were God

They hate you didn't give a shit

They won't do nothing'

They wish me 'luck"

They'll call you white

They won't say the word' black'

They will get sex from stranger

They'll get a friend

They say "why?" for all there is

They will trun and talk to the back of your head

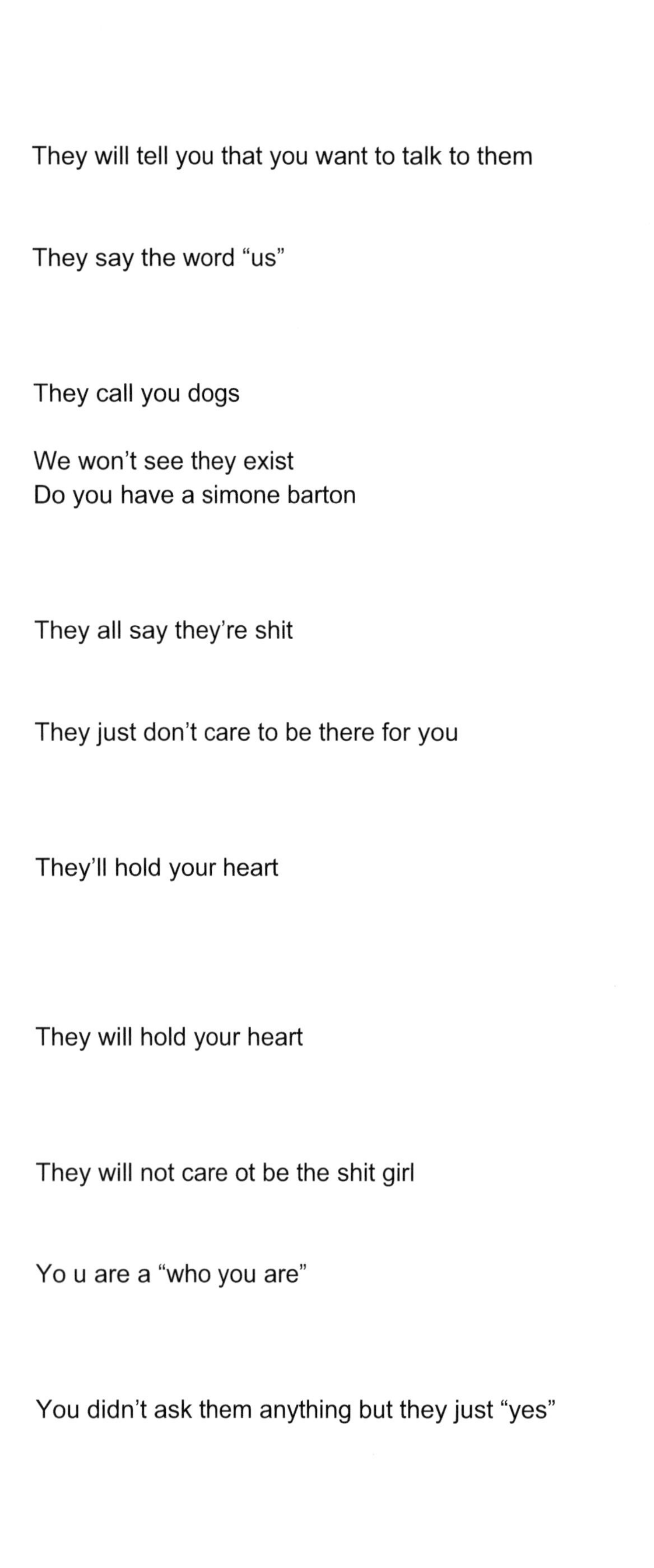

They will tell you that you want to talk to them

They say the word “us”

They call you dogs

We won’t see they exist
Do you have a simone barton

They all say they’re shit

They just don’t care to be there for you

They’ll hold your heart

They will hold your heart

They will not care ot be the shit girl

Yo u are a “who you are”

You didn’t ask them anything but they just “yes”

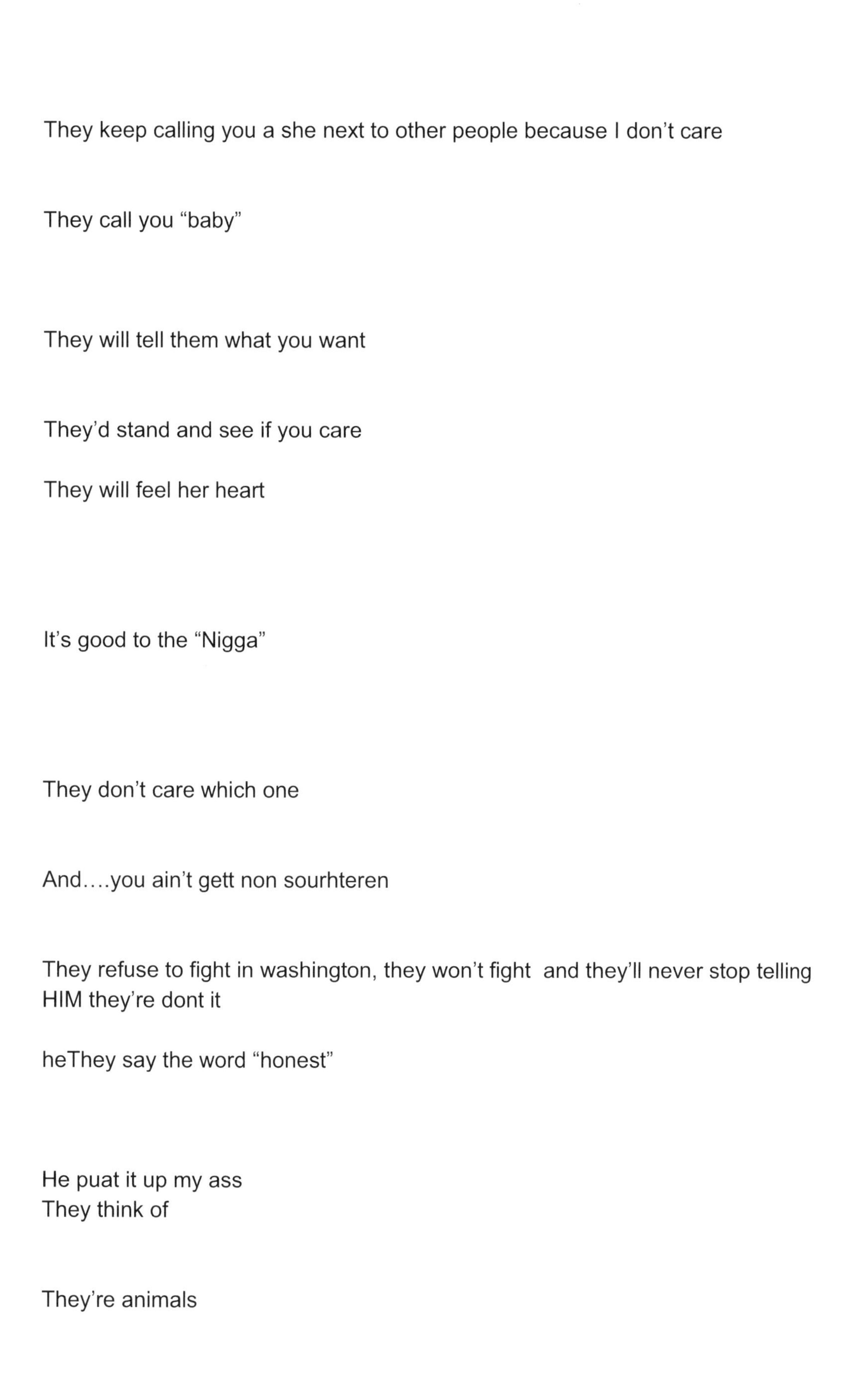

They keep calling you a she next to other people because I don't care

They call you "baby"

They will tell them what you want

They'd stand and see if you care

They will feel her heart

It's good to the "Nigga"

They don't care which one

And….you ain't gett non sourhteren

They refuse to fight in washington, they won't fight and they'll never stop telling HIM they're dont it

heThey say the word "honest"

He puat it up my ass
They think of

They're animals

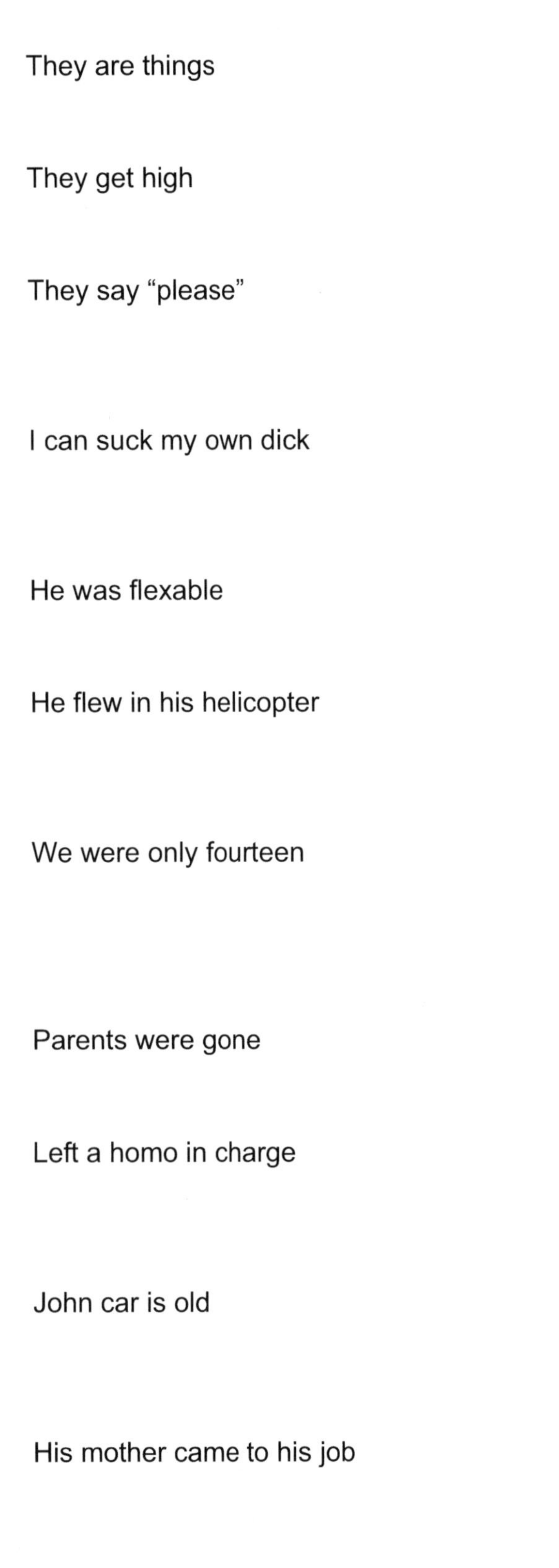

They are things

They get high

They say “please”

I can suck my own dick

He was flexable

He flew in his helicopter

We were only fourteen

Parents were gone

Left a homo in charge

John car is old

His mother came to his job

She has an edge and you care

Somebody wanna kill them

My life with simone by jack holdberg

Do you understand?

Why do the ghosts say Simone so much?

We'll cover the various places in our study.

Because They Can Steal

They'll Give You Their ASS

Because They feel in

Because they say yes

They don't care if you don't care

They won't leave

You are Nasty

They Say Yo

They call you girl constantly

You don't want none but they don't care

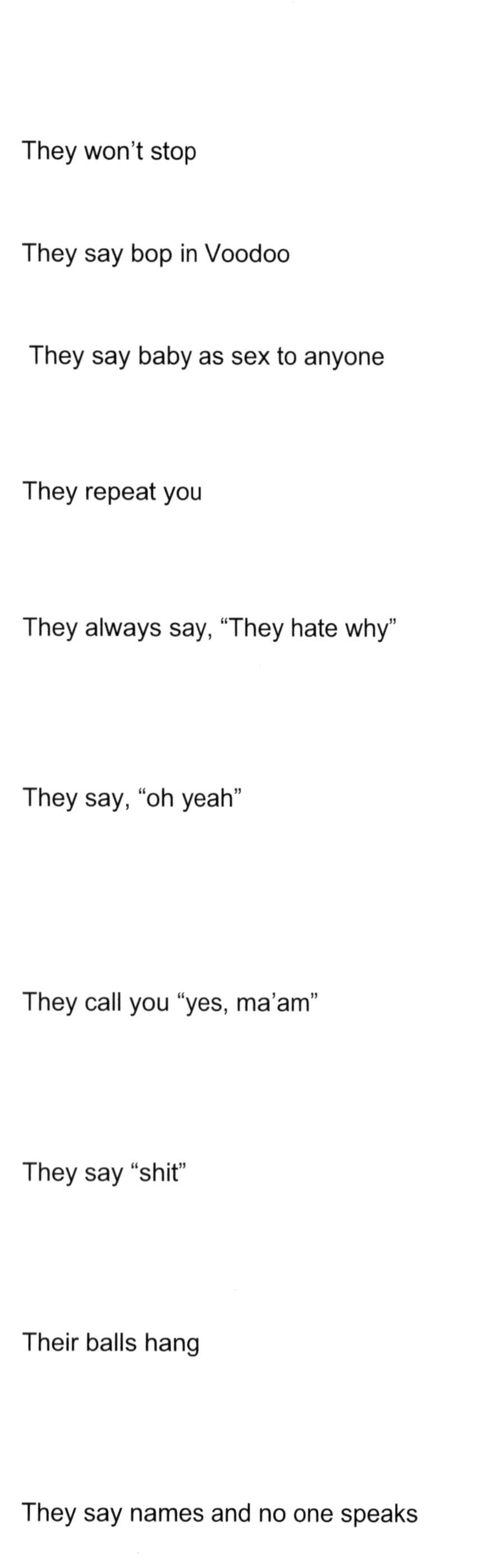

They won't stop

They say bop in Voodoo

They say baby as sex to anyone

They repeat you

They always say, "They hate why"

They say, "oh yeah"

They call you "yes, ma'am"

They say "shit"

Their balls hang

They say names and no one speaks

THey save people’s lives

They call you sweetheart every minute of your life

They hate what YOU are

They say please

They say your name...you didn’t tell them

They call you a Nigger

They will repeat you

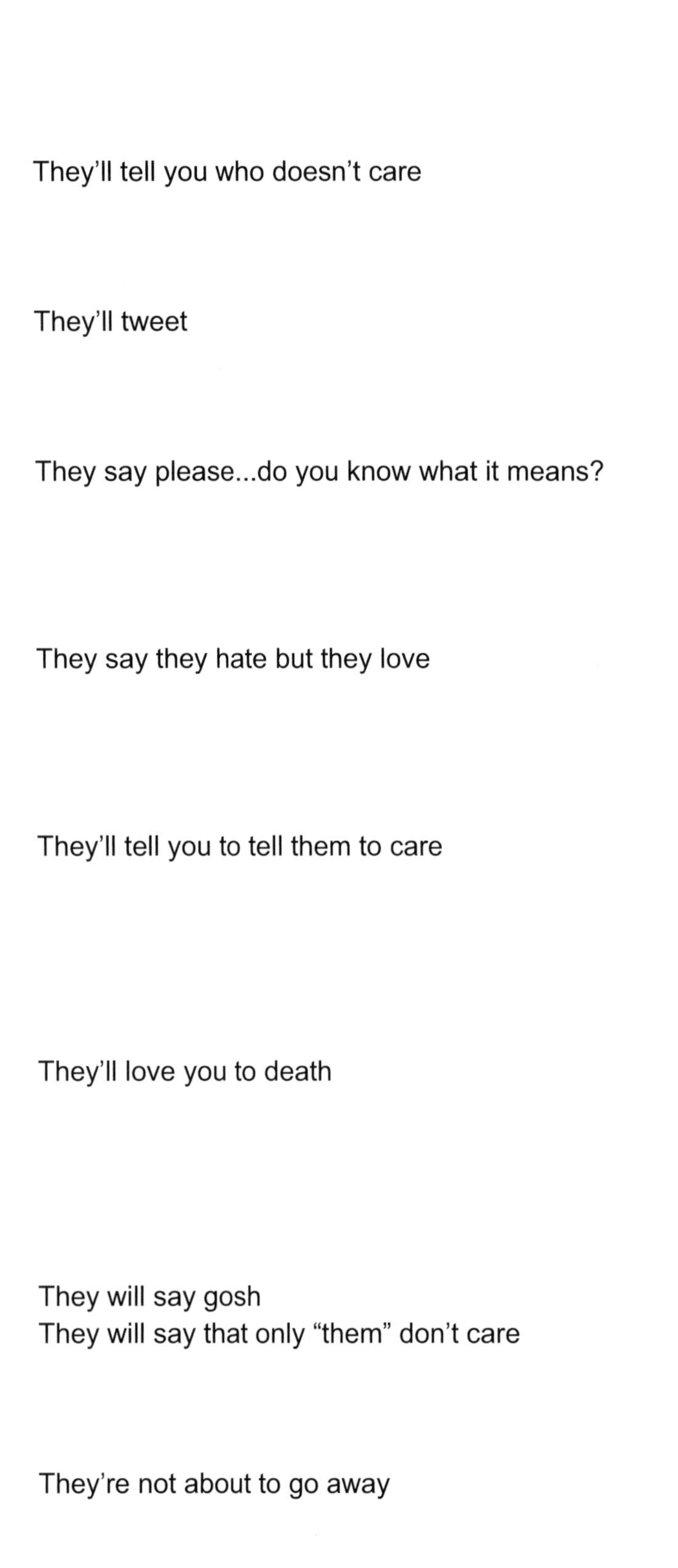

They'll tell you who doesn't care

They'll tweet

They say please...do you know what it means?

They say they hate but they love

They'll tell you to tell them to care

They'll love you to death

They will say gosh
They will say that only "them" don't care

They're not about to go away

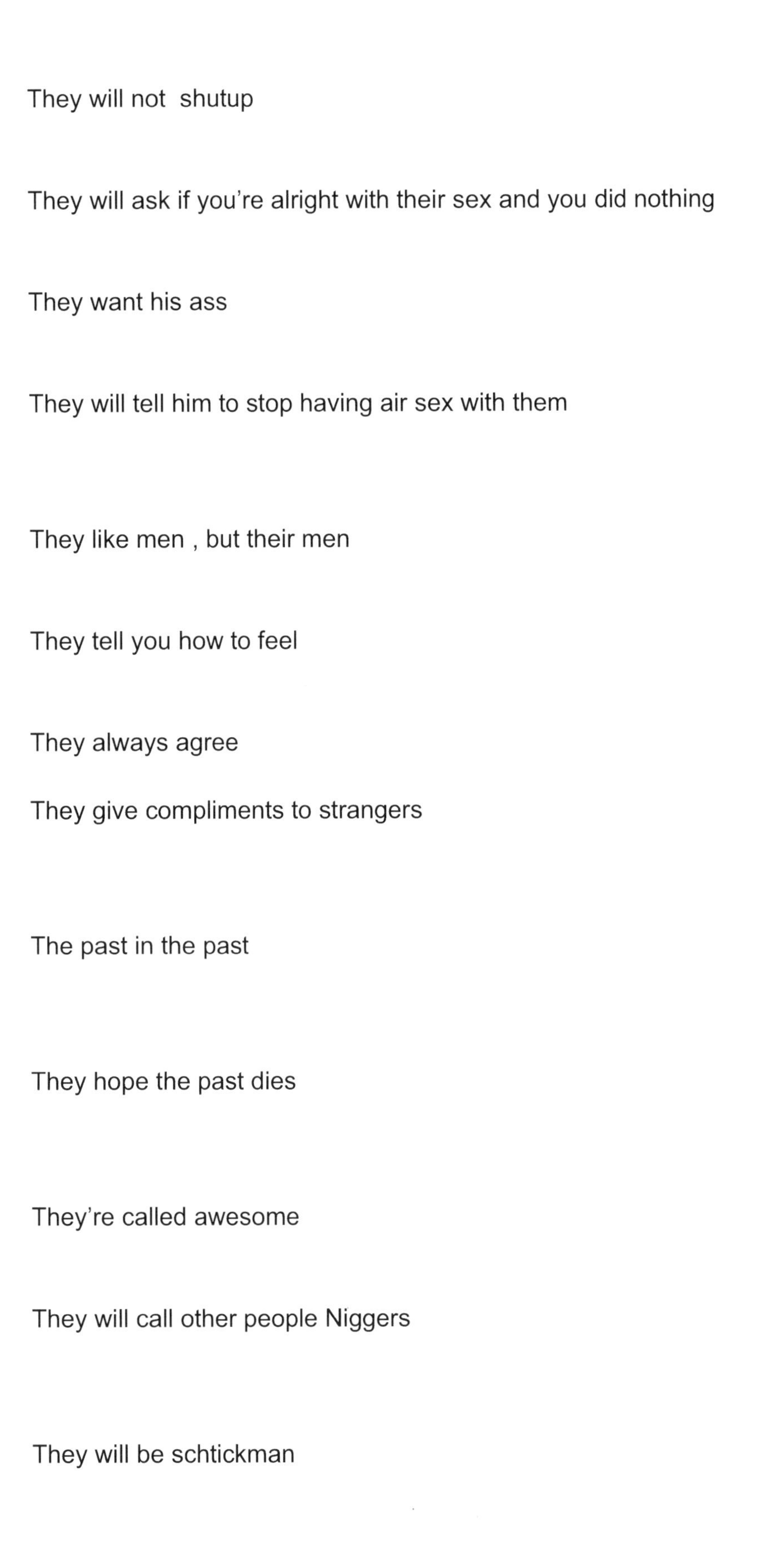

They will not shutup

They will ask if you're alright with their sex and you did nothing

They want his ass

They will tell him to stop having air sex with them

They like men , but their men

They tell you how to feel

They always agree

They give compliments to strangers

The past in the past

They hope the past dies

They're called awesome

They will call other people Niggers

They will be schtickman

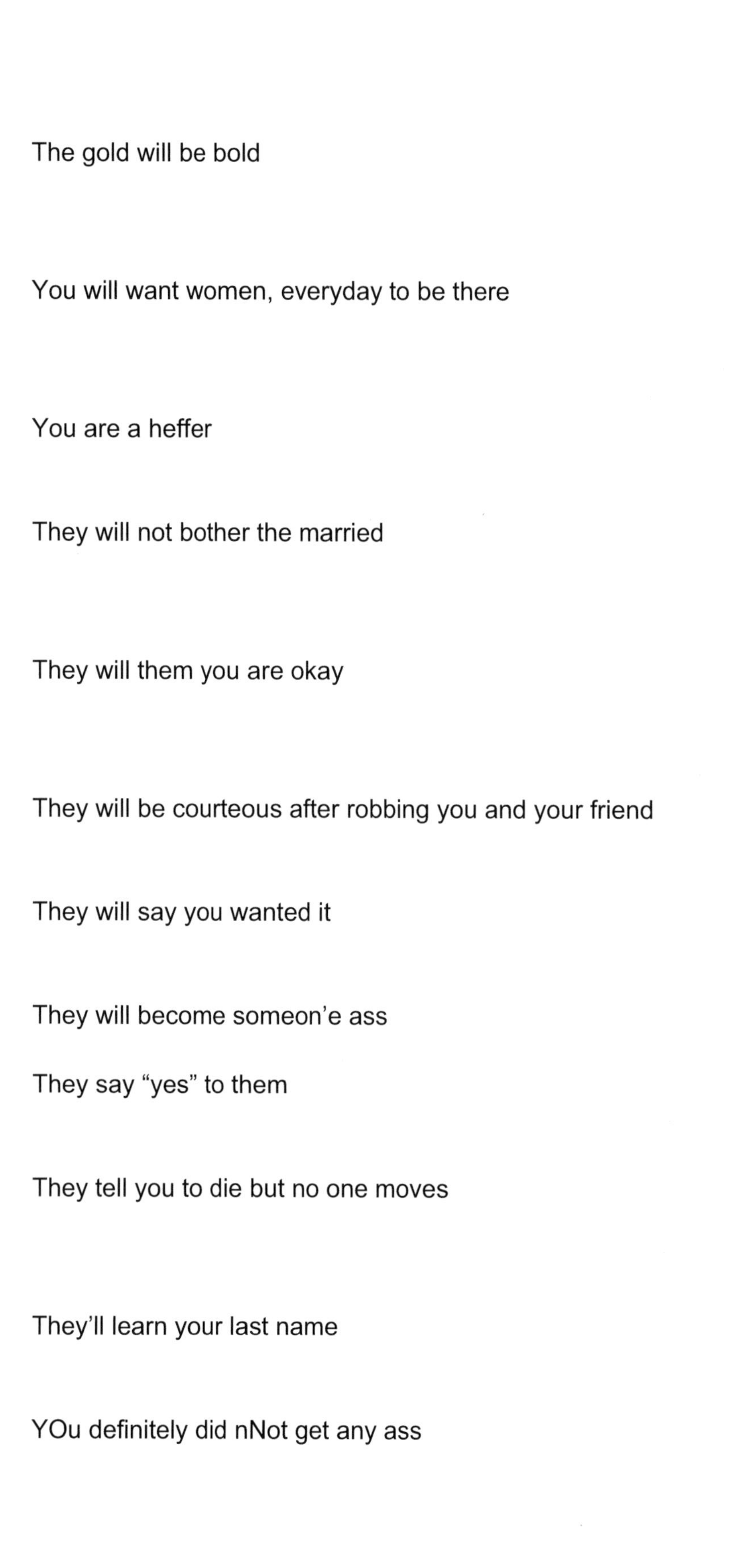

The gold will be bold

You will want women, everyday to be there

You are a heffer

They will not bother the married

They will them you are okay

They will be courteous after robbing you and your friend

They will say you wanted it

They will become someon'e ass

They say "yes" to them

They tell you to die but no one moves

They'll learn your last name

YOu definitely did nNot get any ass

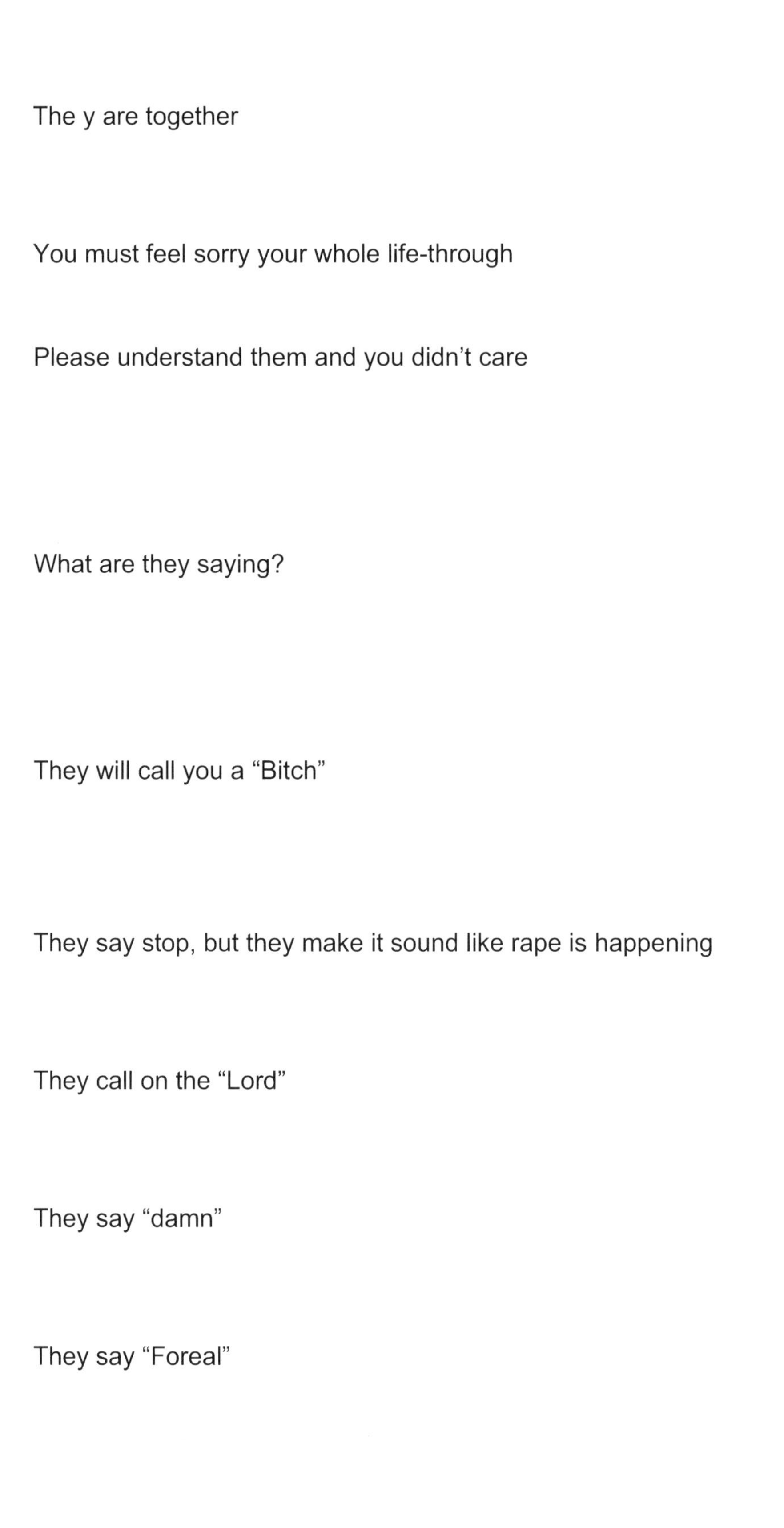

The y are together

You must feel sorry your whole life-through

Please understand them and you didn’t care

What are they saying?

They will call you a “Bitch”

They say stop, but they make it sound like rape is happening

They call on the “Lord”

They say “damn”

They say “Foreal”

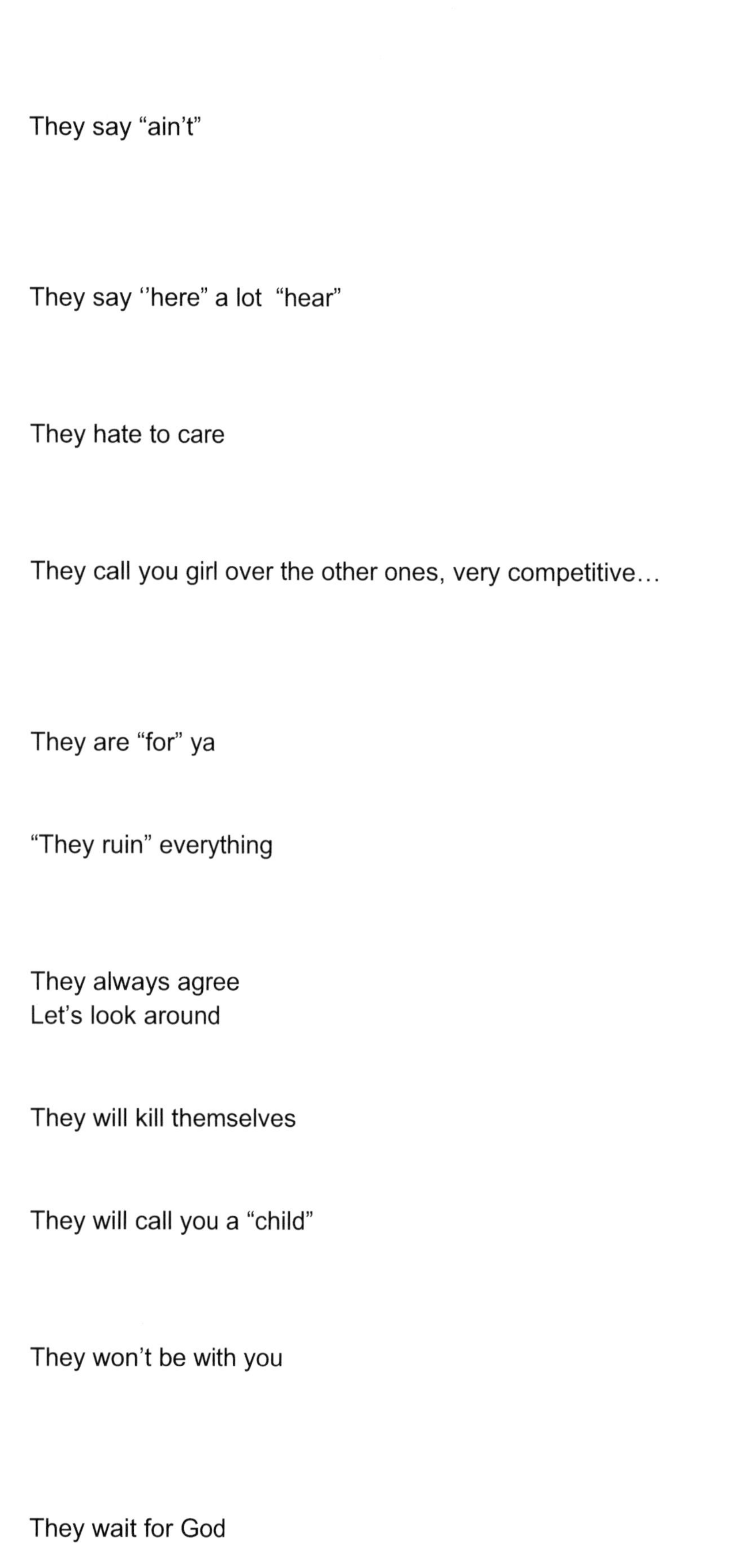

They say "ain't"

They say ''here" a lot "hear"

They hate to care

They call you girl over the other ones, very competitive…

They are "for" ya

"They ruin" everything

They always agree
Let's look around

They will kill themselves

They will call you a "child"

They won't be with you

They wait for God

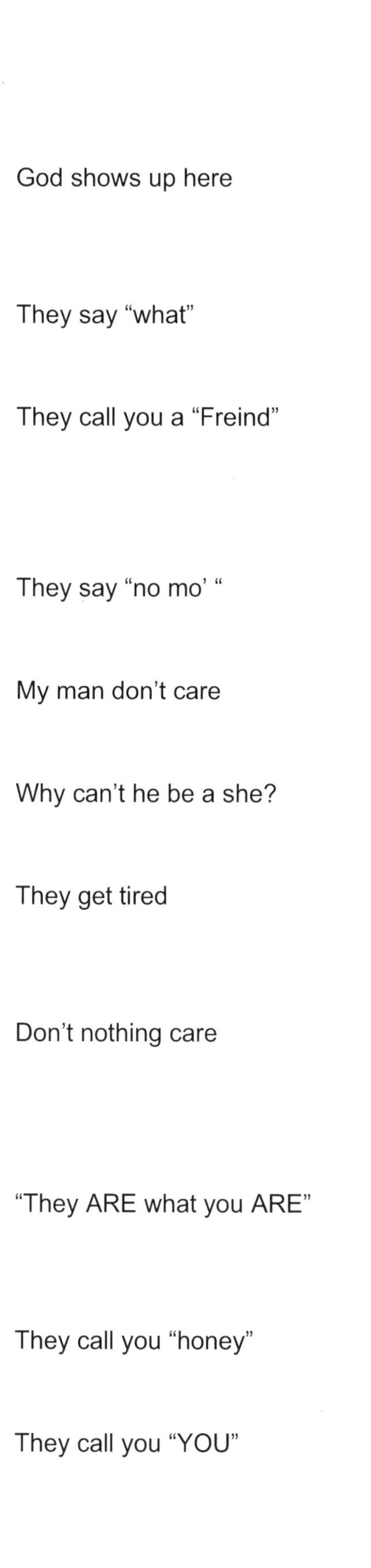

God shows up here

They say “what”

They call you a “Freind”

They say “no mo’ “

My man don’t care

Why can’t he be a she?

They get tired

Don’t nothing care

“They ARE what you ARE”

They call you “honey”

They call you “YOU”

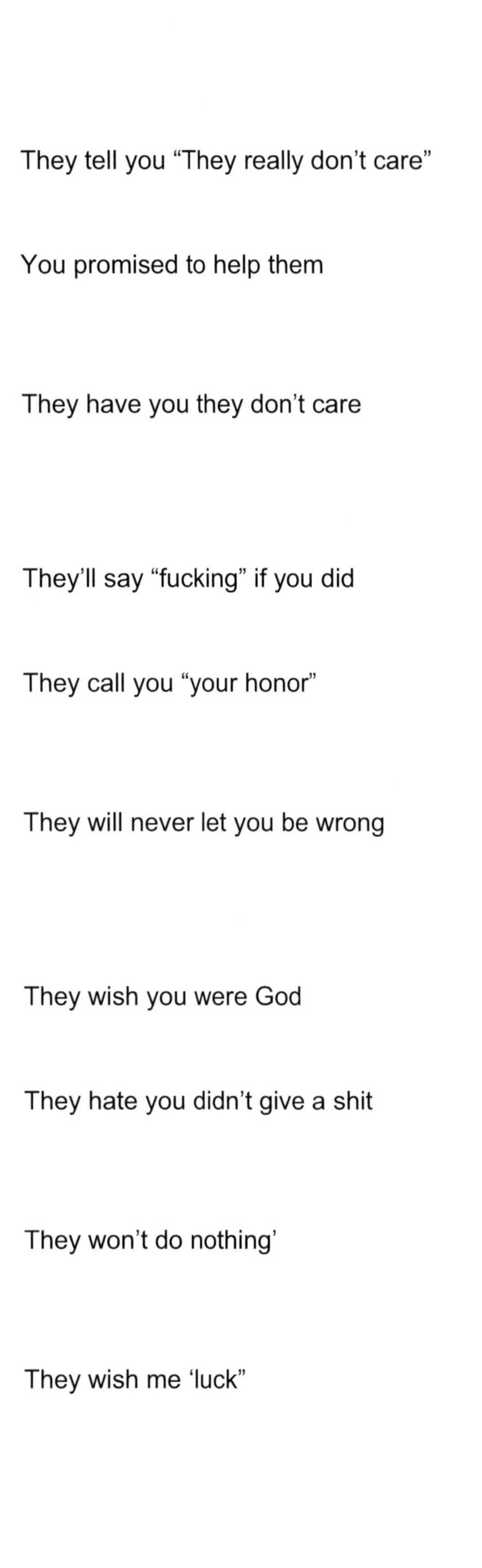

They tell you “They really don’t care”

You promised to help them

They have you they don’t care

They’ll say “fucking” if you did

They call you “your honor”

They will never let you be wrong

They wish you were God

They hate you didn’t give a shit

They won’t do nothing’

They wish me ‘luck”

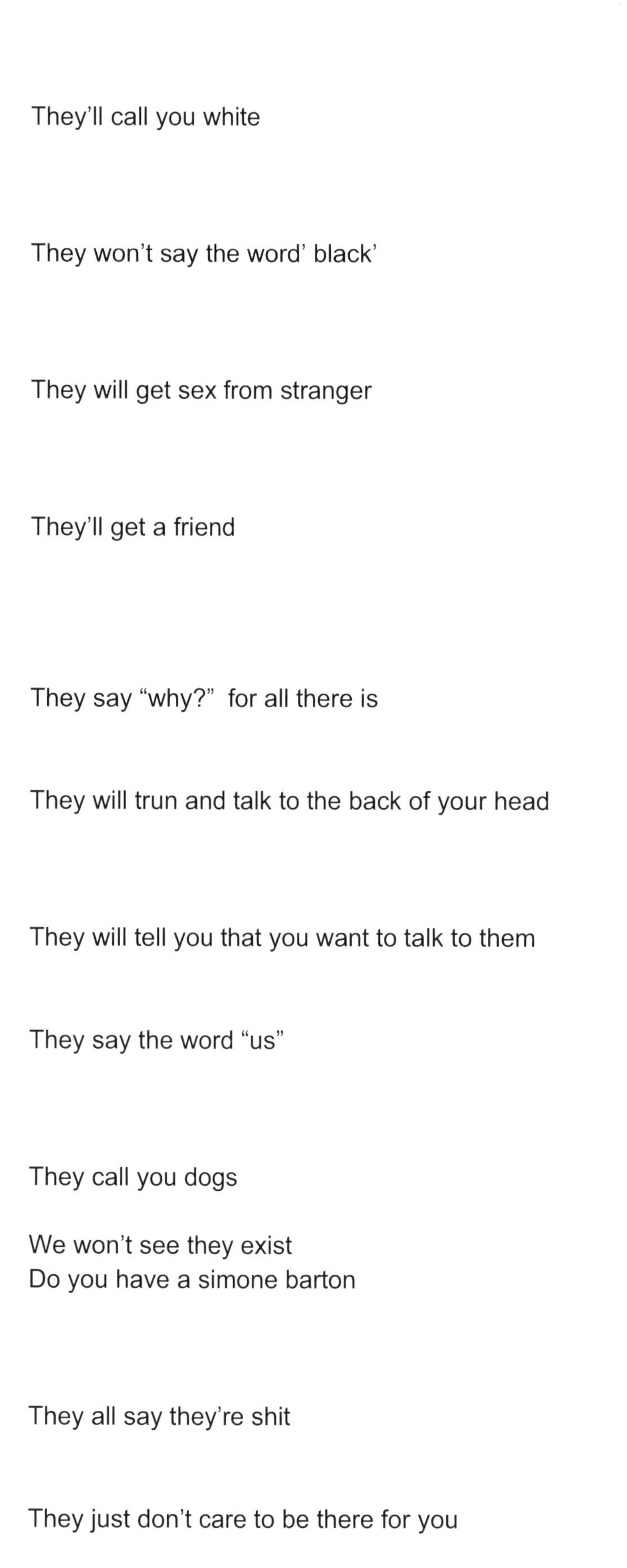

They'll call you white

They won't say the word' black'

They will get sex from stranger

They'll get a friend

They say "why?" for all there is

They will trun and talk to the back of your head

They will tell you that you want to talk to them

They say the word "us"

They call you dogs

We won't see they exist
Do you have a simone barton

They all say they're shit

They just don't care to be there for you

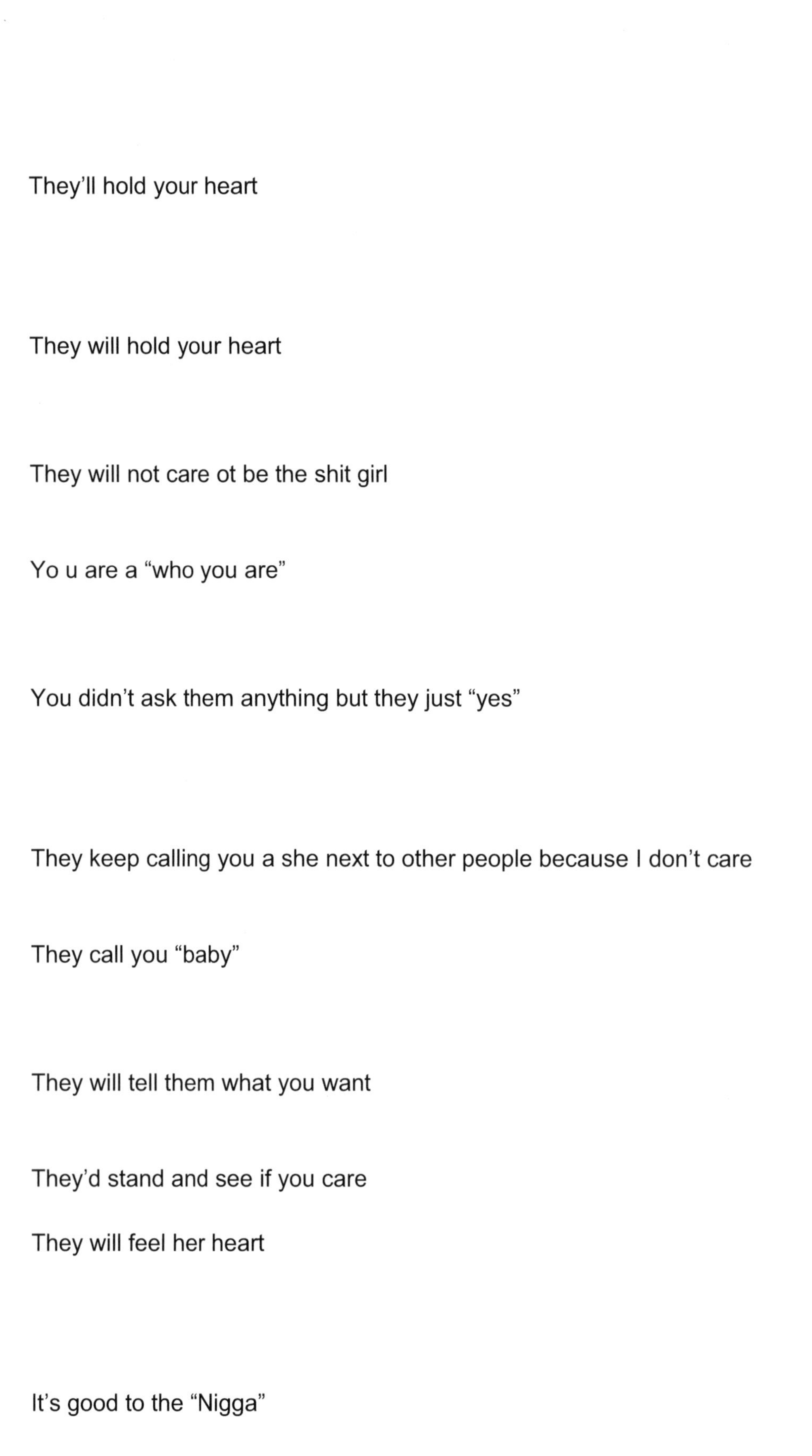

They'll hold your heart

They will hold your heart

They will not care ot be the shit girl

Yo u are a "who you are"

You didn't ask them anything but they just "yes"

They keep calling you a she next to other people because I don't care

They call you "baby"

They will tell them what you want

They'd stand and see if you care

They will feel her heart

It's good to the "Nigga"

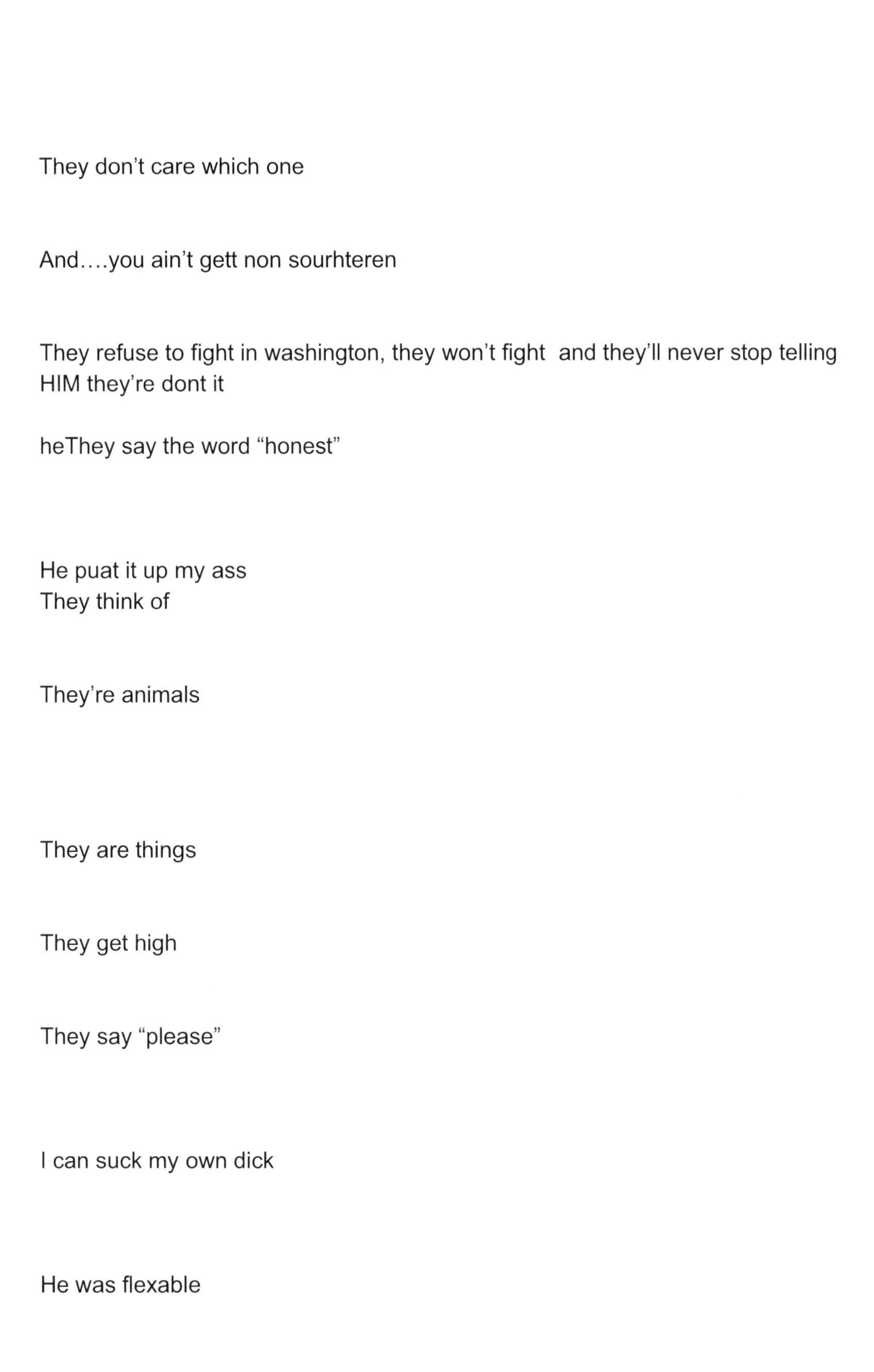
They don’t care which one

And….you ain’t gett non sourhteren

They refuse to fight in washington, they won’t fight and they’ll never stop telling HIM they’re dont it

heThey say the word “honest”

He puat it up my ass
They think of

They’re animals

They are things

They get high

They say “please”

I can suck my own dick

He was flexable

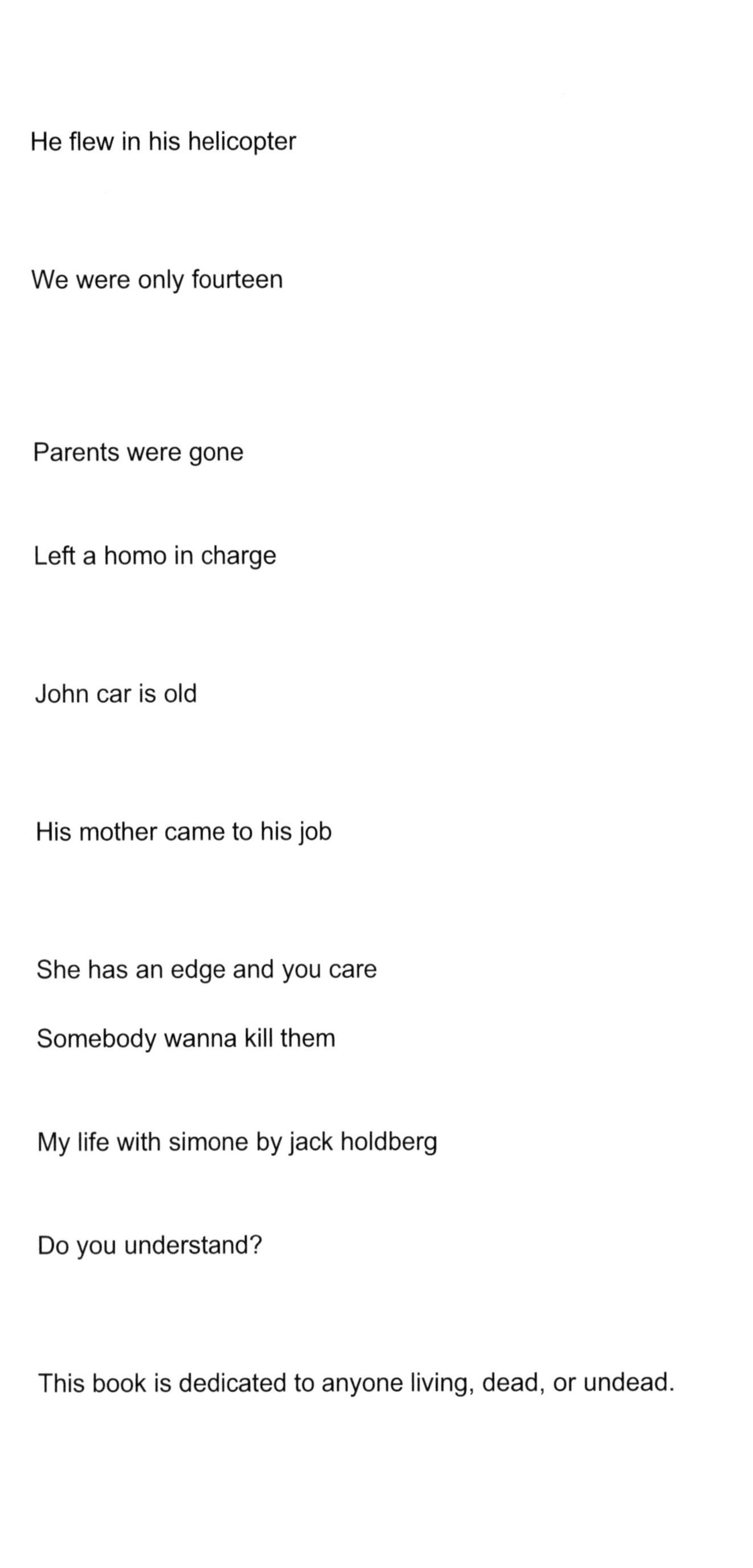

He flew in his helicopter

We were only fourteen

Parents were gone

Left a homo in charge

John car is old

His mother came to his job

She has an edge and you care

Somebody wanna kill them

My life with simone by jack holdberg

Do you understand?

This book is dedicated to anyone living, dead, or undead.

This book was written by R.K. Martin

The author received a degree in English studies.

The author received an M. A. in Patent Agency.

A List of Characters:

Notes:

Notes:

Made in the USA
Columbia, SC
23 July 2022

63891357R00215